Praise for *The Braided Path*

"This rich and beautiful tale of a ropemaker and her family twines the quest for self-knowledge and the need for love into a moving tapestry full of wonders and fiber arts!... *The Braided Path* presents strong, engaging characters in an unusual world full of well-realized details, especially graceful depictions of craftsmen at work. Along the way, Williams explores almost every aspect of fiber, from spinning, twining, dyeing and weaving, to retting linen, plying cord, testing fiber strengths, and constructing nets and hammocks. These details are never intrusive, but rather reveal layers within her world, and explore metaphors for relationships among the characters."
—Elaine Isaak, review for *Handwoven*

"*The Braided Path* is a quiet book, full of good characters trying to discover their path. In fact, the metaphor of the path runs throughout the book. The path, the rope, the braids that bind individuals together into couples and couples together into communities. It is a love story, a coming of age story, and a fable. Mostly it is about characters seeking their place in their world."
—Scott T. Barnes, winner Writers of the Future,
    editor *New Myths* online magazine

"Donna Glee Williams' luminous debut novel, The Braided Path, invites readers to travel with Len Rope-Maker, her son Cam, and his sweetheart Fox as they set out on a path that will lead them further from home and yet closer to each other. In this tale of a utopian craft society whose inhabitants are named, defined by, and relied upon for their gifts, the power and necessity of community and collaboration are beautifully rendered. Williams' lyrical, earthy prose and sensitive characterization wove a spell that transported me to this world and brought it to life."
— Pamela Duncan, Assistant Professor,
    Department of English, Western Carolina University

THE BRAIDED PATH

DONNA GLEE WILLIAMS

Betsy,
Thank you for the
work you do in our
Village!
Donna Glee
2014

EDGE SCIENCE FICTION AND FANTASY PUBLISHING
AN IMPRINT OF HADES PUBLICATIONS, INC.

CALGARY

The Braided Path
Copyright © 2014 by Donna Glee Williams

Edge Science Fiction and Fantasy Publishing
An Imprint of Hades Publications Inc.
P.O. Box 1714, Calgary, Alberta, T2P 2L7, Canada

In-house editing by Ella Beaumont
Interior design by Janice Blaine
Cover Illustration by Neil Jackson

ISBN: 978-1-77053-058-4

EDGE Science Fiction and Fantasy Publishing and Hades Publications, Inc.
acknowledges the ongoing support of the Alberta Foundation for the Arts and
the Canada Council for the Arts for our publishing programme.

Library and Archives Canada Cataloguing in Publication

Williams, Donna Glee, author
    The braided path / Donna Glee Williams.

Issued in print and electronic formats.
ISBN: 978-1-77053-058-4
(e-book ISBN: 978-1-77053-059-1)

I. Title.

PS3623.I4634B73 2014   813'.6   C2013-905012-4   C2013-905013-2

FIRST EDITION
(N-20140107)
Printed in Canada
www.edgewebsite.com

DEDICATION

For Dortha Dell Meade Williams.
She held my hand and let me go.

ACKNOWLEDGEMENTS

Though only one name is on the cover, this novel has been a group effort. Without the gifts of my friends and teachers, it could never have come into being. And now I get to offer my thanks to some of my partners-in-art:

First: To Kathy Panks, who has been along for the ride, uphill and down, since that school-bus to our first day in junior high school. Passing notes in class grew into her listening over the phone to every single page of the first draft of this story, so that I could hear it and I could hear *her* hearing it. The quality of her breathing as she listened told me everything I needed to know about the work I'd done that day and sharing the story with her did a lot to soften the essentially solitary process of writing. A writer can't do better than to have a BFF like Kathy.

To Patricia Lee Gauch (and to the benevolent Path that brought me to her) for her wisdom, skill, kindness, and supernatural understanding of Story in all its facets. What a teacher!

To Frank Parker, who taught me most of what I know about language. I don't know why more writers don't study linguistics. (Oh, wait—I do; because it's *hard*.)

To Jeanne Cavelos, who taught me most of what I know about the world of speculative fiction. Aspiring SF writers can take a huge shortcut by investing in a summer at Odyssey.

To Richard Curtis, best agent in the history of history, for helping me, with patience and courtesy, to find my feet in the business.

To Brian and Anita Hades, for making a place for this little oddity of ambiguous genre and for welcoming me so graciously into their family of authors.

To Steve Brooks for getting me to Brian and Anita and for long decades of steady friendship.

To Jeremy Taylor, my dream guy, who got me down to the sea. For rational thinking about the irrational, Jeremy is King. If you hanker to dance closer to your subconscious, check out his books, classes, or online dream "toolkit."

To Jed Hartman. I submitted "Limits" the short story from which this novel was born, to him at *Strange Horizons* back in 2007. His generous, respectful feedback brought that story to the level where it earned an honorable mention from Gardner Dozois and appeared on several "best of the year" lists. Jed, a man I've never even met, started the pebble rolling.

To Sophia Stone, Poetry Editor at *The New Orleans Review,* for coaching me along the way as the story grew into a novel.

To Lynn Morgan Rosser, whose powerful intuition helped me to find Fox and the core of my story.

To Michael "Cecil B." Caudill and Julia "Prop-Girl" Fuog Caudill, for Waterrock Knob and for the kind of friendship that's about as important as oxygen.

To Don and Dortha Williams, who first gave me Story.

To John Highsmith, for the photo and for the smile.

To eagle-eyed Barbara Macon and Connie Hanna, who were there just when I needed them.

To The Hambidge Center for the Creative Arts and Sciences in the hills of North Georgia, where this tale was born on a long, sweaty, uphill walk one July. For many writers, tackling a longer project requires space and time to sink deeply into the work. Places like The Hambidge Center offer us that haven. If we want to see excellence in the arts, we should all support these creative hatcheries with our money, time, and energy.

To the thousands of menders who betook themselves to our beloved New Orleans after Katrina to help put the world back together.

And to the readers who venture out with me onto The Braided Path:

Thank you!

—Donna Glee Williams, 2013

THE
BRAIDED PATH

THE BRAIDED PATH

ALWAYS IN FRONT OF YOU AND ALWAYS BEHIND, sometimes trailing over the rich, giving soil of the village shelves, but mostly over stone. Some of the stone is the color of those roses that can't decide between red and yellow. Some is motley gray. Some is black, with bits of crystal that twinkle like something in a clear night's sky. Some is almost the color of cream. Some of it breaks into chips so sharp they can cut flesh. Some grinds underfoot into a powdery sand that can slide beneath your boot. Sometimes the path travels not over solid rock, but over an accretion of bits that have rolled downworld from somewhere high above.

Sometimes it is so broad, this path, that two can walk side by side, shielded from the great fall by a hedge of wind-wizened trees. Sometimes it is narrow steps, chipped out of the living stone. Sometimes it is just a rope, dangling across a wide rock face, where walking becomes a matter of trust: in your grip, in your boot-soles, and in the rope as your own weight presses you to the wall of the world. And there are some places where it can be nearly flat, startlingly so, making for easy walking for a time. Always changing but always itself, the path wanders across the rippling curtain of the world, stitching together the whole.

The villages are there, along the path. In the villages, walkers can find their rest at the end of a long day's travel. They can throw down their packs, take food and drink, tell their stories, then sleep and dream.

When did Len first see how far the path would take them on the great wall of the world? With all the switchbacks on the path, who can see ahead?

No Far-Walker had been born under the apple trees of Home Village for many years. But everyone knew Shreve Far-Walker, from Third Village Down, who often passed through as she carried loads between High and Low. When nightfall caught her near Len's Home Village, she would stay over, taking dinner and giving back news. She wasn't by nature a talkative person, but she understood the duties of a guest. Len would crowd in with the others to hear Shreve's account of the Far Villages and the strange stories they told there.

So Len had some notion of the life of a Far-Walker, though her own range was a modest seven villages. (Climbing up beyond her limits made her pant for breath like an old woman; going down past them left her sweaty and sticky.) When Cam began to show unusual aptitude for climbing high and descending very low along the path, she wondered. Like all parents, Len had observed Cam closely from his earliest tottering steps as he followed her to First Village Up. She had shared discreet smiles with the other parents as their young ones tried on the new costume of adulthood to see how it would fit them, daring each other to range ever farther from Home Village on spurious errands

There would be a jaunt proposed, a clamor of assent, and a rush like a group of startled goats when Cam and his friends hurried off. No packing or planning was needed as they carried no real loads and it was understood that they would stay in whichever village they were closest to when night fell. Families who housed a youth from another village tonight knew that their own children would find food and a pallet where they needed it tomorrow, and the balance would be kept.

Len was a maker of rope and twine. She prospered on the fiber of a certain nettle that grew all along the path near Home Village, thinning out above Second Village Up and abruptly disappearing in the shade of the trees around First Village Down. Her house was full of this little plant: baskets of stems, waiting to be broken; fringes of washed fiber draped everywhere, waiting to be plied; and coils of finished cords and ropes of all sizes, waiting to be carried up or down the trail for trade.

Len was a fine crafter, with powerful, knowing hands that meted out the strength of the fiber smoothly and evenly. She did a good business from Fourth Village Down to Second Village Up, selling her rope and cordage and the intricate knots she created as ornaments and symbols.

Len knew her ropes were much valued in the lower villages because they resisted rot so well, but she did not care to take them there herself; she knew her limits. She would have been glad to find her son's range ran a little lower than her own. But it would be selfish for a mother to push or wish a thing on a child for her own convenience. So Len Rope-Maker held her heart open, and waited to see what would emerge from the clouds.

When little Cam let go of her hand and ran off to explore the world without her, she watched after him and waited. (It was a safe place, a place where a knee-high stone rim had been built between the path and the long fall.)

And Cam ran back to her with sparkling eyes, crying out, "As far as the big rock! I went that far, Len!" And she set aside the long, blond fibers she was plaiting and swept him up and made much of him ("As far as the rock!") and solemnly asked him for news.

It was bittersweet for Len when Cam and his friends got older and began to be away more. Len's little house was too silent at night without his breathing, so she got herself a cat. She named it Goose because she enjoyed standing at her door at dinner-time, calling "Goose! Goose! Oh, Goose!" and having the little gray cat run home to her.

Like other parents — maybe more than other parents — Len worried, as the jaunts got longer and Cam was away for days at a time. Days and nights with no word, only her trust in him to rely on. Sometimes there were dreams of a foot slipping on rolling gravel, and then a wailing fall. The world was steep and it happened sometimes.

But there was no need for her to say, "Be careful." Every child had been a part of the sad gift-giving when some son or daughter of Home Village did not return. Many youngsters wore shirts or coats or hats they had received on these occasions. Some had already shared the work of building the cairns that marked where someone had fallen off the path, of piling up the stones: the black stones, the orange, the chalk-white, the gray. Around Len's Home Village, the stones were gray. Granite gray. The shoulders of the world were steep and a fall was almost always equal to a disappearance. The cairns were raised in memory and warning.

The young people of the villages planted their feet carefully and took the dangers of the world in stride.

As the months and years of youthful questing passed, limits began to emerge, a dim map of how far each person was willing to go. One of Cam's friends might decline to join an expedition to gather ice near a certain far Up village, because they could never stay warm that high, or because the thin air made them breathless.

And then someone might refuse to go along on a jaunt to a party far Below, saying that it got too hot down there at this time of year, and who could sleep properly with the heat and the racket of the frogs?

How to feel about these limits was a great riddle to Len. On the one hand, a person with many villages had more choices in every way. Such a person might gather feathers near a Low village, and white ore up High, and still enjoy the apples and the good potters' clay near Home Village. A person with many villages could choose his work based on what brought him delight, instead of on what was close at hand. That person could live where he wanted to, and travel up and down trading his wares without bleeding away the profits in carriers' fees. And, just as important, that person would have many villages to visit to look for a partner if he wanted one.

On the other hand, there was a lot to be said for finding that your son would have few villages, for then he would be much more likely to settle in Home Village or nearby. With family close at hand, there could be visiting and working together and sharing grandchildren— when it came to washing diapers and keeping babies fed, you needed all the help you could get. And, as the years went by and her legs would carry her to fewer villages, Cam and she wouldn't lose each other— or not so fast, anyway.

So what should a mother wish for? And did it matter? Children and wishes went their own ways.

So Len waited and watched her son avidly. He was her only; his father had fallen off the world when Cam was three and the young widow had never found another partner, although she liked to dance with Fane Soap-Maker when dancing was afoot.

Of course, Cam still came home between journeys — it unraveled her heart to think of the day when soon he might go home to someone else's house — and his mother would set aside the knot she was weaving and he would wash at the spout and they would cook dinner together and she would ask him for news. This was no longer just a courtesy. Cam had grown tall and strong and he was walking to villages that she had never visited, even in the vigor of her first youth.

Sometimes now, Len met Cam coming or going on the path itself as she carried her ropes and twines and knots from village to village. It always startled and delighted her to see his form materialize out of the mists that ranged up and down the world, sometimes cloud overhead, sometimes cloud way down below, and sometimes fog right where she stood. The fogs could make the well-known path mysterious, strange, hard to predict, but Len could always recognize that one long stride, her son's stride, unmistakable among all others, coming towards her at the head of a dim line of walkers. She would greet him sedately, because he was with friends, and they might walk together for a while, if they were going in the same direction. But she would be slower, carrying a load, and soon she would step off the path to let him go ahead with his friends. He would kiss her cheek and she would dust the dew from his hair, and then the youths would file politely around and leave her behind to continue on her laden way.

It came to her that whenever she saw Cam on the path, he was always at the front of the group. She could not remember that it had been that way among her own age-mates, that one person was always in the lead. But Cam was.

As Cam's friends found their ranges, many of them settled on their livelihoods as well, and began to carry real loads up and down the world. There was some excitement at shouldering their first adult freight, especially when this involved something fragile. (Much teasing would be visited upon a carrier who slipped or tripped under a pack of crockery or eggs.)

When a young person began to carry real loads, the challenge of walking changed, becoming more a matter of weight than of distance. And with the question of distance settled, they became less inclined to walk for the sake of walking. But Cam still took to the path, Cam and a handful of his friends still reaching for their limits. Sometimes the old group still walked together to the nearer villages, for friendship's sake. But Len Rope-Maker became aware that Cam's companions for the expeditions to the Far Villages dwindled over time to just a few: Karri and Fox and Hull and Gret. And if they were heading downworld, it might be only Fox and Hull,.

As Rope-Maker, it was to Len that people came when they were ready to be partners. There were many reasons for binding lives together, but when the couple was young, it was usually about one thing only. Len had been young once (so *long* ago!)— she didn't blame them. But she would put on her stern face and talk to them about the knot called the Never-Ending Braid. "This isn't easy, you know. It's not *supposed* to be. And it has to be done right, so that it lays flat and neat on your partner's arm. You have to get it tight enough so that it won't slip off and get lost, but not so tight that it's going to constrict when it swells up in a rain." She told them that the Never-Ending Braid chafes sometimes, no matter how well-tied, especially when it is new. But, she admitted, "It does get softer as time goes by." She showed them the one on her own wrist, tied there by Cam's father. She ran two fingers over the smooth, interlocking cord, and remembered.

"Don't squander my time and twine on the Never-Ending Braid unless you are sure and certain," she would say severely. "Once tied, it's like two rat's nests to undo, unless you use a blade, which would be a wicked murder of fine cordage." But if the young people seemed sincere and their ranges overlapped enough for a fair chance at a happy life together, Len Rope-Maker taught them the secret of the Never-Ending Braid, and checked their work, and helped them until they got it right, finished with the ends tucked hidden in the weave. Len would stand at her door and watch as the young couple walked away. Holding hands, usually. And they would be seen to wear the knot, and it would be known that there was a new partnership on the world.

So Len Rope-Maker knew when some of Cam's age-mates began to partner and she wondered whom Cam might choose. She thought sometimes it might be Fox, because they still walked far together even after many of their friends settled down. But then Fox would sit down to share a stew with them, and they would laugh hard, and Len would think, "No, it is friendship." And then the two would stride off together side by side, where the path was wide through Home Village, and one of them might take the other's hand, and Len would think, "Yes, it is love." And then they would be out of sight, and gone for many days, leaving her to wonder.

Love. Friendship. Friendship. Love.

In this way, work and walking and waiting braided together the life of Len Rope-Maker as her son came near to being eighteen years old. Hull found her limits, and Karri too, and now it was only Cam and Fox who pushed higher and lower on the path, always together, going further than they'd gone before.

One afternoon, Cam returned after being away for many days. Fox was not with him, which was a unusual. The two had the habit of eating together at Len's house on their first night back in Home Village. But on this day, Cam came alone. Hmmm…

He leaned his hickory walking stick against the side of the house and threw down his pack, and then himself, onto the steps of the little porch where Len was washing nettle-fibers. She rose and dried her hands, and sat down beside him, giving him a quick one-armed hug in greeting. The speckled hen pecked gently at the stones around their feet, searching for some overlooked thing.

"What's the news, my traveler?"

Cam looked at his feet. He looked at his hands. His fingernails were grimy from the trail. He didn't look at Len, but spoke to the wood of the bottom step.

"Fox turned back."

Len started to speak, to ask for more, but she saw her son slumped there on the steps. Something had happened. Be still. Wait.

He went on, low-voiced. "People told us there was a hot spring just up the path, three hours above Seventeenth Village Up…" Seventeenth Village Up. As high as that. Len felt a kick in her heart, like when Cam had been inside her belly. Even then, his legs kicked out, striding, reaching into the distance his mother had never dreamed of.

"…and I wanted to see it, but Fox wouldn't go on. It was snowing some, maybe a little ice on the path, and she said it was too late in the day and…, oh, it doesn't matter. Fox *never* turns down a chance for a wallow. But she did this time, Len. Fox turned back. And I came with her, and didn't get to see the hot spring. Just think of it, Len, hot water that bubbles up in the snow. It's up there. Just a little way further."

Len studied her son's profile. His face was tense. Real adult misery crimped the skin around his eyes.

"Fox is dear to you," she observed.

"No," he snapped. "Or, yes. Maybe. But that's not the real point, is it?"

"Of course not," she agreed. "But, remind me again: The real point is…?"

He jumped up and began to pace, his head just clearing the lower limbs of the apple tree. The green fruit was just beginning to take on hints of yellow, the glimmer of the ripeness to come. "I told you: Fox turned back. She's beginning to find her limits, Len. I'm not. Steep pitches don't tire me. Scree doesn't trip me up. The long hauls between the Far Villages don't wear me out. Friends younger than me are finding their limits every day, youngsters not even in my age group. But not me. Never me. I walk and walk, but I can't find any end to it. The world is a string of villages, one after another, and I'll go to all of them, one after another. I can do the business of a Far Walker; of course I can. I can carry the news and arrange trail-tending chores between villages and broker trade and, and, and…." He stopped in front of her, his hands hanging slack and empty. "But where are my limits, Len? Why can't I find them?"

Len pulled him down onto the step beside her. "And what's made this all seem so terrible? What's changed? Just a little while ago, the prospect of visiting a new village would make you grab your pack, forget to shut the door behind you, and rush off with Fox."

"With Fox," Cam echoed softly, leaning into her. "When Fox finds her limits, who will I walk with, Len? Will I walk alone?"

Len was silent. She thought about the many miles she'd walked in her lifetime, and the long hours on the path. Seven hours to First Village Down, nine more to the next, the villages spaced like uneven beads along the path. (A flash of memory: Yarrow's back on the path in front of her under a heavy trade-pack. Yarrow's stick swinging with his long, strong legs. Yarrow's voice, blown back over his shoulder, a question.) The path had unrolled like a spool when she had somebody to walk with, but how the hours could drag when she was alone. What would it have been like if those hours had been days, the long days of a Far Walker among the distant villages, where people spoke strangely and there would be no easy, relaxed conversation at the end of the day. Unless you walked with a companion...

"Shreve walks far, too, Cam. If you need someone to talk to... About that life, I mean. She must have—"

"Len, Shreve doesn't even *believe* there are villages beyond Seventeenth Up." His voice went a little shrill at this. "That's just silly; anyone with eyes can see that the path keeps going. And we could go on, too. But we turned back." He took a breath. "We call Shreve 'Far-Walker' because her range is longer than anyone we know, but the path goes on and on. How far, Len? How far does it go? Shreve has never even seen the ocean! What can she tell me — what can anyone tell me — about the life of a Far-Walker, if they've never even seen the ocean?"

"But I thought it was only a...."

"No, it's real and I've seen it. Fox and I, together; we saw it below us, a long way down, when we got off the path..." Len started to say something about this, but restrained the mother-impulse. "...and scrambled out onto a rock overhang to take a nap in the sun away from the ants. The clouds below us broke apart and there it was, very far down, flat, like the bottom of a pan. It's blue-green and shiny like that jade that Tel Jewelry-Maker got from Seventh Village Down. The ocean is real, Len. It's down there, below all the trees and mists and clouds, and it's as big as the sky. It made Fox cry, just from the bigness of it. You could see it, too, if you wanted to. It's easy. We could take you. We could show it to you."

"Not me, Cam!" she laughed. "I get heat rash if I go below Fourth Village Down. But I'm glad to know the old stories stay true. It pleases me that the world has a bottom. I wonder if you'll go there someday and walk on the jade ocean."

"And if I'll do it alone." Cam added somberly.

"Fox turned back one time, Cam. One time doesn't mean she's found her limit for life."

"But she will, Len. Everyone does. Everyone but me. I have to walk, Len. I have to keep going. The path goes somewhere;

I have to see it through to the end. But, Len— I don't want to walk alone."

They sat on the step together, mother and son, and the nettle fibers soaked in pots of cloudy water. A rising breeze stirred the apple tree.

"Maybe," Len said carefully, "that's your limit, Cam."

He was silent for a long moment, looking up the stony path that ran past his mother's doorstep and on towards the upworld villages. Len shivered.

"No," he said, "it's not."

And her son got up and went to wash himself at the spout where the bright chilly water broke out from the wall of the world.

That night, Len dreamed that she was saying goodbye to somebody, a man. She did not know him, didn't even know his name, but he was unspeakably precious to her. After everything was said, he turned away from her and took one step. Before he could take another, her hand flashed out with speed beyond human to save him from a fall, and fastened on his arm.

But her fingers sank through the heavy wool of his shirt, through the heavy muscle of his arm, through the sweet softness of the child's arm within, and closed on nothing at all.

She woke with her hands clenched in tight fists.

Cam stayed near Home Village for a while, helping Len gather nettle stems from the rock face beside the path. It was autumn and the plants had done their growing and were dry and gray. He walked with Fox to villages where they had been before, carrying news and rope. Len wondered if, in spite of what he'd said, Cam was finding his limits. Was he settling?

He was in Len's house a good bit during the wicked weather of winter, sleeping and eating a lot. He was taking on more substance, Len saw, filling out the frame of a man. He had no great talent for rope-making, she admitted to herself; his big hands were impatient and he was too restless for tasks that took long sitting. But he was much help with breaking the fibers out of the stems, and teasing them free from bits of bark and old dry pulp.

Fox was often in the house too, the tightness between the two seemingly relaxed. Fox also took a hand at the work and seemed to enjoy the way the thin dense cords emerged from the soft hanks of fiber. Like blond hair, she said. Just like braiding a child's blond hair. It warmed Len to see that Fox, too, took pleasure in how the twisting and twining multiplied the strength of the fibers. Maybe there would be another rope-maker in the village? But it was hard to really tell what Fox loved.

When spring had settled on them and the sun grew stronger every day, Cam asked Fox if she would walk with him to Seventeenth Village Up and beyond, to see the hot spring they had missed in the fall because of the snow.

Fox looked down into the roots of the apple tree that shaded Len's porch, as if she were listening for something far away, some sound she could only hear if she didn't look at him.

"Let's not, Cam. Let's go down to that pool below Twelfth Village Down, where the water jumps out of the rock in that big waterfall. Let's walk hard and get all sweaty, and then jump into the cold water."

And Cam agreed.

They stuffed their packs with dried apples for eating and rope for trading, and started down the path, side by side, sticks in hand. Len watched them until they got to the bend, and wondered how far they would go.

They left their heavy woolen Home Village overshirts and trousers at the house where they guested in Seventh Village Down and walked on gaily in bright linen clothing that would be thought barely decent in Home Village. They offered rope and news at every village, and greeted old friends, congratulating new partners, exclaiming over the babies that had come since they had last passed through.

They got flatbread and new fruit at Twelfth Village Down, and carried it with them to the pool, which wasn't so far below as they remembered.

They shrieked and splashed in the icy water, ducking under the small powerful waterfall that gushed out of the rocks above and letting it pound them hard on the shoulders and back. Here in the heat of the lower villages, the water that burst from the wall of the world was cold; Cam pushed away the thought of a hot spring steaming in the snow and they feasted by the pool, curled close while the late afternoon sun dried their skin.

They could have gone back to Twelfth Village Down to spend the night, but the downhill path pulled Fox along, and Cam followed her. They left the pool and went further down. Down, down, to the rock overhang that jutted out from the vertical green forest. Once again, they ventured off the path and out onto the rock. They peered over the edge, hoping to see again the place where the world ended in the great jade flatness, but clouds lay across the shoulders of the world like a white shawl below them.

So Fox and Cam did not get to share the marvel of the sun sinking into the ocean that day. But because they had come so far already and twilight was on their heels, they stayed that night on the rock, shared other astonishing things, and were not disappointed.

The rock held the day's warmth for a long time.

When he went, Len did not tell Cam to be careful, but she did give him his father's warmest wool shirt. She had taken it for Cam at the sad gift-giving, though it had been far too large for him to use. But it fit him now, and she asked him to wear it in memory of Yarrow, his father, and in warning, because Yarrow had fallen off the world on a steep talus slope where the yellow gravel was small and rounded, and rolled beneath his feet. They had not been able to build a cairn where he fell, because the rocks were too loose. But they raised one as near as possible, where the path came again onto solid rock. Len added a stone to it each time she passed; Yarrow was not forgotten.

Len also tried to give Cam a load of rope to carry, to trade for warmer clothes when he got to the High villages. But Cam told her that up where people needed wool and fur to stay warm even in the summer, nettle fiber became stiff and brittle. Len Rope-Maker had not known this.

So she gave him instead a bag of her most intricate knots, which she hoped would be of some use to him in trade. (And Reny Leather-Worker at Thirteenth Village Up took some of these knots from Cam for a pair of sturdy boots lined with fur. Reny studied Len's knots and worried out their secrets and learned to work them in narrow strips of goatskin. And that is the way Len Rope-Maker's knots became known in the High villages where she never walked.)

So Cam went away, not like a startled goat, but like a thoughtful young man, taking what he needed and saying goodbye to his mother and his friends. He traded some days carrying apples downworld for a present for his love, a raindrop of watery blue-green jade hung from a fine braid of nettle-cord. Then he said goodbye to Fox, who was distressed and undecided and didn't want him to go alone and didn't want to go with him, but let him drape the pendant around her neck. When all that was done, Cam set out to find either his limit or the top of the world. And he was happy on the upward path, knowing that he would come back. Knowing that he and Fox would take the path together some day, down, down, towards the sea.

And Len Rope-Maker's life continued to braid together work and walking and waiting. She moved the workbench on her porch and the chair where she sat, so that she could watch the upworld path while she plied her nettle ropes. Len did not believe her son was dead, though he did not return. Some day he would come again, if only to pass through Home Village on his way to the sea. Cam was a Far-Walker; he would see the bottom of the world some day, and there was only one path.

Len did not know that high above the tree-line, above the snow-line, above Twenty-Third Village Up, the world becomes less steep. The incline eases, until suddenly a walker finds himself on flat ground.

Fox didn't know what to do with herself. Everyone thought it was because Cam was gone, but the truth was that she had never known. Her friends had found their trades easily, naturally, like pebbles rolling downworld. Gret knew since he was tiny that he cared for bees and honey and wax above all things. Tanen discovered his passion for baking when he was eleven. How did a person find a love like that?

To Fox, everything was interesting, in a mild sort of way. Ever since she could remember, Stone and Becca had always told her she could learn any trade she chose and she believed them. Her hands were good. She knew this from helping the grown-ups at their tasks around Home Village. She was strong too, strong enough to be a climber or a hunter if she wanted. And she could get along with people and animals; she could become a healer or a midwife if she set her mind that way. She was smart enough to learn the craft-lore of any job that called her.

But she had never heard that call: "This! *This* is the work that will bloom in your hands. This is the work that will earn your food and your joy and your name." Was she deaf? Was she missing some sense, like sight or smell, that points a person to their craft? She knew she could do any job. She just didn't care which.

So maybe it didn't matter. (But what if it did?) Maybe she should just settle down and give her life to making ropes. She liked it well enough, she supposed. She knew Len would take her on as apprentice if she asked. They got along well, laughed a lot. Going to Len would get her out of her parents' house and away from their anxious nudges to try this and try that. "Maybe you'll like…" "Grada is looking for a helper, I hear…" "Have you considered…?"

Of course she'd considered. She'd considered everything, including the possibility that walking with Cam might be all the passion she would ever find in life. She should have gone with him. She should have just ignored that stubborn backward lean of her heart, the niggling voice that whispered, "No, *that* way is not for you." But she had let him go and maybe the best she could do was to make her peace with the ration of pleasure she got each day from steady friendship and work without heart-fire. Holding out for some uncertain dream kept her unsettled, striving. She could learn to be happy in Home Village, doing the work at hand.

But what if she was wrong? What if there was something she hadn't found yet, somewhere further down the path, in some village she had never seen? If there were, then settling down would be giving up, closing the door on brightness. She felt the urge to walk, to see. But there was nobody to go with her now, not to the Far-Below villages. Not towards the sea.

So the moodiness that Fox's parents spoke about in low voices was not (as they thought) grief for the foolhardy Far-Walker who had launched himself at the sky. It was Fox's divided heart, debating whether to stay or go.

Cam stops to catch his breath, gasping in the thin, cold air. He pushes back his fur hood and squints against the ice-sharp wind and the sun that glares off the white, white world. It is flat, as flat as a village terrace. He begins to laugh. He has come to the top of the world.

But the path goes on, a clear groove in the icy snow in front of him, showing the way, showing where other feet have trafficked.

He pulls out a handful of dried goat-meat from his pack and chews it thoughtfully. But there is never really any question. Cam Far-Walker pulls up his hood again and gathers it tightly to protect his ears and cheeks. His world narrows to a little window, framed in fur. Cam walks on, along the path as it begins to slope downhill again, and still Cam walks on, down, onto the other side of the world.

And what Cam does not know is that Fox dreams of walking also, with a pack full of rope and knots from Home Village, down and down, all the way to the ocean. And in her dream, Fox finds the ocean is not jade and cannot be walked upon. There is no path. It is restless living water, though salty, like tears.

What should she do?

She thought of following him.

She thought of waiting for him, but she hated to wait. She'd always hated it.

She thought of taking the path downworld, of walking until she got to where people talk strangely and you can see the polished ocean far below.

She thought of asking for an apprenticeship, though she had never found her limits, and apprentices can't be running up and down the path like children.

She didn't know, she didn't know, she didn't know, and she found herself just waiting. Waiting to know what she should do. Waiting to hear that Cam's body had been found (or not found.) Waiting to see his easy rolling stride bring him to her door.

She grew sick of waiting. She grew sick of her parents worrying about her and sick of her friends inviting her to do things and go places. (What should she do? Where should she go? And why?) Only in Len's house did she find the quiet to wait and fume about waiting.

Because Len was waiting, too. Somehow, that comforted Fox. She could feel the waiting, though she couldn't see it because, on the outside, Len was the same. She rose early, made her bed, washed, dressed, worked, walked, talked, cooked, and ate.

How could she eat? Fox couldn't understand. The roiling bubbles of waiting made food sit uneasily on her stomach. Even the smell of Len's stewpot made her queasy.

She despised waiting, but she didn't know how to stop. She spun like a windmill: I am waiting for something. I hate waiting, so I should do something. But I don't know what to do, so I do nothing. I have to wait to know what to do. But I hate waiting.

She became unpleasant to be around.

Then, one morning, after she had turned away from another offer of porridge she didn't want, Len asked her if she might be pregnant.

Len sat on a stool by the fireplace with Fox cross-legged on the floor in front of her. Fox kept the drop-spindle turning by brushing it with her hand whenever it slowed while the older woman struggled to feed out the wispy fluff from the thick hank of wool in a steady, even stream.

They had arrived at this awkward two-person style of spinning after a certain amount of hilarity. Len Rope-Maker, known for making the best cordage on the path, simply could not spin yarn worth a damn. People up and down the world, small children even, mastered this simple chore so naturally that they could spin while they talked, while they walked, while they carried loads from one village to another. But Len, who boasted that she made "everything that holds the world together," who could knot, braid, and twist two-ply, three-ply and four-ply cord, the best on the world, had never learned to spin. And neither had Fox.

They had reasoned, though, that spinning could not be very difficult, as so many people managed it. So Fox had given a hundred feet of heavy rope for some wool, spindles, and a quick lesson while she was in Seventh Village Up. The trade had seemed expensive to her, for a bag of fuzz from the hind end of a sheep and two notched dowels stuck through stone discs. But she had been made to understand that the shearing and washing and carding of wool, and the grinding of perfectly centered holes through perfectly round water-stones required skills undreamed of, as well as prodigies of effort. She shrugged off the cost. The baby would come in the winter. The baby would need to be kept warm. The baby. Cam's…

Her baby.

If it had to be, maybe winter wasn't such a bad time for it. Carrying the weight and heat of it wouldn't plague her during the summer months. And by the time the sun came round again, the little one would be ready to enjoy it. *He* would be ready, she thought to herself. Or *she* would be ready. Fox felt the baby both ways— sometimes male as if Cam still rang inside her like a bell, sometimes female as if only a girl could fit into the life of a mother without a man.

At any rate, he or she, the baby would need to be kept warm until spring came again. So Fox brought wool down the world to Len and they began to learn to spin.

They started after dinner. By lamplight. Inside the house, not on the airy open porch where Len did most of her work in the warm months. Fox was a little amused that Len Rope-Maker preferred privacy for her first efforts with this new fiber, so soft and crinkled, so unlike the stiffer, straighter, springier nettle strands. Len was not vain about many things; still, she clearly didn't want her first tries at spinning to be public comedy.

But she and Fox had laughed until they panted. The cream-white wool acted like a living thing possessed by a malicious intention to make fools of them. Their yarn swelled until it was as fat as rope, then shriveled to hair-thinness, then broke altogether, sending the spindles rolling on the floor to the great delight of Goose. Goose viewed the whole proceedings as a performance for her benefit and obligingly chased after the runaway spindles, unwinding, snarling, and chewing on their hard-won yards of eccentric, uneven yarn.

"That beast was never much of a mouser," Len groused. "I don't see why she should discover this sudden passion for the hunt now."

"Maybe she's never been around such spirited prey before. These things are pretty lively, for wood and stone." Fox disentangled Goose from spindle and yarn. "Let's start over."

Eventually they arrived at a sort of teamwork, with one of them managing the spindle and one of them managing the wool. They began to find a rhythm in the work, and something like evenness in the gauge and tightness of their yarn. Len reflected ruefully on the teasing she would get if her neighbors saw her and Fox working one spindle between them. Oh, well. They would get better with practice.

"You would think twenty years with fibers and cords would count for something," Len sighed as she teased back a wad of wool that wanted to join the yarn all in a bunch.

"And we haven't even gotten to the knitting yet," Fox said darkly.

"Ah, yes: the knitting."

They spun for a long time like that, seeing the coil of yarn around the spindle grow. Their yarn did become more smooth and regular, more like something that could indeed be rolled into balls and knitted up into warm caps and wraps for a new baby. (Her baby. Hers, alone.) Then Len offered to change places with Fox, who took over the bundle of wool, while Len settled onto the floor to keep the spindle turning. It took them a while to find their rhythm again.

After a long spell of silence, Len asked, "The baby, after you've weaned it... Will you leave it with me sometimes? When you are out on the path, walking?"

A rush of wetness prickled at Fox's eyes. She concentrated on keeping the flow of the wool smooth, steady, and even.

"Do you want me to?"

"Yes. Very much. I'd like to help raise it— if you want."

"I would like that, Len, if you're willing."

"I am. More than just willing— eager. Maybe because I only ever had Cam, and one wasn't enough. Yarrow fell off the world too soon." She was silent for a few moments, then went on. "It would make me happy to think of a little one in the house again. All that noise and activity. It's getting too quiet for me sometimes, and too orderly. I don't want to be old, yet, Fox. Babies help with that."

"You'd get less work done," Fox pointed out.

"I know. Cam was a handful in those years between when he found his feet and when he found his legs."

"Maybe sometimes it can stay with Stone and Becca, too, when both you and I are on the path. Their first grandchild. They'll want some time, too. But mostly with you and me, I think."

"But..." Len said carefully, "you'll still be living with them, won't you?"

Fox fumbled a bit and the wool fed out thin. Len slowed the spindle to match. This time the yarn, though slim, didn't break. "I'm thinking to share the work with you, Len. I'm thinking, what if I came into your house?" There. It was said.

"You mean as an apprentice? You're good with the work, but I didn't know you had settled..."

"I was thinking... No, stop a minute. Let the blighted spindle rest." Len obligingly stopped the spindle between her palms. Fox took it from her, and fingered the reel of new wool yarn they had made. Rough and whiskery, but real. "Look what we made, Len: real yarn. It was just a puff of wool before."

"Definitely yarn, I'd say. I wouldn't want to offer it for trade, but I think it will do to keep a body warm."

Fox set the spindle and the wool, joined by a strand of almost-yarn, down on the table.

"What I was thinking, Len, what I was wondering was: Would you like to be partners? Share the baby? Share the work? Share the life?"

"You mean, until Cam comes back?"

"Yes," she said, with just a little catch in her voice. "Until Cam comes back."

Len picked up the spindle and wool. She rolled the fibers between her fingers in the old familiar movement with which she plied cord. "He's not dead, Fox. I know they say he fell off the world. But he didn't. I would know. With Yarrow...

I knew. In my bones, I knew. In my fibers. In every part of me. Cam is still walking, Fox. I *know* this. He'll come back to Home Village someday. He'll find you. And this child. His child. And he'll tie the Never-Ending Braid on your wrist."

Fox inhaled deeply. She was already beginning to feel a little something that took up space inside her, something to press against when she breathed. "Maybe he will, someday. Some days, I think that, too. But some days I don't know. He could walk up to the door tomorrow. Or never. In the meantime, there's this baby, and there's life. I love my parents, but I'm ready to be out of their house. And they're ready for me to be gone, I think. It's time for Becca to take on apprentices; she's getting a very good name. But I'm no potter. Potters sit in one place all day long and their hands are always dirty. And I can never, ever get the clay centered properly on the wheel." She sighed. "Becca's daughter will never be Becca. Kel from Third Village up has asked for the place. She and Stone told him he would be welcome, as soon as I got myself settled." Fox laughed, a little chokingly. "And now there will be me *and* a baby— no room for apprentices, unless a neighbor suddenly feels the call to pottery." She took another great lungful of air. "So: Would you like to be partners?"

"Fox, if it's a matter of needing a place to go, you're welcome in my house, always. We don't have to tie ourselves to each other for that to be true. You can just move in, and move out when you want to."

Fox squeezed her hand. Her eyes glistened. "Thank you. I'll settle for that if you don't want more."

"You mean that, even knowing that you have a place to be, you'd still want the bond?"

"Yes, I do. I... I want to be part of something. I need it."

"Knowing it might not be forever? When Cam comes back... Or if you settle on another... You're so young."

"But not a child, Len— I know nothing lasts forever. Nothing but the path."

"Well, the Never-Ending Braid *can* be undone. It's not easy, but I've untangled enough, I should be able to find my way out of my own..."

"And this, Len?" Fox touched the weathered knot that bound Len's wrist, the Never-Ending Braid that had been placed there so many years before by Cam's father. Len looked at it blankly, as if she had forgotten it for a moment.

"It's very old," she said. "But the cord is good. We can use it again."

And Len used that same cord, Yarrow's cord, to weave the Never-Ending Braid around Fox's wrist. But Fox plied fresh cordage, into which she twisted a strand of their new-made yarn among the nettle fibers. Len told her this was silly and sentimental, and probably wouldn't do the cord-strength much good, but once the knot was woven she rather liked the odd piebald look of it, with white fuzzy wool among the smooth russet nettle-strands. It gave her the idea to visit Bren Dyer, to discuss staining some fibers so she could make cords of blended colors.

And it was seen that Len and Fox wore the knot and it was known that there was a new partnership on the world.

That is how Fox came into the house of Len Rope-Maker, as partner, daughter, and apprentice. On the coldest nights, the two women shared Len's big bedstead and all the blankets in the house. But mostly, Fox slept in Cam's single bed, where the pillow-smell still hinted of his hair.

It was all new. Cam threw back his hood.

He had come down out of the snows to a strange tilted land of grass and small streams. Not up-and-down like the wall that carried the path of the world he knew, nor table-flat like the terraces that sustained his villages and their gardens and orchards. This was something in between: a slant land, like the slope of a roof. Trickles of snowmelt joined, braided together, and unraveled again. The path wandered and curled around them, circling the boggy bits and winding its looping way ever lower.

As he walked, he spotted small furry animals he had never seen before, brown, about as long as his arm, low like groundhogs, never close enough to see clearly. When he came upon them, they sat bolt upright like squirrels, then trundled off and disappeared into the grass. In shape, they reminded him of the large water-rats that played in the falls at Fifth Village Up, but they were nowhere near as quick.

"It will be wet sleeping out tonight," he thought as he squelched along the muddy path, "unless I come to a village."

Although he was below the snowline, he was still very high and it would be cold when the sun went down.

He had half-resigned himself to cutting grass to make some kind of nest that night when he came to such a strangeness that his eyes almost refused to see it.

He knew what it was; in a village it would be no oddity. In a village, not every door opens directly onto the path. Fields may be set back quite far on the larger village terraces. So it happens that grooves are worn in the ground as feet pass from one house to another, or make their way back and forth to an orchard. These may look like little paths, but are not paths of course, just ruts that cross and join, well-worn choices in the traffic of the village. There is only one path.

But Cam was on that path, with no village in sight, and still right at his feet, there was a crossing. What he could only think of as a second path sloped downward off to his right and continued to his left as well, while the path, the real path, the path he had been walking all his life, continued downhill directly in front of him.

A second path. A crossing. He felt a little queasy as his mind stretched to hold the possibilities. He tried to think. The path meant traffic, meant villages, meant direction, meant destinations. Two paths crossing meant... His mind shied away from the thought, back to the familiar, back to the walking, the planting of one foot in front of the other, the swing of weight from one leg to another, the distance eaten up one bite at a time.

He made himself step over the strange place, the crossing, the choice that was part of no village but of the path itself, and he walked on, down the slanted world towards the tree-line.

"Expecting," they called it. That was just a nice word for it; it was waiting, pure and simple. Babies were nothing but waiting.

She had always hated the last blizzard of winter, when one final fall of snow would drift over the door and halfway up the windows. The walls that kept them cozy all through the cold months would begin to feel like a very small box and she would nearly perish of impatience, knowing spring was coming but it was not yet here.

Hating to wait made her a very bad cook. When she was hungry, she wanted to eat. Her roasts were pink and bloody, her loaves were heavy and yeasty, and her porridges were what Stone gently called "chewy."

And now, this business of the baby. The baby was coming but it wasn't yet here. Her breasts and belly were rising like loaves, but she had to wait. Something was in the oven, but she had to wait.

She *hated* waiting. She really did.

The excitement of moving out of her parents' home helped for a while. Carrying her things to a new place. Carving out space for them in Len's house, amidst rope-gear and Cam's old clothes. (Cam: the other waiting, for both of them.)

She settled into a new routine. The change did her good. Len treated her like a grown-up, as long as she ate "properly," whether she felt like it or not. Even Becca was different when they met, talking to her like a newly-minted adult with her own place in the world. She liked not being treated like a child, though she still had the old bright hunger to stretch out on the path. Walking soothed her restless mind. Sometimes, walking the path, she could even forget about waiting for a while. (Until the way her balance now was different on some ladder or set of carved steps reminded her: the baby. Yes, the baby.)

Work helped with the waiting, too. It distracted her from the mystery of what was coming and focused her on what was *now*. Rope-making was good for that. A lot like spinning that way. If you let your mind wander, things would get away from you. Suddenly one ply would be much fatter than the other. Then you would catch yourself and have to undo your work and make it right. Rope kept her thoughts from rolling away.

Laughing helped, too, and stories. She and Len shared many house-hours now, working and eating. Fox's fingers grew strong and tough from twirling the fibers into the twist that made them strong. The two women also walked together, trading rope and cord up and down the path for food and rope-stuff that didn't grow near Home Village, dogbane and leather-root and the inner bark of the trees that found a toe-hold on the steepness of the world— Len loved learning new fibers. There was a lot of time for conversation, and many tales to tell. Len had loved and partnered, borne a child, become a widow, mothered Cam, and earned a great name on the world. Fox, though young, had walked farther up and down the path, seen many things, and heard the stories of things beyond what she had seen. Both women enjoyed good talk and good listening. They had a lot to say to each other.

But for all the working and walking, laughing and talking, at the end of the day Fox lay down in the little bed — Cam's bed — alone and in the dark, to wait. Something was coming: a birth, a baby. Being a "mother." It was coming and it was not yet here. Cam was coming back, or he wasn't. But not yet here. Not yet.

Not yet.

She wished that she could knit in the dark like blind Gertha, because in bed, here in the dark, there was only waiting.

Nothing brought home to Cam how new this place was more than walking into... what should he call it? First Village Below Snow? How could he be in a place and not know its name?

All his life, the geography of his world had been gauged by two things only, direction and distance. Were you above or below the village you called Home? And how many villages were situated between? Knowing the answers to those two questions told you all you needed to know about where you stood on the world.

But here he was, coming into a large village he had reached by going both up and down. Where was this place? What name did it carry for him? Twenty-Fourth Village *Over*? Cam took it for granted that people would either call it Home Village if they lived there or some numbered reference from their own Home Villages if they did not. He could not imagine there being anyone to ask what *he* should call it, even if he could have made himself understood, which he could not.

Cam was a Far-Walker; he was used to the language around him changing as he walked. Since boyhood, he had delighted in the different turns of phrase he noticed, the different words for common things, the changes in rhythms and pitch, the way certain sounds became flattened and clipped as he walked high or became rounded and drawn out when he went low. He expected to have to listen with care when he was far from home. And always, before a trade in the Far Villages, he would say back the terms slowly and precisely — "Ten yards of heavy cord, we agree, for that fine, fat piglet?" — to make sure there was no misunderstanding.

No chance of misunderstanding here, he thought. No understanding of any sort.

Distance was difference, he knew. Children learned that early as they explored the tall wall of the world. But the path connected them all, held the villages like beads on a single string, and he had never before walked anywhere patient attention could not tease out the sense of what someone was telling him, whether it was a barter offer or directions to where a walker could find food and a roof for the night.

Never before this day. As he walked into the village without a name, he greeted the people he passed and if their answers bore any kinship to the language of his world, he couldn't hear it. How lonely would he be, he wondered. And how hungry, too, unless he found a friendly house to offer him a traveler's due?

He had come into the place feeling like a man who had done a new thing, an enormous thing— he had crossed over the roof of the world, a thing you'd think people would be interested in. But no one rushed to the windows. No children came running to see who he was. In fact, a little gang of seven- or eight-year-olds hustled past him with barely a wave of greeting.

He felt deflated and homesick for the shouts of welcome he was used to: offers of hospitality and queries about what his pack held to trade. He was tired and hungry and weighed down by the heavy furs that had gotten him over the peak of the world, but were now no more than a load on his back. They were all he owned, but couldn't be used as trade-goods; he would need them if he ever hoped to go home. He had finished up all his pack-food the day before.

He strode on into First Village New World, and wondered what was wrong with these people. Didn't they see him? Didn't they see that a traveler had come from far? But other than a passing nod and a few words of casual greeting that he didn't understand, no one seemed to notice.

Just being there, after such a feat of effort, seemed astonishing to him. "Look at me!" he wanted to shout. "I'm from another place! An altogether *other* place!" A world that is different from here, a place where people know how to welcome Far-Walkers. But these people calmly went about their business as if the most remarkable thing had not just happened, as if having strangers walk into their village from the other side of everything was commonplace. A dim haze of worry began to gather: If people didn't care for travelers in this strange tilted land, what was he going to do?

He began to search the faces of the people he passed for some possibility of being received, some opening. But though the eyes that met his eyes were friendly enough, none seemed to see his need. None offered him the hearth-fire of warmth and welcome he sought. Not even a cup of water.

His footsteps slowed in front of a house where a tall old woman was piling wooden shingles into neat stacks at the base of a ladder. This was a story Cam understood without language.

"Can I help you?" he asked.

She smiled up at him, and he saw that she was not so old after all. No older than his mother; he had mistaken her age because of her silver hair. She said something he didn't understand. It sounded friendly, so he tried again.

"Can I help you?" He mimed lifting a stack of shingles up towards the roof and then hammering. She laughed and nodded and went back to her work. Cam stopped her and carefully strung his pantomime question together: He pointed towards himself, then lifted an invisible stack of roofing up high, then hammered the air. For emphasis, he pointed to himself again, flexed his muscles to show how strong he was, and looked at the white-haired woman.

She studied him for a long thoughtful moment, and then nodded. She said something that sounded affirmative to his hungry ears. He threw down his pack, grasped her hand, and thanked her in the only words he knew, hoping that she would understand some part of how grateful he was. She patted his arm; he thought she understood. She asked him another question, then mimed putting something in her mouth. She pointed to him.

Cam nodded enthusiastically and grasped her hand again. "Yes, very hungry. Very, *very* hungry. Yes. Thank you."

She started towards the door of the house, but turned back. She pointed at herself. "Lalileh," she pronounced.

"Lalileh," he repeated. "Lalileh, I'm Cam."

"I'm Cam," she echoed.

He laughed. "No, just 'Cam.' Cam Far-Walker. Cam."

"Cam," she nodded, and went to get him a bowl of soup.

The whetstone ran smoothly down the blade. After the stroke, Fox tilted Len's paring knife in the sun so she could see if she'd done it right. The slenderest ribbon of bright metal glinted down the cutting edge, flat and even. Good! She'd held the blade and stone at the correct angle to each other. She turned the hilt in her hand to do the other side.

"You sharpened that yesterday, Fox."

"I know. I like sharpening things. You want me to do your shears, too? Hand them over..."

"No, thanks. I think you just did them last week. They don't really need it that often."

"I don't mind. I love seeing that little shiny strip the whetstone leaves. And getting the edge back— going from blunt to sharp! I can get it to where it'll shave my arm-hairs now, just like you showed me."

Len snipped off a tassel of nettle-hair from the rope she was trimming. Each time she added a bundle of fibers to fill out the ply, she left a little tail hanging out. These had to be trimmed away before the rope was ready for trade. "Neatening up," she called it.

"These seem pretty sharp right now," she said, laying down the scissors.

"I bet I can get them sharper."

"The thing is, Fox, that if you sharpen something that's already sharp, you'll wear it out faster that way."

"Why? I don't get it— I thought you *liked* having your tools sharp. You said, 'Blunt breaks; sharp slices.'"

"I did. And it does. It's great to have all my tools nice and sharp, and I appreciate how you've been keeping up with them. But we don't need them shaving-sharp every single day. That's the goal when you pull out the whetstone; if you're putting an edge on something, make it a keen one. But then don't do it again until you need to."

"But I *like* to do it. And I'm getting good at it, too. Look at this." She handed over the knife, handle first as Len had taught her.

The older woman dutifully thumbed the razor edge. "It's perfect, Fox. But tools aren't for sharpening. I mean, they are, but that's not their *purpose*. Their purpose is to work, and to last. Sharpening isn't just something to do. It's about what's good for the tool. Remember the whetstone doesn't so much *add* sharpness as *take away* bluntness. Every pass with the whetstone rubs some of the metal away. And if you keep sharpening every blade in sight, my tools will be thin as toothpicks in no time."

"Oh. Sorry. I didn't think. I'll stop."

"Don't worry about it. Just wait 'til things lose their edge, that's all."

"Okay."

Two days later, Len surprised her partner with a present: her own belt-knife.

"It's beautiful!" Fox stroked the curves of the smooth white grip. "Thank you, Len!"

"You're welcome. I got you one with a plain bone hilt, so you can decide for yourself how to decorate it. All you have to do is etch in your pattern with a sharp nail, then rub it all over with oak-gall. The color gets caught in the scratches, but barely stains the smooth surface. Like this." She laid her own old knife down by her partner's new one.

Stained smoky gold by sweat and use, Len's knife-handle was decorated with fine dark lines. Now that she was looking at them closely, Fox saw that they traced lacy, delicate outlines of ropes that twined around the handle and looped themselves into some of the same knots that she had seen Len weave, some she'd even learned to do herself.

Next to Len's old knife, Fox's new one looked pale and raw. "I love it just the way it is."

"You want to leave it plain like that?" Len asked.

"For now. It's too beautiful to mark up. And I wouldn't know what to put on it, anyway."

"All right," Len said doubtfully.

"It's wider than yours."

Len laughed. "That's what a lifetime of sharpening will do. It's getting as thin as a flensing knife. I have to take care of it; it has to last. I'm too old to break in a new blade at this point in my life."

Fox thumbed the much broader steel in the moon-white hilt. She understood now why Len didn't want her working the whetstone just for the fun of it. "I've never had my own knife before."

"Your parents never gave you a knife when you were a child? What were they thinking? Sometimes I wonder about Becca and Stone. I really do."

Fox giggled. "Knives aren't that useful, working with clay. You know how we cut clay, don't you, Len?"

"With a knife, I suppose."

Fox was pleased to know a bit of craft-lore that Len didn't. "With a piece of string, held tight between our hands."

"Really? How odd. Why?"

"Because it works, Len."

"Hmmm. You learn something new every day." A string. For cutting. Len pondered the strange ways of potters for a moment, then shook her head and laid more gifts on the table.

"But look, Fox, look here at what else I got you: Dary Cutler had some old blades broken off at the tang, so I brought them for you to sharpen to your heart's content. Twice a day if you want to. You might even get a handle on them and get some use out of them, I don't know. But they're yours and you can do anything you want with them. Only…"

"I know, I know; I'll leave your tools alone. Unless you ask me." And she hugged her.

"Now let's get this table cleared for supper." Len was a little embarrassed by gratitude.

After that, sometimes, in the evenings, after the day's work was done, Fox would sharpen one of her blades to a miracle of keenness and sit shaving long strips of wood from a stick until the metal was satisfyingly blunt again. Then she would happily sharpen it and start over. This mystified Len, but her firebox always had plenty of woodchips for starting the coal-stones. And Fox began to learn to carve.

Fox woke to an empty house. She'd let the fire die.

Len was up the path somewhere, trading for bacon for the winter. It was pig-killing time up above Home Village, with the first freezes working their way down the world. It was cold in the morning, too cold to give up the warmth of the little bed. With no cheerful voice to roust her out for breakfast, there was no real reason to get up. But if she stayed in bed, in *his* old bed by the wall, she would start to think. She should get up.

She was supposed to eat, of course, but she didn't feel like it, and there were things she was supposed to do — gathering the eggs, for one thing, and changing the water in the soaking tubs and the never-ending baby-knitting — but she didn't feel like doing them, either. She tried to think of something she would enjoy, something that would be *fun*, like fun used to be.

Apple harvest had come and gone. With the baby still ripening, they hadn't let her go up on the ladders, so she'd kept herself busy with the slicers, readying the bruised fruit for drying. After the cider-pressing, she'd stood along the wall and watched the dancing until her bones ached and she went off to find a chair.

Now a pillow over her face kept the morning out of her eyes. She considered going looking for one of her old friends, but she didn't really want to talk to anyone who would ask her about the baby, or Cam, or anything at all. She could go by Stone and Becca's for breakfast. They would welcome her with hugs and hot cider. But then there would be the worried eyes and the feeling that they were still waiting for her to figure out what to do with her life.

No, being alone was hard, but being with people was harder. Except Len. It would be good when Len came back. She rubbed her rounding belly and gave herself up to day-dream, just a little, about Cam: walking together, talking, holding hands, laughing, dancing at the apple-harvest, kiss-ing on the rock above the sea, coming together at last. But it was a sour daydream; it ended, like they all did, with him walking away from her. Leaving her. He left her with a baby and went so far away that she couldn't even fight with him, not even in her head. If he were with her, she would have yelled at him, maybe slapped him, too. But he was fallen, maybe, or frozen....

She *had* to get out of bed, even if there was no joy in the day. Doing was better than thinking, even if she didn't know what to do. Getting up— and then there it was, that flutter under her heart, like butterfly wings waving urgently at her: "Get up, get out. Throw back the covers." Wonderingly, she obeyed.

And one thing led to another. It always does. Throwing back the quilts meant she had to wake up the coals in the fireplace to warm the house. Getting the fire going again led to putting the kettle on, which led to eating breakfast, which led to feeding Goose, which led to...

And so, by a series of small stumbles, falling from one thing into the next, another day was gotten through. Work was done, enough work so that Len wouldn't raise her eyebrow in that questioning way when she came home, enough work to keep sorrow, anger, fear, and hope at bay. And the flutter under her heart stayed with her throughout the day. Even when it was still and quiet and she could feel nothing at all, it stayed with her.

The girl was afraid. Jumpy, but not panicky. Able to do what she was told. That was a good sign. She looked strong, but was far too thin. Worrisomely thin. And younger than Lia Midwife liked to see, a child. Well, childhood is over, Lia thought to herself. It ends tonight.

The midwife helped Fox out of her walking clothes, wanting to give a good shaking to whomever had let the little doe out on the path alone at night so late in the year. Why, she was seven months gone if she was a day. Someone was going to get a good talking to.

But that would be later. Right now, between the squeezes, she got the story. The girl's name was Fox, she was from Sixth Village Up, and the baby's father had gone upworld on some errand that wasn't very clear. That was a long time ago, and now she lived with the boy's mother and partnered with her in making rope. She'd come downworld when her village ran out of salt and her water had broken on the path. She'd tumbled into the Singers' house, and they had brought her here and would send word back to her partner.

Lia helped Fox into a loose gown, soft from many washings, and felt her belly, round and tight as a board but nowhere near big enough.

So. A first baby, too small and too early. A scared mother, away from her own place, too young, too thin, and alone.

Lia Midwife put the kettle on for tea. It was going to be a long night.

So the baby came early, while Fox was away downworld.

Len and Goose were eating supper by the fire. There was a pounding at the door, and a man's voice bellowing her name. "What on the world...?" Goose flashed under the bed and Len jumped up to let in Brant Fast-Walker, come to tell her that Fox had been taken in labor at Sixth Village Down. Len cursed. "When? When?"

"Four days now. Lia Midwife said you were to come and bring the necessaries, but not to rush yourself and break your neck and leave her with a new mother to care for until spring. Very forceful she was about it, too, the not rushing and breaking your neck. And, by the way, it's a girl." Brant grinned at her. "Congratulations, Rope-Maker! A baby is always good news, even if it lands in the wrong village."

Idiot man, Len thought as she practically pushed Brant out the door. It's not the where, it's the when! It's too early. More than a month too early.

Her first impulse was to snatch up her stick and start out instantly. But she was a sensible woman. Not like that impossible Fox who had to set out on the path, at this time of year, heavy with child, just because Home Village had run out of salt. Salt! Risking her life, risking the baby, so that everybody's soup would be tasty. Idiot girl. Brant had come to her in the dark, it was cold, the path was already icy in spots, and somebody had to take thought of what they would need. What the baby would need. If it lived. If only it lived. It would be tiny, and they would not soon be bringing a less-than-eight-month infant home on the winter path. Not for weeks, maybe months. If ever. Oh, if ever.

She got out her heavy trade pack and began to fill it with all the woolens Fox had knitted for the baby. On top of the caps and wraps and mitts and leggings, she laid a suit of clothes for Fox and one for her. Then she crammed in all the food she had in the house and all the rope and cord she had ready for trade— they would need something to live on for awhile. Ordinary hospitality to travelers didn't extend for weeks and weeks.

Len filled her water bottle and hung it from a loop on the pack, which she heaved over to rest by the door until dawn, under the hook where her heavy coat waited. She leaned her two winter walking sticks with the sharp iron points against the wall, her heavy high-topped walking boots below them. Goose stropped against her legs, troubled by all this packing.

Len sat down and gathered the cat into her arms. "You know, don't you, Goose? This is no time to be starting down the path. You can smell the snow in the air. But silly Fox had to go, didn't she? Had to get out on the path. Couldn't just sit still by the fire and let it grow inside her, could she? Not our Fox. And now here we are, and I'm going to have to go down the path without you: you, my other partner." She blinked away a wetness in her eyes. Goose peered into her face. "You know that, don't you? You're our other partner, Goose. And we'll come back, but it will be a while. You'll stay here and take care of things for us, won't you? Now let's go see Mel and Thera about looking after you while we're gone."

Just before dawn, Len Rope-Maker started down out of the first snows to look for her partner at the house of Lia Midwife in Sixth Village Down. As the sun came up, it glittered off the curtains of rippled ice that flowed from frozen springs across the rock. The path was slick and tricky right at the beginning, before Len moved downworld from the ice. She walked slowly, bracing her steps with her iron-shod walking sticks where she could; she realized that she walked more carefully today because someone who needed her was waiting. Soon, though, it warmed up and she could relax into walking. A granddaughter. If she lived. Oh, if she lived. The midwife had said not to hurry. That must mean something.

After five days of walking and hoping, overnighting with old friends in villages along the way, Len stooped under the neatly trimmed thatch of the house that had been pointed out as the midwife's. She knocked at the cane-and-wood door, calling out that she'd come to see Fox.

A sharp little woman opened the door to her and was rude, grumpy about Len "letting" a first-time mother walk so far, so late, carrying such a heavy load. "And winter coming down on us, too!" Lia huffed, although as far as Len could tell, "winter" in Sixth Village Down meant nothing more than a pleasant briskness to the air. Len forgot the midwife's testy welcome when she saw, over Lia's shoulder, Fox sitting by the fire, smiling at her, with a very small bundle in her arms. And the baby's name was Jade.

And so it was Fox's reckless and unseasonable pursuit of salt (*Salt!*) that brought the partners to winter six villages closer to the sea — two villages below the rope-maker's ordinary limit — where Len learned a great deal.

First, she learned that not all midwives were soft, motherly souls like Home Village's Deen, who had helped her with Cam. Lia was everything that Deen was not, small and stern and snappy, with strong opinions about everything having to do with babies and no patience for anyone who strayed from her rule. Len was grateful to her, for she was tender and careful with baby Jade and, in a rougher way, with Fox. Len also knew that it was hard to have guests underfoot for a long time, so she did her best to help out around the house, but whatever she did seemed to irritate. If she was rocking the baby, then she wasn't close enough to the fire; what, did she want the little flea to perish of the cold? If she did the laundry, Lia refolded the linens to her own mysterious specifications. She learned to stay out of the kitchen when Lia was there; the clang when Len banged her head on the low-hanging pots seemed to enrage the older woman. *Just as if I might carelessly break them with my skull, instead of the other way around,* Len thought— but kept her thought to herself. The midwife found Len's cooking bland, her housekeeping lackadaisical, and her childcare— well, it was a wonder that her son had survived his first year.

Not that there was ever any question of Lia sending them away. Because of her work, the midwife's house was actually better ordered to receive guests than most village homes, with a large kitchen and two spare rooms hung with hooks for the hammocks used for sleeping at this level of the world. Len admired the craft and color of the hammocks, but the swaying unsettled her. She missed her bed badly, with its cozy comforters and Goose to warm her feet.

Though there was tension in the house, the midwife made it clear that they would not be going anywhere until Jade was at least as big as a normal nine-month baby. And it was obvious that Jade needed Lia's expert care; she was small enough to fit entirely into Len's two big hands, with skin like a newborn mouse. She slept most of the time, with Fox gazing down at her doll-sized face, and had to be coaxed and cajoled to nurse.

That was the second thing Len learned at Sixth Village Down: how to take care of the little ones who are not yet ready for this world. Lia taught them little tricks about how to help Jade's tiny mouth to suck without working too hard and how to keep her warm. "But not too hot! Do you want to cook her?" Lia was a terror about the baby's temperature — "What, you want the child to burn up its food in keeping warm instead of growing?" — and the newborn did thrive under her care. Len watched Lia rubbing nut-oil into Jade's filmy skin and had the fancy that the midwife's firm hands were tamping the life down into the bony little body, insisting that she stay with them, grow, and be well. Len resolved to be pleasant and tried to make herself as small as possible. At night, when they lay down in their hammocks in the midwife's spare room, Fox teased her a little about her unwonted meekness, but quietly. Very quietly.

They had all settled in for a long winter together when one day Lia came back from attending a birth with a coil of smooth silver-white fiber that she had been given in payment for her work. She threw it down in Len's lap. "Make yourself useful, Rope-Maker. I'm running out of twine for tying off the cord."

Len picked up the silky fiber. "I'd be glad to make you some," she said as she rubbed it between her fingers. "Tell me what kind of twine you want. I mean, how thick? How stiff?"

"Not so fine that it will cut when you tie it tight." She rooted in her kit for a sample. "And as to size, about like this. Flat would be better, but I don't reckon that's possible."

It was possible for Len Rope-Maker. Instead of plied cord, she worked a fine flat twelve-strand braid. It took a lot longer, but it kept her occupied and out of her host's way. When she had a few inches to show, she asked Lia if it was what she had in mind. Lia studied it closely, as if trying to find a fault, but finally grunted in approval. "That'll do," she said. "That'll do well enough. I could use about as much of that as you can make."

And so it was Lia Midwife that first introduced Len Rope-Maker to the sweet, soft fibers of the green creeper that grew below Sixth Village Down, creeping down the walls of the world to who-knows-where, far outside Len's limits, though not outside Fox's, for Fox's limits were still unfound.

Lalileh brought Cam a generous bowl of spicy stew. Inexplicably, she didn't invite him to her table, so he ate standing in the yard. Neither did she offer him water for washing nor a cloth for his hands. He was beginning to have some thoughts about the hospitality of the people of First Village New World.

Still, shingles didn't need clean hands and he was glad for a full stomach on any terms. He ate with gusto and handed back the bare bowl, which shone with a bluish glaze he admired and had never seen before. Then they went to work.

Cam and Lalileh were a good team. Roofs speak their own language and this one they both understood.

They started by carrying their materials up, with Cam on the ladder handing the fresh-cut shingles, smelling of cedar, up to Lalileh on the roof, from which the old ones had already been cleared away. She deposited the bundles at intervals up and down the pitch. Soon, Cam joined her up above. She shared out a bag of nails with him and they began to hammer, starting on each end of the lowest line of the roof, working inwards, and meeting in the middle. They were almost a match in speed, so they began to tease each other about whose line of shingles reached farther before they met.

Now hammering is no great time for talking, but by the time the sun went down, Cam had made a five-fold increase in his vocabulary, which is to say he had learned the words for "hammer," "nail," "shingle," "thank-you," and a curse that was appropriate for accidentally dropping something off the roof, splitting a shingle, or hitting your thumb. In all, a very fruitful afternoon.

But the late autumn sun set early. Too soon, they were climbing down the ladder as the first stars appeared in the clear evening sky. It would be cold but dry that night.

Cam had been giving some thought to what he would do if Lalileh did not invite him to stay with her. He was beginning to realize that he could not take even the most basic things for granted here.

Lalileh had been friendly and easy to work with. She seemed kind. Cam was fairly sure that, if he could make her understand his need, she would take him in for the night. What he wasn't certain about, though, was whether he preferred sleeping outdoors one more time to asking for something that was not offered. He rather thought it would be better to sleep under a bush than to impose on his new friend. Unless she invited him, of course. That would make him feel happy, make him feel at home.

But what Lalileh did was this: She gave him two metal disks, like game-markers, or buttons without holes. They were pretty things, finely engraved and shiny, and he thanked her, though he would have preferred a bed and a meal. Then, as he was pulling on the jacket he'd shed when the work warmed him, almost as an afterthought, Lalileh asked about his arrangements. She acted out sleeping and gestured interrogatively. He shrugged and pointed vaguely back down the path, towards the outskirts of the village. She looked concerned, signaled that he should wait, and stepped indoors to get her coat. When she came back, she took his arm.

She pulled him down the path, which broadened as it passed some very large houses— weathered wood, with steep-pitched roofs like Lalileh's. She turned into one of these, without knocking. Ah, a relative no doubt. Here she introduced him to a big man named Keptha, who welcomed him warmly and took him in.

It was with regret that Cam said goodbye to Lalileh. She was the first person to really see him in this new place. Perhaps he would find her tomorrow and help her finish that roof. But for now, he was glad to be in the house of Keptha, who knew how to welcome a traveler.

Keptha led Cam up a small stairway to a long, bare, extremely narrow room with several doors leading off it. Cam had never been in a house with so many rooms. Keptha must have a very large family. Or perhaps his family was simply very hospitable?

At any rate, Cam was extremely grateful when Keptha showed him where he might bathe and a room where he might sleep, all to himself. But Keptha was not through.

After Cam put down his load, his host pulled him back down the stairs. Where was he taking Cam now? The big man pointed through a low doorway into a warm, crowded room with many tables, where men and women ate and drank. An extravagant wood-fire burned on a huge hearth. The clatter of crockery and the chatter of conversation filled his ears that had been tuned to silence by his long walk alone. But here was hospitality indeed! This house was positively made to welcome travelers.

He retired back up the stairs to make himself as presentable as possible, shaving for the first time since coming into the cold, and then went back to the eating room, where he was jovially welcomed, fed, and plied with a sentimental cider that reminded him of home.

Keptha was not so warm the next morning, when Cam said goodbye to him on his way out the door. He was going to look for Lalileh, not at all certain that he could find her house in this village of many crossing paths. But Keptha blocked his way and expectantly held out his hand.

So Cam shook it, which seemed to annoy him. Keptha then said a good deal, unfortunately not about hammers or nails or thanks. But his guest thought, several times, that he could pick out the curse-word that was appropriate for hitting your thumb with a hammer.

Cam listened carefully, politely, trying to show by his face that he was willing to understand, if only Keptha could show him what the problem was.

Finally, his host opened an old wooden box and dug out a handful of metal disks like the ones Lalileh had given him. He held them out to Cam, pointing at them with his other hand.

Cam reached out to take the offered gift, and then Keptha became angry indeed. He snatched back the coins and dragged his guest to a steamy backroom where a mountain of bed-linens, a large sink, and a washboard told their tale. Cam understood perfectly.

"Of course! I'd be glad to help out. After all your hospital-ity, I should have thought to offer." He smiled at Keptha, who turned on his heel and left him, slamming the door harder than was good for it. Cam shrugged out of his coat and rolled up his sleeves. By the end of the day, he had learned the name of Keptha's partner and two daughters, as well as the words for "soap," "clothesline," "clothes-pin," "help me," and several new curses, useful in a variety of situations. He had also heard, if he had but known it, several excellent and detailed explana-tions of commerce, the theory of money, and the principles of dealing fair with honest merchants. Unfortunately, he had understood none of this and so remained ignorant of these important matters and the two coins Lalileh had given him clinked in his pocket along with a perfectly round pebble he'd picked up on the path and a blue feather that glinted with a strange rainbow sheen.

Besides the temperament of midwives, the care and feeding of the small and unready, and how to work with the sweetest, longest, finest, strongest fibers she had ever met, Len also learned something about her partner: It was actually possible for Fox to be still.

A new tranquility had overtaken quick, jumpy Fox and she happily lolled away the mild downworld mornings in her hammock with Jade lying skin-to-skin against her breast, which Lia told her would be furnace enough as long as the two of them were well covered. "But don't you smother her with the blankets, for pity's sake— the child needs to breathe." If she got up at all, it was to sit for hours by the fire, rocking the baby and crooning walking songs, which Lia said were all wrong for lullabies, but Fox sang them anyway.

Len remembered this same rosy tipsiness from nursing her own baby. She had complained to Yarrow that her brain turned to milk after Cam was born. It was as if when her son drank, his mother became drunk, in a mild and mellow way, like after a glass of mead.

It was her partner's new milky serenity that prompted Len to consider Fox's darting, busy, continual bustle over the last months.

Since she had been in Len's house, Fox had rushed from one thing to the next without a pause. Much of the stir had to do with getting ready for a new baby: spinning and knitting, building a cradle, reorganizing Len's tools on high hooks so that nothing sharp could get into little hands. "Little hands won't be reaching for them for months," Len had protested. But Fox had been relentless.

Len wondered about the busyness now. Why had Fox been so driven? Had she been trying to keep her mind off something? If so, what? Had she been that fidgety before, before Cam went away?

Less than a year had passed, but Len found it hard to remember who they had all been, back then.

Fox had been just a girl, and Cam just a boy. They had had no particular responsibilities in Home Village except to help with the work when they weren't stretching out to find their limits on the wall of the world. And maybe to find their partnership, too. They'd walked the path together since they'd first found their legs; had they been questing after *each other*, exploring what lay between them, seeing just how close they might come? Had Fox found in Cam what Len had found in Yarrow?

Found, and then lost?

It was hard to remember Fox, before, with so many things changed in their lives: Cam gone, Jade here, and the three of them wintering in the house of a stranger. But when she was as honest as she could be, Len thought that, yes, truly, Fox had been restless ever since Cam had said goodbye. She could see that now.

But even if this was true, what did it mean? Did all the frantic whirling cover the unhappiness of a heart that had found its true partner, but had been forced by the switchbacks of the path to walk without him?

Len remembered the year — years, really — after Yarrow fell, how she had set the tasks in front of herself, one after another: Now, breathe; take this one breath. Now make breakfast for the child. Breathe. Now wash this spoon. This dish. Breathe. Button his jacket. Breathe...

Time had seemed very slow to her, like an inchworm, crawling across one thing at a time: Keep your focus on this job right now. Don't look up. Don't see the path in front of you. The endless chain of days. All the things that must be done, without Yarrow.

She'd put one foot in front of another in what had felt, from the inside, like a slow trudge down the path of her life. But looking back, she realized that, from the outside, she must have appeared very busy: working, cooking, keeping Cam tidy, dragging him up and down her range as she carried and traded, probably too far for such a little boy. The busyness had gotten her up in the mornings, had anchored her like a strong rope, and kept her from falling off the world. Was it that same need to be pulled back from the edge of loneliness and grief that had driven Fox to work so hard and walk so far? Now that she thought about it, had there even been a bit of relief in the way Fox started down the path when the word went around Home Village that there was no salt to be had, and how could such a thing have happened?

Fox hadn't really cared how it had happened. She only cared that it gave her a good excuse to get up and go down-world to find a village that had salt to trade.

But thinking about Fox and the salt started Len musing on another thing: What if Fox wasn't so much afflicted by losing Cam to the path, as by losing the path itself?

From what Cam had told her — the hot spring in the snow that went unvisited — Fox had seemed to find her upper limit, clear enough, and a high one, too. But had she ever truly found the low end of her range? She had gone astonishingly far down on the world; she had seen the ocean; how many could say that? But had she ever really reached her limit? Was her restlessness, perhaps, that of a young Far-Walker whose exploring had been broken off by an early pregnancy?

Len had never heard of such a thing. You walk; you find your limits. You find your limits; you find your partner, if you want a partner. You find your partner; you have your babies, if you want babies. Then your babies walk, and that is the order of things.

But had it been the order for Cam and Fox? They had found each other before they found their own limits. Maybe that was the trouble: Love came too soon. Like Jade. Was love a limit too? Then Cam was gone and Fox had come into his mother's house with a baby on the way, perhaps still feeling the drive to push down the path and see how far she could go. What a tangle. Who could blame her if she'd tried to keep herself busy, to keep her mind off the stirrings of her heart? It was nobody's fault.

And now, the rosy glow of nursing let Len see for the first time who Fox might be with a peaceful heart. And Len liked her, too, this new Fox, serene in her body, swaying in her hammock, humming little walking songs into Jade's ear.

But a baby doesn't nurse forever. Len wondered what could be done about a young mother who still had not found her limits.

Keptha was a loud man, but not a mean one. When midday came, he took Cam a plate of bread and cheese, along with a cup of water and a bright yellow apple that appeared to delight the young man to an unreasonable degree.

"Thank you! Thank you! Thank you!" It was one of the few words the young vagabond appeared to know and he seemed disposed to say it as often as possible.

"You're welcome, you're welcome, you're welcome; it's just an apple, boy," Keptha grumped, setting the meal down on the folding table. But it was Cam's emphatic gratitude that, in spite of everything, began to disarm the innkeeper.

He was also impressed when he fingered the wet sheets in the big basket and found that they had been well rinsed. It's easy enough to rub soap into a thing; the real work comes in getting it out again.

So Keptha tentatively classed the scruffy stranger as a good worker, though he was ready to change his mind at the first evidence of sloth.

"Leave it there, on the table; you can eat after I've shown you the drying yard." He pointed, then led the way through a little door at the back of the house.

Cam blinked in the bright noon sun of a cool autumn day.

The back door opened onto a flat space between the two halves of the house, unfolding outward like the wings of a bird. Such a *large* house! Between the wings, there was what Cam would have to call a yard, because it had no roof, but it was also like a room, because it had a floor. Slabs of slate were sunk into a sheet of green— not moss, he realized when he stooped to study it, but a low flat plant with tiny leaves. His hands came away fragrant after stroking it.

Keptha noticed him sniffing his fingers appreciatively. "It's thyme, and very good in soups and stews, if you don't overdo it," he told him. "Never mind," he added, at Cam's blank look. "Thyme."

"Thyme," Cam said back to him.

"That's right: thyme. But the word you really need to know is 'clothesline,'" and he showed him what it meant.

The baby had smiled that day. Fox had shaken the little gourd rattle and Jade had smiled, really smiled, and turned towards it.

But Cam wasn't here and Cam didn't know and Fox couldn't tell him that Jade had smiled her first smile.

She lay in her hammock, trying not to let Len hear her cry.

Cam admired the good sense and efficiency of the arrangement: The walls of the two wings of Keptha's house held metal rings at intervals. These rings supported neat, taut parallel cords that were strung from wall to wall across the paving stones. The slate would keep the dripping laundry from making mud underneath itself, while the green cracks between would drain away the wetness, which would water the sweet little herb. But what a prodigal use of flat space it was! It seemed that in this tilted world without walls, people could afford to pave over tillable ground and let it produce nothing but laundry.

And why shouldn't they? He reminded himself that most of the lands he'd crossed here were workable, if a person gave some thought to which way the water would run when it rained. When he had come out of the brushy forest into the plowed country around the village, he had been staggered by the sheer abundance of space. Among fields that had already been cleared after the recent harvest, there were also many patches that had obviously been lying fallow. In a world so rich in acreage, why *not* have a room, a yard, just for drying laundry on nice, orderly clotheslines?

He remembered with a pang of homesickness the way that drying lines festooned his mother's porch and trees, for hanging her rope fiber after she'd washed it, and their clothing too, so that sometimes stray nettle-fibers worked their way into itchy places in their underwear. "Ah, the perils of rope-making are many," she would say when he complained. "It is not a life for the faint of heart."

He grinned at the memory — he missed her — as he ducked back into the warm, steamy wash room to eat the bread and cheese, and the apple that was just like the ones that grew in the orchards of Home Village.

When Keptha came to check on him again, he found Cam sitting on the flagstones, the laundry half hung and half still in the basket, and one of the clotheslines undone and drooping. The innkeeper gathered himself for a roar, but as he stepped closer, he saw what the young man was doing.

Cam had noticed a place where one of the clothesline cords was coming apart, wearing away on the metal loop that fastened it to the wall. He had untied it, cut away the frayed portion, and was re-attaching the tail. He held up the splice.

It was the neatest join Keptha had ever seen, and all in the service of repairing a clothesline that wasn't even broken yet. That evening, Cam ate at Keptha's table, with Anani, Keptha's partner, and Dixa and Rudily, his daughters.

Although he was not invited back into the guest room where he had spent his first night, Cam was given a cot in the back room where he had washed the sheets.

Where Cam came from, guests were usually bedded down on pallets on the floor. He very much admired the ingenuity of the folding cot, though it was tippy and tricky to sleep on. But he was glad to be in the house of Keptha and Anani, where he had learned the words for "apple," and "water," and "bread," and "thyme," although he had never seen this plant before and could not say in his own language what its name might be, if it had one.

Ounce by tiny ounce, the bundle that was Jade grew a little heavier in Fox's arms in the slow pendulum swing of the hammock and the rocking chair. Len filled the long, rainy days of late fall by making yards and yards of the tight, flat, creamy white braid for Lia, who told her it was the best thing she'd ever used for tying off the baby-cord.

The whole business had been something of a breakthrough between the midwife and her guest. Len had appreciated Lia's thoughtfulness in offering her something really useful she could do. The rope-maker enjoyed a little idleness as much as the next person, but it was good to have work in her hands again and good to be learning the ways of a new material.

For her part, Lia was grateful to have her guest out of the way; now, Len was either rocking the baby by the fire, or out braiding in the better light of the breezeway, and not underfoot in the kitchen, "helping." And it was good to have her tying-twine replenished; she had to admit the rope-maker did good work.

The braiding cut down on the friction between the women so much that Len was saddened when she ran out of the baby-hair fiber, as she had come to think of it. She asked Lia where she might get some more.

"It was Sand and Mack Basket-Weaver gave me that bunch, for seeing after their daughter Mel. But the vine grows everywhere below the village." She gestured vaguely. "You just start down the path and you'll see it soon enough."

"Would anyone mind if I harvest some? I mean, well away from the village?"

The midwife snorted. "Take all you want, and take it from as close as you find it. It's a nasty nuisance if it gets into the gardens, hard as a ringworm to get rid of. They say that in the summer it can grow a foot in a day. But folks will say anything; I've never actually taken a ruler to it myself. Take as much as you like, and welcome."

So one day during a break in the rains, Len went out to look into this nuisance vine that yielded up such a strong, soft fiber. She left Fox rinsing out the baby's cloths one-handed while she held Jade in her other arm, and took her pack and stick and knife with her down the path through Sixth Village Down.

Len had not actually explored the village much in the weeks she'd been living there. Her attention had been too fixed on the little world inside the house of Lia Midwife. But on this day, her eyes were fresh.

Maybe it was that her anxiety about her grandchild was beginning to abate, for it did seem that Jade wanted to stay on the world. She was nursing better and beginning to fill out her skin, which had hung at first like a too-large suit of clothes. She opened her eyes more often, though never for very long. Her lips were pinker, and the slightly yellowish tinge was leaving her cheeks. Len's heart was lighter about Jade than it had been since the night Brant Fast-Walker had pounded on her door.

And, for once, it wasn't raining. Winter at Sixth Village Down was mostly a matter of fog and wet, Len had come to understand, although when Lia Midwife went out, she layered on as many sweaters and shawls and coats as if she were on her way to attend a birth in a raging blizzard. Len understood that living this low in the world thinned the blood, but she had to admit that she was enjoying a season away from cold feet and the survival chores of winter.

It lifted her spirits to be on her way to gather fiber for her craft again. Not the nettle-stems— something different, but today that difference didn't seem disappointing; it excited her. She felt awake to her own senses again and enjoyed walking through this village that was not her own.

People she didn't know greeted her by name. They, like Lia, were dressed as if for extreme cold, she noticed, while she was comfortable walking in her overshirt. In a noticing mood, she took in the different colors of the rock here, less black and gray, more orange and rose. Unfamiliar cooking smells drifted from the houses, which were, most of them, split like Lia's with an open air gallery running between two walled-in portions, the three segments covered and held together by one large, gently-pitched roof. Len saw that the roofs were all thatched like the midwife's and not shingled, which hardly seemed sanitary. Night-rustlings in the thatch told of small lives lived out there, but "distance is difference," as her father used to say. Nobody was more of a stickler than Lia about cleanliness and *she* lived under thatch, so it must be survivable.

As she walked, she noticed a different feel to the way the houses were set back amongst the trees here. Not like Home Village. She had a hard time putting her finger on what was strange until she realized that of course the trees themselves were different here. No oaks or apples grew this low, nor was there any holly. All in all, the trees were bigger here, and more green. There was a lot of the long-needled pine that she knew was used to make baskets; she had a number of them in her own house. But she didn't know the name of the tall handsome trees with the smooth reddish trunks and the flat leathery leaves, still green in spite of the season. She laid her hand on one and the bark felt like skin. There were many of these giants towering over shorter, bushier trees with their leaves turned copper but still aloft, so that the treetops were layered, brown capped by green. When the wind stirred them, the copper leaves rattled strangely.

She walked on through the village. The clouds that held the rains were down below her now, watering people in villages even further downworld from where Len walked, admiring lush gardens and big flowers brighter than any that ever grew in Home Village. Things were different here, and she felt young.

Whether to head homeward or to press further into this new world, Cam had not yet decided. But whichever he chose, he reckoned he would need to winter here in First Village; the roof of the world had been a harsh frozen place even in the summer. He couldn't even imagine it colder or more deeply buried in snow and ice, which it would be if he started home now. When he did turn back, he wanted to live to tell the tale on his mother's porch, with all his village pressing close around to hear the news.

On the other hand, if he went forward, deeper into this place, there was a lot he would need to know and First Village New World might be a good place to learn.

For one thing, this matter of direction would have to be sorted out. Not only had he passed a number of paths cross-ing and joining his way down to the village, but he knew now that there were several routes leaving it as well. Where did they all go?

In this world, a person could get lost.

When he was a boy, he had once borrowed his mother's awl to pick the tiny garnets out of the stone by their spring. When he drifted off with his playmates to other games, he'd left it there, forgotten on the ground.

Then Len needed her tool but couldn't find it, and Cam had cried because he remembered taking it but couldn't say where he had left it. And so he had learned that objects could be lost, and grieved.

Weeks later, the awl had been found and returned to the rope-maker, but Cam never lost the lesson. You had to be careful with things, and not misplace them, because then they would be gone. But it wasn't until he came into this new place and found paths wandering and crossing promiscuously in all directions that he ever had a notion that a person, too, could be lost.

In his world, the idea would be silly. There was the path and everyone was on it, unless you fell off, and then you were dead and it didn't matter. But if you were alive and walking, how could you be lost? Up or down, you were still on the path. But here... Here was different. Here, if he were to leave the village, he would have to *choose* a direction. And then at every crossing, also, he would have to choose again, and remember his choices so that he could find his way back. It made him dizzy to think about it.

How would a person make decisions like that? Some of the paths that left the village were narrow, just tracks in the dirt. Others were so broad that five could walk abreast. Some inclined downwards, while others climbed back towards the snow. Others wandered off in an indeterminate direction, neither up nor down, which he could only describe as "across." How could he choose among them?

He wished he could ask Keptha and Anani; they would know. But this question was so far beyond his meager word-hoard that he couldn't begin to think how to phrase it.

That was another thing he would need before leaving First Village New World: more words. That was vital. He had collected many, mostly the terms for things around the inn, but he needed more, many more. Keptha, Anani, and the two girls made a game of teaching him, pointing at things and quizzing him to make sure he remembered. But he was hungry to be able to understand the news that the other travelers brought to the inn and to tell them his story as well. For that, he would need to know more than the names of the different utensils for eating and the different coins for exchanging.

And the business of the coins. To the two he had from Lalileh, each week he added the three that Anani gave him for no reason he could discern. He would need to understand that, too. They seemed to serve as a sort of trade token. He could tell they were important from the persistent way Anani tried to teach him the subtle differences in size and color among them. Each had a different name; he was able to follow her that far. And, in the eating room, two of the smallest could be traded for either a large glass of beer, milk, or cider, or for a tiny glass of stinging liquor. Yes, he could see that as well. But when it came to receiving large coins and giving back small ones, Cam's fragile understanding of the game broke down, and Anani set him back to washing the pots. (Anani could always tell when he'd reached his limit and had to stop learning and do something familiar for a while.) Clearly, the coins were another mystery he must master before moving on.

Cam resolved that First Village New World would be his learning place, and he would stay for the winter with Anani and Keptha and Dixa and Rudily, if his welcome held.

"Don't knock, woman; you live here! Don't make us get up— just walk in and… What happened to *you*?" Lia demanded of the mucky, disheveled Len standing on the threshold. "Were you in a fight?"

"You could say that. I won, too, and here's my trophy." Len grinned and wriggled out of her bulging pack. It hit the floor with a solid thump. She patted it affectionately. "Yards and pounds of the stuff. But that blasted vine doesn't give up easy." She rubbed the small of her back.

"Oh, Len, are you all right? Did you fall?" Lia had drummed into Fox that she must never interrupt "the little flea" when she was having a good suck, or Fox would have jumped up to see to her partner. For Len was filthy from hair to heels, covered with twigs and leaf-litter and smeared with green leaf-stains and red mud.

"I'm fine. Now all I have to do is tease out the fibers and I'll be…"

"But, Len, how did you get so *dirty*?"

"Ah. Now that's a tale that doesn't want to be told."

"No, don't sit there," Lia interrupted her. "Get outside and dust yourself off first. Talk later."

Len obediently stepped back outside; Lia followed her, snatching up a stiff whiskbroom from its hook as she went. Fox heard cries for mercy mingled with orders to stand still, and soon a much-improved Len was sitting by the fire, with Lia muttering, "…and what we can do about your hair, I don't know. I suppose there's nothing to be done but to wash it. I'll put the kettle on."

"Lia, please don't go to the trouble; I can wash it under the pump easily enough."

"What, cold water on your head at this time of the year? Do you mean to die of pneumonia and leave these two for me to take care of? No, I don't think so."

"Len, please tell us," Fox interrupted Lia's rumble. "What happened to you? You were going down to find some of that plant…?"

"And found it, too, just like Lia said, heaps of it, just below the village. Great snarls of it as tall as trees, an amazing sight. But I guess you've seen it, haven't you, when you were on the path here? The thickets are so thick with it — is that why they call them thickets, I wonder? — that you can't rightly walk through them at all, just throw yourself on top of the stuff and heave yourself through, hands and knees and feet all pushing and pulling and getting tangled." She laughed and stretched. "It's a wonder it doesn't eat up the path itself."

"It tries to— you're right enough about that," Lia said darkly. "Everybody who passes is supposed to do their part, snipping off the shoots that try to overgrow the path. Sometimes I skip it, if I'm called to a birth below the village. If you are in a mortal hurry, you can be excused. But otherwise, you're expected…"

"But how on the world did you get so *dirty*?" Fox broke in.

"Well, I wanted to get really long, unbroken streamers of the stuff, like what Lia gave me. The length of the fibers is part of what makes them so remarkable…"

"Len, dear, stick to your story."

"Yes. Like I said, I wanted to get…"

"Yes, we know, really long strips of creeper. Go on."

"Well, yes, and I thought I could just grab a vine and follow it back and cut it off at the root. But that would never work, you see, because it was all in this most amazing knot, over and under and around itself and other vines and anything else that got in its way. Nobody could ever follow one branch of it very far, unless you were a snake, and I couldn't even see my own feet— did I mention how thick the growth was?"

"So what did you do?"

"Well, I grabbed a nice fat strong vine and just pulled and pulled and pulled some more until something gave way and I fell over on my back side. Then I stripped the leaves off, and wound it up into a nice loop. And then I did it again and again until I had a pack full, and frankly, I'm glad there were no witnesses, because today I used up all the dignity I will ever have in this life."

"Oh, I wish I could have seen it. But you didn't hurt yourself, falling down so much?" She rearranged Jade, settling her on her other breast.

"Not at all. That's one good thing I will say about the green creeper: It's very springy. I never hit the ground, not once. I don't think I ever *saw* the ground, and as for my idea about following one of the vines to its root: I can say for sure and certain that I never, ever, found a place where that plant went into the ground. As far as I could tell you, it lives off air and rain alone."

"And strangling the other plants, poor things," Lia added.

"There's that. I can't say I would want to sleep too near one of those thickets, for fear of waking trussed up like a spider's dinner." About this, Fox couldn't tell whether or not Len was kidding.

Cam had been a baby the last time he slept in the same place for an entire season. Even before he began to take the path on his own, his mother would take him with her, holding his hand when he was very young, putting him in front of her with strong arms encircling when they climbed a ladder, always standing between him and the long fall. Only in the iron heart of the winter would they stay home as long as weeks at a time, hunkered down, doing work that could be done by firelight while the snows fell outside, almost erasing the path.

In the cold dark of the year, the people of Home Village turned inward, guesting and hosting more with each other than with travelers from below and above. And the wildest weather might keep them home altogether, behind shuttered windows with their own household, talking, telling over their maps, and sharing stories with the family that was often scattered during the gentler seasons, coming and going up and down the path.

So Cam was used to the idea of a mid-winter stillness like that of the squirrels in the oak trees when the icy winds came. But it was strange not to walk at all for so many months.

He could have gone out. He had good furs. They had seen him over the top of the world and would have been more than good enough for short walks out of what he still thought of as First Village New World, though he had learned its people called it High Town.

But Cam was scared. In this strange place, there was no sharp drop-off that would claim your life if your foot slipped on a bit of ice, but the idea of branching paths disturbed him. What if he started out on a bright sunny day and a storm came in? He might miss a turning in the snow and wander lost in the endless white and slanted world until he curled up and froze alone.

So he waited out the winter months working in the inn. His arms grew strong from pumping and carrying water, for in this place water did not spring out of the walls of the world on its own and gush through pipes into the sinks and troughs of the houses. No, in this world people had to work hard for their water, drawing it up from wells on chains so cold they could freeze your palms or pulling it up with pumps. He had never had to deal with the weight of water before and, truth to tell, water's heavy.

He split and carried logs for the fire; with patches of forest so easy to reach on the gentle slopes around the town, wood was abundant here and people burned it instead of coal. Wood fires left a lot of ashes, which he swept up and carried to the barrel under the rainspout. He cleaned and mopped and washed dishes with an earnestness that would have amused Len; neither she nor Cam relished these chores. He also helped in the kitchen, although neither Keptha nor Anani were about to put their reputation in the hands of a novice by trusting him with cooking or baking on his own.

His life seemed busy to him, though there was time for talking lessons. These became a sort of hobby with the girls, now going beyond simple pointing and naming games to "playing Keptha," although they did not call it this when their father was around. "Playing Keptha" involved giving complicated commands that the other players would have to obey exactly: "Now pick up the blue mug, fill it with water, set it on the table, and touch your left shoulder," Dixa might say and Cam would do as he was told, saying, "Now I pick up the blue mug. Now I fill it with water. Now I set it on the table. Now I touch your left shoulder."

"*My* left shoulder," they would roar, laughing at him. (They were boisterous girls.) Then it would be his turn to "play Keptha," and give orders to Rudily.

Rudily was going to be partnered in the spring, he learned, although he never saw her talking to anyone like Cam would expect of a person soon-to-be-partnered. That was because her Frameli lived down in the valley — a low place between two high places — and she would join him there. Cam understood that. Sometimes people came from different villages and, when they partnered, they would have to decide where would be Home.

It was good, Rudily told Cam, that he had come to High Town so that he could take her share of the work when she was gone. This startled Cam; with the five of them working together, there seemed to be more than enough to do. Perhaps Frameli should come to the inn instead?

No, Rudily laughed, she would go to Frameli in the valley. And Dixa teased her about leaving in the springtime, just when the real work would begin. And Cam blinked again, because it seemed that this busy life of serving and washing and mopping and tending the fire wasn't the real work at all. The real work, he learned, started when the snows melted and the passes opened and there was travel on the roads again, guests needing lodging and a meal. Winter was the quiet time, just giving the people of the town a warm place to gather and pass the gossip around.

This made Cam thoughtful and a little worried. He had assumed that when the winter weather cleared he would be able to wander as he wished. He had thought, without thinking, that it would be like it had been when he was a boy in Len's house: freedom to come and go, to find his feet at his own pace. He had imagined short jaunts growing into longer ones as he explored the length and breadth of this new world. It had been a comfortable plan, but now he felt uneasy: Had Keptha and Anani taken him in to replace Rudily? Were they expecting him to stay?

They were kind. He liked them. And he did not know whether he would go forward or go back. But he didn't think this was his stopping place; he had not yet reached his limit.

The house of Lia Midwife had settled into a kind of order.

Jade was healthy, still small, but growing. Her mother was shrinking, all except her milk-filled breasts, back towards the far-walking leanness that had been her shape before the baby. Lia had finished with her busy season, nine months after the long nights of winter. And Len was trying to talk the green creeper into giving up its fiber.

It was not easily persuaded.

She hung the long tendrils of vine to dry in the open air, leaving a scraggly curtain hanging from Lia's eaves. But she was impatient, and also tried drying a few samples by the fire-place.

It made no difference: Whether after a few hours by the fire or a few days in the open air, the dried vines resisted being peeled. They snapped in her fingers like icicles, leaving nothing but a few shreds of fiber shorter than her fingernail.

Perhaps she had let them get too dry? So she soaked a few in the rain-barrel, which turned them to mush entirely.

Perhaps she had let them get too waterlogged? She took some of the dried stems and wrapped them in a damp sheet, checking them often until they were springy again, and then failed one more time to coax them apart.

After explaining to Lia about the sheet, which now had an interesting brown pattern running up and down its length, Len admitted she was stumped. Lia told her to hang the sheet out to bleach in the sun, if it ever shone again, and if she really wanted to learn a thing, then she should go see the people who knew the thing— that being the Basket-Weavers in this case. They were the ones who had given her the stuff in the first place and they should be able to teach her how to tease the fiber out of the stems.

"But why the Basket-Weavers? I thought all the baskets from these parts were made from the long pine needles?" Len said.

"Yes, but pine needles won't tie themselves; you need the creeper fibers to bind the bundles and then to stitch them to each other." She picked up the solid, tightly-lidded container in which she kept her pine-nuts, and pointed out the buttery stitching over the brown coils of pine, just the same as on the baskets that Len had in her own house.

"That's the creeper?"

"That's it. And it's in your hammock, too, of course, only dyed to make the pattern. It takes a flower dye pretty well."

Pretty well, indeed, thought Len, for the hammocks were as brilliant as the blooms here. She would dearly love to learn to ply cordage with colors like those.

So Len went to Sand and Mack Basket-Weaver and arranged to come into their house for a brief apprenticeship. It would just be for the winter, they understood, and she would still sleep at Lia's house.

Sand and Mack worked her hard, and fed her, and showed her the way to harvest the pliant silver floss from the obstinate green creeper.

It was a stinky business, based on soaking the vines, neatly coiled around huge wooden spools, in open barrels until the plant flesh had rotted and could be rubbed away by hand. By Len's hand, to be exact, because that was what an apprentice was for, wasn't it? Then the slimy lank strands were washed in a small waterfall behind the Basket-Weavers' house, draped over a cane frame so they wouldn't tangle in the water. (Basket-weavers and rope-makers share a loathing of tangles.)

After washing, the fibers were dried in the sun, which lightened them to silver-blonde. In the winter, when the sun might not show for days at a time, sometimes the fibers were dried by the fire, which brought out a more amber tone, a lovely color to Len's eye, but not as valued. It was said not to be as strong but, as to that, Len could never tell any difference.

The Basket-Weavers took apprenticeships seriously. There was chat and banter in their workshop, but they expected Len to work hard, and not just on tasks that interested her. (She spent a great deal of time sorting and cleaning pine-straw.) Basket-weaving was like rope-making in that the actual time spent doing the skilled craft was tiny compared to the long hours spent gathering and preparing materials. It was during those long hours that Len learned a great deal about the lower villages. It struck her that the Basket-Weavers spoke of the sea matter-of-factly as a place that was real though very far away, while they seemed to regard snow as a creation of winter-crazed upworld imagination. They were startled to hear that she had seen it and walked in it and, yes, even shoveled it off her roof so that her house would not collapse under its weight. They hadn't known that snow was heavy.

Sand and Mack were glad to have her with them, for the extra pair of hands at the work as well as for her stories. They gave her long days, as Sand got up at dawn and worked 'til sunset, while Mack lay abed until mid-morning and then worked late into the night. Len was old for an apprentice, and she sank into her hammock each night limp and tired. But she discovered that she enjoyed working with new materials and making new mistakes. It had been a long time since anything in her work had surprised her, and a long time since anyone had scolded her for a fault in her technique. It was odd, because she was hardheaded and knew it, but she found that she enjoyed being a beginner again.

After creeping into the house late at night, trying not to wake the others, she wriggled into a comfortable lie across her hammock and went to sleep with a little smile around her eyes. She dreamed of silvery fibers growing out of the tips of her fingers, branching out, reaching far, questing up and down the world like a vine that could grow a foot in a day.

All Fox wanted to do for the rest of her life was to hold Jade and look at her. It was like a hunger in her eyes. Mostly, she made do with gazing at the baby's face — that nose, those eyelids fine as butterfly wings — because Lia said she must be kept wrapped up for warmth. But Fox always longed for the next time she got to unwrap the baby to change her cloths and see her naked, snatch a look at her perfect fingers and toes, her tiny perfect heels, and the way her skin — once as thin as a peach's — was filling out with the substance of her mother's breasts. It was as if all the beauty on all the world was packed into that precious little doll-body, and Fox loved her beyond words.

And nobody seemed to expect her to do anything except what she wanted to do, which was to sit by the fire and rock and feed and look at her baby. And eat, of course; they kept bringing her things to eat, which was fine, because she was always hungry now.

The best was when Jade opened her eyes. It was happening more often now: With her small mouth stretched wide around Fox's nipple and perhaps one arm escaped from her swaddling blankets to lie along the breast as if embracing it, Jade would open her eyes and look up at Fox as if she knew just who she was. Her eyes were clear, deep bluish green, the green that water would be, if water were green.

It was those moments that made Fox melt. She became liquid and flowed into a new form.

Cam was puzzled about what he was being shown. It was a tangle of random lines, inked onto a thin square of pale hide, a picture that was no picture at all. He knew about maps, of course, and understood the concept of scale, because your map could not be as long as the path or you would never be able to carry it and then what would be the point? To map the world you had to shrink it, so that maybe a hundred or a thousand paces might be shown as the length of a finger. A person's entire range might be worked onto a piece of cord no longer than an arm-span. But this flat picture that was no picture, hanging on the wall in Keptha and Anani's eating room, looked nothing at all like a map.

Maps that Cam had known varied in style and purpose and scope, but their essential *mapness* was obvious: lengths of string or rope or braid that represented some segment of the path, marked to show where various significant features appeared in relationship to each other. Many maps were simple and pragmatic; Jass Beekeeper used nothing but knots to mark where the hives were hidden because knots can be tied and untied as restless bees swarm and settle. Jass's map covered a fairly small segment of the world, the path that could be walked, up and down, within one half-day from Home Village.

Other maps took a much wider view. Craft households often owned maps of where on the world certain materials could be found. The Carpenters of Home Village treasured a map, handed down through generations, with tiny pendant samples of all the types of wood that could be had from Twelfth Village Down to Twelfth Village Up. (During her apprentice years with Rize Rope-Maker, Len had made a similar map, though not as wide-ranging, of the homes of plants that yielded fiber.) Such a map might be the work of people with different ranges, who used the same scale and the same sorts of markers and symbols, splicing their maps together to show a more complete picture of the world than could be offered by any one person working alone. Some of these maps were things of great beauty, as were the old people's maps. When people knew their days of walking were drawing to a close, they might map the part of the path they had traveled, with beads and knots and tiny pendant carvings to mark their lives' adventures.

Maps were regarded as highly educational; it was thought that they helped to give young people perspective on the world. Len had not neglected Cam's upbringing in that way; he had made and contemplated maps, but nothing in his experience had taught him that a map could look like anything other than a string that represented the single path. The thing on the wall in the eating room stumped him.

On this particular day, his friends had undertaken to help him understand the picture that was not a picture, interrupting each other in their jovial attempts to explain, pointing forcefully at the marks on the hide, then at the floor below them, and repeating the same words more loudly, as if Cam might be hard of hearing. Their explanations were as opaque to him as the thing they were explaining.

Finally, one of them broke through the chaos by drawing with his finger on the steamy pane of one of the windows, sketching out a simple floor-plan of the eating room itself, with its tables and bar and doors and hearth.

Yes, Cam could see that it was a sort of picture of the eating room, although it didn't *look* like the eating room. And yes, he could understand that this square stood for the table and this long thing was meant to be the high counter over there where the drinks were served.

Yes, yes, his teachers nodded eagerly but held themselves in check while Jonavi, the one who had thought to draw the plan of the room, pulled Cam's attention back to the hanging picture that was not a picture. Cam followed him willingly enough.

Jonavi pointed back at the plan of the room and then at the room itself. Cam nodded. Then he indicated the flat mess of squiggly lines that hung on the wall and wiped away all the steam on another pane to point, with a flourish, at the world outside. Everything. The whole world.

And Cam understood! All in a moment, he saw that the thing on the wall was a *map*, not long like the path, but broad, like people would need in this place of many paths. Not just up and down, but *across*. "This," he said carefully of the picture that might be a picture of the world, "is like this," pointing now to the hazy floor-plan of the eating room, "but bigger.

And more…" he fumbled for a word meaning "details," but finally settled on "…more tables."

Yes! More tables, indeed! They slapped him on his back, gave him a drink, and taught him the word for "map." They explained about east and west, north and south. (So *many* kinds of across!) They showed him where on the map their village was, and where the river was, and the way the river ran: towards the sea.

Jade's mother's urgent craving to spend every waking minute gazing at her baby settled down over time. Right at this moment, Fox's eyes were closed and her head lolled back in the rocking chair. Jade lay quietly at her breast, awake but still.

Fox was daydreaming. She was remembering springtime when she was a girl, the first walk after winter. Her friends would meet on the path in their newly-waxed boots, shivering a little because it was early but nobody wanted to wear their heavy coats. "We'll warm up when we get moving," somebody always said, and they always did.

Cam would lead off, downworld, away from the ice that still gripped the world above them. They would slosh through the mud and…

Lia clattered in through the door. "What on the world are you doing inside on a day like today, girl?" she demanded, throwing down her bag on the table.

Fox woke up. "What do you mean? You said 'Always by the fire.'"

"Well, my stars and sunbeams! It's *spring*, child. That baby needs some sunshine, and so do you. Pale as a cloud, that's what you are. Get out of here."

"But you said…"

"I know what I said. That was then; this is now. So, scat. Go. Take a walk. And mind you shade the baby's eyes from the sun."

So Fox carried Jade out into the new spring day and walked on the path again. Only, not far, because she was caught in a child-swarm before she got to the lower edge of the village.

"Are you that girl, the one from the Up place that came down here and had a baby and can never, ever leave?"

"What's your name?"

"Is that your baby?"

"Jalla had a baby, you know, and guess what? It was *me*!"

"Will you come to my house and let me show you…?"

"Can I see your baby?"

So Fox sat down by the path and let them meet Jade and learned their names and how old they were. Then they left her and ran off to see how far they could go.

Jade drank all of this in, the voices and the blue sky and the green and brown that waved over her head. The world was turning out to be more interesting than she had supposed.

Later, Lia showed Fox how to wrap and tie a long strip of cloth around her chest that would carry the baby and leave her hands free.

"Are you sure this will hold her?" Fox asked doubtfully. Lia hmphed and didn't dignify the question with an answer.

With Jade in the sling, and her walking stick in hand, Fox began to find her legs again. Lia was pleased.

"She's getting some color back in her cheeks," the midwife mused. "It's been a long winter."

Cam, your daughter went outside today. We walked in the sun and met the children. There were birds in the trees, those big ones with the long blue tails hanging down. One of them cawed when we passed and Jade looked around for it. She's fine, Cam, she's little but she's fine. She's healthy and we're going home.

But Cam wasn't there to hear her.

"Take it slow," Lia counseled them on the early spring morning when they left for Home Village. "Stop for a few days at each village along the way to see how the little one is faring with the travel. And if it looks like bad weather is setting in, stay put! You don't want the little flea…"

"…to freeze to death," Len and Fox chorused obediently. Lia laughed with them.

But just before they started out, while Fox was nursing the baby one last time in Lia's rocker by the fire, the midwife pulled Len aside for a private word in the breezeway.

"You've all done well; it isn't easy, fattening up a little early hummingbird like that one. And I wouldn't want to say this to Fox, because sometimes a mother's worry can make itself come true, but there it is. You need to know that sometimes things come a little more slowly for babies born before their time. Don't be too surprised if Jade is late sitting up, or walking, or talking. Fox isn't likely to notice, Jade being her first and all, but don't you let other mothers worry her about it, if it happens. It may not mean much in the long run; these babes usually catch up with themselves in time.

"But one other thing: Remember that Jade had to learn to breathe while she was still meant to swim. Her little lungs may never be strong. Go on home to Sixth Village Up, and enjoy the spring and summer there. But when the chill weather comes down on you in the fall, if Jade seems to catch a lot of colds, and if they settle in her chest, you get yourselves back down here before the snows lock you in for the winter. Remember: This is Home Village for Jade, and there will always be room in the house of Lia Midwife for her and for you two, also." Lia's strong old hand reached out, brushed back a lock of hair from Len's cheek, and straightened the set of the younger woman's collar.

Len's eyes were suddenly wet. "Oh, Lia... After all the trouble..."

"Hush, now. You were good guests. And it was nice to have someone in the house. After a long labor, or when things don't go so well, it's good to come home and find the fire lit and the place... not empty. It was good to hear you sneaking in late at night, trying not to wake us. You were a good guest, Len," she repeated, squeezing the rope-maker's shoulder.

Just then, Fox and Jade came out to find them sniffling and hugging as they said goodbye.

Cam knew that joining two lives in a partnership was not a simple thing, but these people had raised it to a level of complication that was new in his experience.

The way it would go, he was given to understand, would be like this:

There was to be a certain day, a day planned and agreed upon, when Rudily's new partner would come and get her to take her to the valley. But he would not simply come for her and go; no, there must be a great meal for everyone, and they must all dance and drink and toast the couple. There must be gifts given and words said and music played, and only after all this was done would everyone see that there was a new partnership on the world.

Cam tried to explain how much simpler it was where he came from, but it seemed that his new friends could not take seriously the idea that a partnership could be undertaken with nothing but a braided bracelet to show for it. "Ah," he answered, "but it is a *very* complicated bracelet, very hard to tie, very hard to untie. You see? Just like a partnership."

But in this new world, much more was needed. They must all have new suits of clothes, and these new clothes were not to be worn while doing chores around the inn before the appointed day. And there must be great mounds of food — pickled, roasted, baked, and smoked — prepared ahead but still perfectly fresh when served. Then there was the inn itself, which must be cleaned and polished to a fever of perfection, the windows burnished to invisibility, the floors as sparkling as dinnerplates. Then the whole place must be decorated with vases of evergreens and early spring blooms that would drop needles and blossoms on every surface. And there was the packing and fierce discussions of what Rudily would take with her from the inn.

Also, in the days of preparation, a good deal of loudness seemed to be required: the girls, shouting at each other and at their parents, Keptha and Anani shouting at each other and at the girls, and everyone shouting at Cam. But poor Cam could shout at nobody, because he lacked both practice (Len not having been much of a shouter) and swiftness of tongue.

With the house so stormy, Cam resolved to wait until after Rudily's glad gift-giving to tell Keptha and Anani that he too would soon be leaving.

Little Jade's lungs were weaker than Lia thought. They never got to Home Village.

They had taken the midwife's advice, traveling easy, short days, with plenty of stops for resting. They walked like children, happy to be on the path, happy to be going home, happy that Jade was with them. A skitter of rock drew Fox's attention. "Look, Len! It's the goats; I haven't seen them in five months!" And there they were in the distance, the nimble little beasts that needed no path at all, for they could find a foothold on the very wall of the world. "Look, Jade: Goats!" And she turned Jade a little in her sling so that she could look out at the world they walked. And Jade looked.

Jade was now a respectable weight in her mother's arms. She was beginning to be a real presence at last, with opinions of her own that she expressed through gurgling coos and a good strong cry, so different from the plaintive mewling of her first months.

So there were three of them now, and they were going home to Goose, to friends, and to family. Fox's parents had yet to meet their new granddaughter, for they could not travel as low as Sixth Village Down although they had sent gifts of cheese and dried apples, which Lia had hurried to cook up before they could spoil in the damp. Homeward steps are easy steps, they say — though in truth, both Len and Fox were a little out of shape for the upward way.

That night, they stayed with Remi, an age-mate of Len's who had partnered with the blacksmith of Third Village Down. It was at the house of Remi and Jon that it happened.

After a long uproarious evening of eating and drinking and stories about Len's rascally ways when she was a girl, they had all turned in. Len was surprised to find her pallet by the fire felt hard; her hips pressed uncomfortably into the ground. She sighed and rolled over, missing the hammock that had cradled her so perfectly. But, tired and relaxed from a day of walking, curled up with Fox and Jade in front of the hearth of friends, she fell into a happy dream of going home.

Sometime in the middle of the night, Fox woke her. The fire had burned down; only a dull glow from the embers showed her partner's panicked eyes.

"Len! Wake up! There's something wrong with Jade!"

"What? What happened? What's wrong?" Len sat up, disoriented in the strange place.

"She didn't wake me up to feed her, and then I woke up... I don't know... She's all floppy and won't suck. What could it be, Len? Something's wrong."

"Let's have a look at her. Poke up that fire and see if you can get the candle lit." Len took the baby from Fox, lay her down on the pallet, and undid her wrappings. Fox handed her the candle. Oh, no...

In the uncertain light, Len could see Jade laboring for breath, sucking for all she was worth, grabbing at the air with her belly, her ribs, and even the muscles around her neck.

Fox turned back from throwing a log on the fire and saw her baby, sucking not for mother's milk but for air, and dropped onto her knees with a moan. "Oh, Len— is she dying?"

Kneeling face to face across the gasping baby, for just a moment Len saw Fox and thought, she's too young! She can't possibly be so young. Then she tamped down the panic that was welling up in her own core and said briskly, "Of course she's not dying. But she's sick, Fox, really sick. I think we may have walked outside her range, and the poor thing couldn't tell us. So we have to go down, Fox, now. Fast. We have to get her back down to where the air is heavy and thick, what she's used to. We have to go now."

"Will she be all right, Len?"

"I think so. Now get your clothes on quick and wrap her well, because we're leaving right now."

And they did, though Remi and Jon offered to run for the midwife of Third Village Down, or the healer, or the herbalist— whomever they needed. But Len wanted no help that would delay getting Jade back down the path, so Remi instead carried a lamp, walking with them until the sky whitened, back down the path away from Fox and Len's Home Village, and towards Jade's.

Of the glad gift-giving for Rudily's new partnership, Cam mostly saw the crockery. There were great platters of food to be served, jugs to be poured, mugs to be rounded up from where guests had set them down on tables, chairs, and window-sills. There were dishes to be washed, in great teetering heaps, and dishes to be dried so that they could be brought out once more.

Anani was grateful for Cam's help and gave him a quick hug as she bustled past him in the scullery. And Rudily thanked him for his gift: a rope mat made in the shape of two inter-locked circles. It was based on one of the flat ornamental knots he'd learned from his mother, but the design was his own, new for the occasion.

The circle design turned out to be more fitting than he had known, for among these people circles were a great theme when partners joined. Their dances were circle dances to music blown and pounded and plucked from round-bodied flutes and drums and stringed instruments. Only round trays and platters were used to serve the food, and small, sweet round cakes were handed around all day. When the couple sat down to eat, it was at the big round table decorated with a circle of spring flowers laid around an enormous round pie.

The day passed in a rush of serving and washing and running errands for Keptha and Anani when they yelled for him. He was no longer bothered by their shouting; indeed, he had come to think of it as just part of their language, some-thing different and new, hard to understand, but nothing to be feared. Several times, he let himself be pulled into the circle dances, though he did not know the steps. He caught on quickly enough and danced until he was dizzy, in honor of the new partnership on the world. Then, also in honor of the new partnership, he went off to wash some more dishes.

In the middle of the hubbub, there was a brief moment of stillness when everyone pressed into the eating room. Cam roosted on a windowsill with an empty tray wrapped in his arms. His perch let him see over the crowd to where Rudily and Frameli stood face to face before the window. They held each other's hands, like two children playing a circle game. She said words and then he said words. Then, to the sound of a great affirming shout from the crowd, they each kissed the left hand of their new partner and pressed it to their heart.

That night, Cam dreamed of Fox. They were lying on their stomachs, looking over the edge of a sun-warmed rock. Far below them, wrapped round by two folds of the world, they saw a gleaming circle of jade that opened out into a flatness as broad as the world was tall. Near the base of the world, the smooth surface was pocked by fragments, pieces that must have fallen off the world. But as their eyes reached out into the distance, they saw a perfect line where the sky came down and rested on the sea. Clouds were there, and the sun also, although Cam could not tell if it would rise or drop onto the jade ocean and break.

Then they were lying together, Fox on her back beside him. They wore nothing but cloths wrapped round their loins, and Fox's breasts were free without shame, after the fashion of the very low villages. Cam was lightly dragging his fingertips up and down her belly, watching her eyes. "Go lower," she urged him, laughing. He woke up thinking of the sea.

Jade's air-hunger began to calm as soon as they started down. By first light, she was sleeping in her mother's arms. She was pale and limp, but her breathing was slower and easier, not that shocking full-body gasp that had terrified them so. Remi and Jon left them with hugs, offers to help in any way they needed, and entreaties that they stay with them again on their way home, after the little one got well.

On their way home. Where would their home be, now?

By the time they reached Lia's house, Jade was herself again: reaching for the breast when she was hungry, nursing well, and expressing her pleasure or displeasure with vigor. She'd seemed to like walking and had sometimes wrestled around in her sling until Jade rearranged her so she could watch the world go by.

Len reached out and squeezed Fox's hand before knocking on the cane-and-wood door. A lot hung on the midwife's first expression when she saw them. If she opened the door and her eyes lit up, then they might consider staying with her again. But if she looked disappointed or irritated (or more irritated than usual), then they would really have to make other arrangements. What these might be, Len had no idea. But if her granddaughter could only thrive in Sixth Village Down, then that is where they would live.

Len never even saw the midwife's first expression when she opened the door, so quickly did Lia throw her arms around the three of them and pull them across the threshold into the house that would become their home.

Rudily went away with Frameli in a cart like a giant wheel-barrow pulled by a great animal like an ox, only much bigger — almost as tall as a man — and also different in that its roan hair was short and smooth and its horns were painted red with yellow flowers.

Then there was much to do to tidy up the inn after the glad gift-giving. The family was cheerful and weepy by turns as they settled back into the business of lodging and feeding the travelers who were ever more numerous as the spring opened roads, pastures, and markets.

Dixa was delighted to have her room, and Cam, all to herself for the first time, but she missed her sister more than she had expected. She was a little grouchy, too, at having to take a larger share of the work of running the inn.

The days were getting longer, but Cam decided to wait before announcing that he too would leave them. The snow blanket that had covered them all winter was melting away, leaving patches of white only in the shadows of trees and houses.

With Rudily gone, Anani began to teach Cam to bake. It interested him very much how a person could mix flour and water together and come up with something that wasn't like either. Then, if you could wait long enough (but not too long), the loaf would grow, actually *grow*, and at last you could bake it and it would be transformed. You'd open the oven door to a new loaf of hot fresh bread, chewy, with a crackly crust and a taste no words could describe, in this world or the other. Cam hadn't been raised with the smell of fresh bread in the house; Len always got theirs from Nori Baker. The magic of yeast, the care and handling of doughs, the fine points of crust and oven temperatures— all this was new to him. So much to learn. It seemed to him that baking was a chain of linked mysteries, something beyond his understanding that he might be willing to spend a long time mastering. What would it be like to stay in one place, he wondered, and to try to master a single trade, to try to get to the bottom of just one thing among all the things the world offered?

Cam saw the path dividing in front of him now, as it never had before. Choices stretched out in front of him as clearly as that first crossroad, in the grasses just below the snow-line: He could stay or go.

He could stay with Keptha and Anani, laugh with Dixa, and delve into the secrets of baking and cooking and tapping beer barrels and keeping a house where travelers felt at home. He could do this and be happy.

Or he could go. He could take up the pack and walking stick that had sat for so many months unused in a corner. He could walk with sure and certain steps towards home, back through the fields and forests to the grasses where no trees grew, and then up again and over the roof of the world, and back down again to Home Village and his mother, and to Fox. He could bring the news, as he always had, the stories of where he had been and what he had seen. He could bring the news and be happy.

Or he could go further, down into this world that was not a wall, to learn what it had to teach him.

·And then, as abrupt as that first dizzy vision of the path dividing at his feet, came the solid sense of which path was his own. He knew it, as clearly as he knew his mother's house in the dark, and it led away from the house of Keptha and Anani. He was a far-walker, not a baker or an inn-keeper, and it was time to say goodbye. He knew this. Suddenly, he just *knew*.

So he told Keptha and Anani and Dixa that he would leave them. Keptha and Anani yelled at him, separately and together, on the themes of: "What will we do without you? Where will you go? What will you do without us? How will you eat? How will you get along? Who will do the laundry, with you gone?"

But Cam knew them too well by now to let their shouting worry him. It was their family language, and he was beginning to understand it, like he understood the words for "meat" and "beer." He had seen how they let go of their Rudily, and this was how they let go of him. He was more pained by the way Dixa didn't yell at all, and wouldn't meet his eyes. She didn't even come down to the dooryard to see him off, but watched the embraces and tears from her bedroom window as, laden with some of Keptha's old clothes in his pack and a bag of Anani's hard rolls and cheese in his hand, Cam took his leave.

"Where will you go?" Keptha asked him.

"To the sea," Cam answered, a little surprised because, until he was asked, he had not known this.

Keptha squeezed his shoulder. "Travel safely, son," said. It was either that or "Travel safely, radish"— Cam grip on the word-hoard of this place was still a little loose.

So Jade's first solid food wasn't applesauce, but a paste of the sweet orange yams that grew so well around Fifth and Sixth Village Down. Lia said it would help Jade grow well, if she could only learn to keep it in her maw. The midwife was holding her in one arm and spooning the mush into her, deftly scooping up the food that oozed from her lips and replacing it in her mouth.

"She likes it," she announced with satisfaction.

"If she likes it, why does she keep spitting it out?" Fox asked doubtfully.

"That's just enthusiasm. She's still learning how to use her tongue and lips. Take my word for it, this will help flesh her out. And giving her a bite before bedtime may mean that you'll get to sleep a little longer between feedings. And with a little more sleep, everyone will be calmer and we'll have peace in the house."

They had been going over and over what they should do. As far as Lia was concerned, there was no question: They would stay with her, because that was what was best for Jade. How could anything be simpler? But it seemed more complicated to Fox.

When she and Len had agreed to be partners and care for the baby together, they hadn't known that this would mean living two villages below Len's limit. Fox had felt terrible about Len having to leave her lifelong home and friends and join her in this far village for all those months. She was so sorry. She couldn't ask Len to make the move permanent. It was too much. Living here in the winter was one thing, but summer was something else altogether. Sweat was something you just got used to here, because it never went away. And the damp... Should she mention the damp? Even if the baby could thrive in the warm wet air, could Len? Fox fingered the Never-Ending Braid around her wrist uneasily. The salt. She shouldn't have taken the path that late. And then Jade got so terribly sick. There were others that could have gone for the salt. It was all her doing; Len should just go back to Home Village without her and get on with her life.

Len thought this was all just silly. Jade was her granddaughter and Fox was her partner, and any talk about untying the braid was just upsetting everyone. For her, the question was: What should they do with their house and goods up in Home Village? What should they bring down? She was a woman of means and could afford the carriers' fees, but what would they need? Lia's house was large, but Lia had her own things. What was there space for? The baby's crib? Maybe not, what with Jade being so used to the hammock by now. But certainly Len's tools — she had to work — and the dishes she had from Beda Cook, her mother. And clothing. They would need clothing. But even that was a question, because, this far down on the world, they would need different clothing than up in Home Village. Things without sleeves. Not wool. Linen. And other clothing for walking the path, of course. What else would they need? And what would they do about the house? So much to decide...

Lia slammed the bowl of mashed yam down on the table, hard enough to make them all jump.

"Hush, both of you. I want it quiet in the house, not a word spoken, for as long as it takes for me to burp this baby and lay her down. Then I will tell you what you are going to do."

Len sputtered — she was her own woman and nobody told her what to do — but then she caught Lia's eye and decided that perhaps taking a break from the discussion was not a bad idea. Fox got as far as saying, "But..." before Lia hissed her into silence.

She wiped Jade's yam-painted face with care and put her up on her shoulder, patting her back until the child yielded up a satisfying bubble of air. Then she deposited her into the hammock in the corner of the kitchen, where she hung like a potato swinging in a string sack.

"Now the two of you can just stop this nonsense. Fox, you're acting like a guilty child. Stop it. Things happen. You didn't make Jade come before her time. Or maybe you did. We'll never know, and it doesn't matter. Maybe your crazy long walk for a load of salt caused your labor to start early. Or maybe she would have been untimely born anyway and, high in the freeze of an upworld winter, she wouldn't have survived until daybreak, much less until spring. As it was, she was born where the air is good and nourishing, and in the house of a fair-to-middling midwife. Your little winter stroll may have nearly killed her, or it may have saved her life— and, girl, you will never know. So stop acting as if you have to cut the Knot off your partner's wrist with a paring knife. That's not what being partners is about."

"But *two* villages below her limit, Lia? Isn't that like asking her to do to herself on purpose the same thing we did to Jade accidentally? Dragging her outside her limits?"

"Certainly not. What are limits, anyway? They're just decisions about how far we want to go. Jade didn't want to go up, but she's little and weak and couldn't do anything about it, so she got sick. Len decided a long time ago where her limits are, and now she's changing her mind. But she's no helpless babe; she's got some strength and she's got some sense. She can learn with her mind how to take care of her body. And she's got us to help her and teach her the little tricks of getting along and keeping cool in the hot season. And, I'll say this for her: She's stubborn enough. That can go a long way.

"But, Len, for pity's sake, you don't have to make all the decisions today. Go home. Get your cat. Bring your tools down. You can have the breezeway. Get back to work. Spread out and fiddle with your ropes. But don't do anything hasty with your house until after you've spent the summer here. Find someone, a friend to see after the place. Don't hurry the decision. A house is too big for ordinary trade anyway. Give yourself time to think.

"Well, I've said my say. Now, I'm going to sleep, because the Weaver's baby kept us up all night. I would be grateful if there could be some quiet in the house."

And there was.

Cam's legs pushed off from what was behind him, swung through the moment of balance, and reached forward to what was before him. It felt good to be walking again. His back and shoulders were strong from carrying laundry and heavy trays, strong now under the weight of his pack, the weight mostly of the furs that he had not been able to bring himself to leave behind. If — *when* — he made his way home again, he would need them to help him through the bitter cold at the top of the world.

He was not moving quickly. In this land where hospitality was bought and paid for, each meal and each night spent in a bed had to be bargained for with work or coin. He didn't mind, for he was in no hurry. The jobs he worked along the way taught him the way things worked here. There was a lot to learn.

He learned about sheep, the shearing and the lambing. He learned about spring cleaning and the proper beating of rugs. He learned about planting and weeding. He learned about mucking out the stalls of animals that had been barned up through the winter but now were turned loose to enjoy the pleasures of sunshine, wind, and grass. He collected new words like he had once collected bird-feathers when he was a child— for the simple joy of having them.

Sometimes, after work, he would study the map he had copied from Keptha's wall onto his under-vest. As far as he could tell, he was heading west, towards Rudily and Frameli's valley. West, he understood, was where the sun set, and he had carefully marked his map to show which side was sunset and which was sunrise.

In his old language of direction, he believed he was going down-world. But even that was not obvious, because the path would slant downhill for a time and then slant uphill again, down and up, over and over again, as if it couldn't make up its mind whether to rise or to fall. But it seemed to Cam that he always descended a little more than he climbed. He was going lower every day, towards Rudily's valley, towards the river, the river that ran towards the sea.

Cam didn't think much about *why* he was going in this direction. It wasn't a matter for questioning, or for giving reasons. It was simply that it was his path. While it was true that this strange new place was webbed with many paths and roads, so many that his mind shied away from contemplating them, it was also true that only one of these seemed to be for *him*.

Was this how people here could bear the bramble of choices that tangled their world like green creeper vine? Did they know some kind of trick, some way of squinting, maybe, that kept them from even *seeing* all the mind-melting possibilities in front of them, that kept them focused tightly on the only path that mattered: their own?

Fox dreamed of Cam.

They were kneeling on a rock, face to face, lit by smoldering embers. Jade was lying between them. Fox was weeping, apologizing, telling Cam how sorry she was that she couldn't bring the baby home, that she had taken his child down, down, further away from him. "But closer to the sea," he whispered and smiled at her radiantly. He motioned for her to look around, and she saw that they were on an outcropping of granite high above the sea. Cam touched her face, and she felt the golden, joyous glow inside her. She looked down and saw that Jade was fat and pink, naked and laughing, kicking her feet and flailing her arms, reaching out to catch her toes. "She's trying to find her feet," Fox told Cam in her dream.

At first, Cam thought it was a bee-tree. It had that same steady, hissing hum, not changing of itself, though growing louder as one drew nearer. But as he walked and walked down the broad road under the hemlocks and oaks and trees without names, he neither reached it nor passed it. It just got louder, surely, but very slowly. Could there be more than one bee-tree hereabouts? Perhaps a whole string of hives marching down-world with the road, squeezing closer as the little valley narrowed?

As the noise swelled, it became more textured, rougher, like the roar of many voices heard from a distance. Cam's curiosity grew. The source of the sound, he realized eventually, was down-slope and off to his right, but he could see nothing but trees. No path branched in that direction, not even an animal track.

He looked doubtfully down the sharp incline that fell away from the road towards the droning hive-song and considered stepping off the path.

The ground was steep and rocky as far as he could see, which was no great distance because of the trees that crowded and shaded the road. The canopy of leaves below him cloaked the view completely. All he could see was forest.

Since he had come to understand that a person could get lost in this world of many paths, Cam always paid close attention to his route. He dreaded losing his way, not so much because there was any particular place he wanted to reach, but because he wanted to be able to find his way back. He had made a habit of noticing choices, turnings, and forks in the path.

But here there was no path, not to the mysterious sound that pulled at him. A litter of leaves covered the ground and testified that nothing larger than a squirrel had gone into the forest at this place, not in a very long time. Maybe never. If Cam left the road here, he might be walking where no one else had ever walked. The idea made him light-headed, but the sound called him.

If he climbed straight back up, he'd be sure to find the road again. He couldn't miss it. But still, as he slithered down the slope, whenever he could brake his skid by grabbing a tree, he would pause for a moment and gaze up towards the road, trying to fix in his mind the look of the way behind him.

Of course, the landslide would help a lot in the business of finding his way back, he reflected ruefully, as he rubbed his behind after a long slide. He looked back up at the violence he'd done as he passed, plowing up the forest slope, exposing rocks, breaking branches, and stripping the leaves off tree limbs he'd grasped to slow his descent.

To lighten his load for climbing, he had thought about leaving his pack up by the side of the road, but it was too precious to him. Everything he owned — food and flint and the furs that would take him back over the top of the world to his home — all of it was in that pack. He couldn't part with it, even knowing he would be coming right back as soon as he had seen what there was to see.

So he floundered down the slope top-heavy and laden. The noise, a sort of rumbling drone now, was definitely closer, and he thought suddenly of water, water as it bubbled out of the world — the old world, *his* world — gurgling and chattering as it forced its wet way into the light, then over the edge, leaving a dark trail of dampness on the stone. Or chuckling as it spilled into the pipes that channeled it to his mother's house. Or dripping into hollows, natural and carved, along the path. And the big waterfall where he and Fox had romped on their last walk together, when he had given her his heart but not his promise. And remembering that great spout of water, as massive as his thigh, he suddenly understood that the sound he had been following was water. The many voices must be many springs, all babbling together. No longer attending to the trail behind him, he plunged downward, eager to see what kind of place this might be, this gathering of many waters.

He tumbled again on the rocky slope and slid the last bit on his side, fetching up against a sturdy sapling that snagged his pack. Streaked with mud from nose to toes, he rolled over, laughing at the ridiculous spectacle someone would see if she were here. The sight of the water stopped, stunned, and silenced him.

For it was not water springing *from* the ground but running *across* it, like when Len threw out a pot of wash-water and it rushed over the ground before sinking away. Or when it rained, and water flowed down the path for a while. Only this water was huge, beyond imagining; two or three Cams, laid head to foot, could not span the boiling race plunging through the rocks. It went on and on, rushing down from his right to his left with no end in sight in either direction. Where could so much water come from? Where could it go?

Cam shrugged his pack away from the young tree that had snared him and clambered out onto a rock to study this marvel.

One evening, Len called for Goose and Goose didn't come.

They had finished dinner, the two-legged members of the family, and Len had scraped a pile of juicy scraps into the cat-bowl by the door. "Goose, Goose," she called, "oh, Goose…," but there was no Goose.

She walked up and down the village, calling and worrying. Goose wasn't a wandering cat, and she *never* missed a meal. She was a plump, domestic soul who had always been content to loll about Len's house and take her adventures in their little dooryard. The move to Sixth Village Down had been a harsh break for the cat: the disruption of packing, rugs that belonged on the floor being put into baskets, outsiders stomping through the house dragging the furniture around and moving things that had been in their rightful places since she was a kitten.

But she *had* enjoyed the carrying baskets. They had been scattered all over the floor and filled with all manner of things: clothing, tools, pottery, and coils of stuff that could be pulled, tangled, and chewed on. She sampled each basket, nosing through their contents and napping in them if they were soft. They were like little dens; she was pleased with them.

She'd stopped liking them when someone closed her in one, shut the lid right down on her so that she couldn't get out. She squalled and clawed at the wicker of her prison, sure that Len would come and free her.

But Len said, "I'm so sorry, Goose. We have to go now. We're going to live in a new place. Jord will be staying in our house for a while and we're going down to live with Lia."

Goose didn't accept her apology and ignored the finger Len stuck through the slats to stroke her fur. "I know you'd rather stay here, Goose, but I just can't say goodbye to anyone else. Not right now. You'll like it down there, I promise. It's warm, all year long. You like warm, don't you?" And then the basket had lurched up into the air like a live thing, moved and kept moving.

Goose hadn't liked the swaying, jostling trip down the world at all. She rode on the back of someone she didn't know in the line of carriers bringing the things that Len and Fox couldn't live without. She yowled and threw up and wouldn't eat or drink along the way. Her fur grew matted, and she'd always been such a careful groomer. Goose took her place in the long list of things that Len had to worry about.

But when the carry-line came at last into Sixth Village Down — their Home Village now — Len saw that her cat couldn't have done anything more perfectly suited for winning the heart of Lia Midwife than to show up ailing at her doorstep. Because Lia took one look at Goose and saw nothing but another small creature that needed to be fed and comforted and cared for.

Len grinned at the memory, for she had also been worried about how Lia would take to having a cat in the household. But the two had approved of each other from the beginning,

Goose of Lia's confident, stroking hands and Lia of Goose as
a sort of furry baby. The midwife also cherished the notion of
cats as great hunters of vermin, four-legged members of the
sisterhood of housekeeping, dedicated to maintaining clean
and healthy homes. Len never mentioned Goose's peaceable,
even affectionate, relations with mice and let Lia keep her
belief that the cat would be a fierce mouser, "just as soon as
she'd settled in."

It had taken Goose a long time to settle. The house, the
smells, the people, the plants— everything was strange here.
There were new territorial arrangements with the dogs and
goats and chickens and other cats of the village to work out.
She'd stayed close to Len for many weeks and now, just when
she was beginning to venture out, suddenly she was gone.

Len kept calling, walking up and down the path through
the village, knocking at her neighbors' doors, asking everyone
if they had seen Goose. She asked about dogs and was firmly
told that they didn't know what it was like where *she* came
from, but in *this* village they brooked no cat-killers. Then
she asked about the wild ones, the foxes and wolves, but no
one had seen any such creatures on the village shelf recently.
And, Trand Hunter added, "If a wolf took the path through
this village, it would have to be moving *very* fast."

But other animals were missing too, now that Len mentioned it. No carcasses, no blood— just gone. And the hens
were uneasy and the goats were off their feed today.

After an hour of fruitless pacing and calling, she finally
turned off the path at Lia's door. The midwife was sitting on
her front steps, gazing up into the bland twilight sky. Len
sat beside her, tears prickling her eyes.

"I can try to be philosophical about it. If a fox has gotten
her, there's nothing I can do. If not, she'll come home when…"

Lia wasn't listening, or not to Len, at any rate. There was
a listening look on her face, though, like when she searched
out a baby's tiny heartbeat inside its mother, but she was
staring out over the world, still as stone.

"What is it, Lia?"

"Hush. Listen."

Len listened and heard it. The silence…

"Where are the birds?"

"And the frogs? And the crickets? This time of night, there
should be a righteous riot of crickets."

"What's going on, Lia?"

"I don't know, Len. I've never heard such, or heard *tell* of such. But I'm thinking that whatever the birds and the bugs know, Goose knows too. She's gone to ground somewhere safe. So should we. I'm thinking maybe we should put the shutters up tonight; there may be hard weather coming."

Len looked out at the sky. A few streaks of gauzy clouds caught the colors of the sunset. No thunderheads, no overcast.

Lia caught her doubtful glance and said, "I know. But it's the only thing I can think of. I'll see to the shutters and you run and find that Fox of yours. Tonight's a night to know where your family is."

In her bowl by the door, Goose's dinner sat untouched. Not even a fly settled on it that night.

When Cam stepped onto the rock, which was wet and slick with scum, his feet went out from under him. Suddenly he was in the icy stream. It was so fast that his mind had no sense at all of the moment of falling, just a heart-beat translation from air to water. But his body was wiser, shocked into a great gasp that filled his lungs with air before his leaden pack pulled him under.

He had never imagined water so deep or so powerful— it was bottomless and the rush of it pulled him along, flailing for the surface, for the bottom, for any solid thing. Rocks struck out at him, but were gone past so quickly that they gave him no purchase. He tumbled through a world that was white then glassy green, light then dark, but always and most of all *cold*, so cold that his muscles began to get stupid. As he rolled and caromed off the bruising stones, one clear thought came to him: He could die here, and Len would be very angry.

Cam clamped his throat shut against the water and gathered himself around that thought. He had to get free of the pack on his back. It was pulling him down into the dark, dangerous green and away from light and air. Nothing else mattered.

He stopped trying to fend off the rocks, stopped reaching for air or solid ground. He gave himself to the current while he tugged the pack-strap away from his left shoulder, then wriggled and shrugged that arm free. The weight twisted away from his back. He came close to panic as he felt the strap kink more tightly around his right shoulder for a moment, but then the weight of the pack stripped the loop down his arm and it was gone, taken by the greedy water.

A moment later, his head broke the surface. One gasp, and he was snatched under again, but that one breath made all the difference. He would not annoy his mother by drowning here today.

He pushed himself towards the light again, and filled his lungs before he swirled over a drop and was pinned under it by the sheer weight of falling water. He could not fight against the force of the flow, so he surrendered and let it push him down, down, and down into the watery dark. The weight of falling water crushed him to the bottom and pinned him there.

He squirmed onto his belly and clawed at the rocks, dragging himself along until the current whirled him loose again and finally spit him to the surface.

The water was calmer here, with fewer rocks beating it into a fury. He turned himself in the flow so that he could see down the stream and tried to bounce off the boulders with his feet instead of his head and shoulders. He took his air when he could get it and fought for it when he could not. But this couldn't go on for long. The cold was stealing his strength and the rocks would mince him if he didn't get free from this monstrous rush of water. He had to get out.

He saw the forest was a bit closer on his right. Whenever he could, he threw himself towards that bank, pulling at the water, grabbing at low-hanging branches, angling his pushes away from slabs of stone, always working his way towards the right, until finally a fallen tree caught him and held him.

That tree was nearly the death of him, for the water rushed through its sunken branches like tea through a strainer. It tried to suck him under, to where no strength could escape the current pinning him there until bones and branches rotted away together. But instead, he used his last reserves to pull himself up, clawing at the tree-limbs like a cat, thrashing with his feet as he dragged himself up and onto the trunk, where he gagged and choked and coughed for a long time.

It was an earthquake.

Len woke up with a lurch. Something had happened— she wasn't sure what. It was very dark, but a faint glow outlined the windows. It must be near dawn. The shutters were closed. Where was the wind coming from? Oh— it was the air moving as her hammock swooped from side to side. What...? Then there was Lia's voice from the other room: "Is everyone alright?" She heard movement but no words from the hammock Fox shared with Jade. She pulled herself up and swung her feet onto the floor, feeling wobbly, wanting light more than she had ever wanted it in her life. Then Lia was in the doorway with a candle.

The dim and dancing light showed Fox's hammock to be swinging wildly, Fox just beginning to stir, and Jade wide awake but oddly silent. "Get up and get out," Lia snapped. "Earthquake." Then she was gone, leaving Len in the dark on the quavering floor.

"Up, Fox! Now! We have to get out, in case the house comes down."

"What? What's happening?" That girl sleeps like a bear in winter, Len thought to herself as she fumbled for Jade. Lia could have at least lit the lamp before darting off to who knows where.

"It's an earthquake. Now give me the baby and get your feet on the floor. Come on!" They stumbled out of the dark, shaking house into the lesser dark outside.

The milky half-light that comes just before dawn was dotted by bobbing candles, lamps, and a few torches along the path. The whole village was out, swarming like an anthill that had been poked with a stick. People were calling out, "Are you okay?" "Where's...?" "Is it over?" "What happened?" Families were finding each other, losing each other, running to check on neighbors, and failing to find them because their neighbors had run to check on *them*. Children were crying; they didn't understand what was happening.

In the boiling crowd, Len kept a tight grip on Jade and Fox while the earth shivered. She knew where her family was and meant to keep it that way. Until things settled down, the best she could think of was to get themselves to the green around the spring-pool, the broadest space in the village where there was nothing that could fall on them, neither trees nor buildings. And not unless the world itself came down on their heads would any rockfall touch the green; any landslide that reached that far would have to leap out over the entire village terrace.

So, they made their way to the pool and found that others had gathered there too, particularly parents with children. Mostly to occupy the youngsters while the trembling died away, Len organized a bonfire, which became a cook-fire a little later when people brought food. No one was ready to go back inside yet, not until they were a little more sure that the world was ready to be still again. A makeshift breakfast was served around the fire and carried to the work teams that were dealing with the small rockslide that had come down on two of the houses tucked into the very corner of the village. Several people had to be freed from the rubble; Jee Mason took charge of that effort. As the nearest Healer was two villages away, Lia saw to the injured in front of her house, where she could dart in and get supplies as she needed them. The sun rose, the chaos of the quake gave way to order. People went to their houses to see the damage, then came back to tell.

"All my plates, smashed to crumbs!"

"Hunter's rooftree is down, did you hear?"

"And we'll all be eating pan-bread for a while— Baker's oven cracked and crumbled." That was bad news indeed. The oven was the pride of the village, made from great bricks of the pretty, rosy sandstone native to those parts. Although the sandstone was good for building, the village houses were mostly made of wood and a light, strong cane that grew somewhere downworld. To Len's eyes, they had a flimsy, blow-away look to them, but the truth was that they had stood up well to the great shaking. What had been destroyed was mostly stone: Baker's oven was fallen to bits, Potter's kiln was cracked but could be repaired, and several chimneys had tumbled. It could have been much worse, everyone said, and it probably was, up where everything was wood and stone. The quake had come when everyone would be inside, asleep in their beds.

Len's heart ached to think of her snug little house, maybe nothing now but a pile of ruins. And Fane? How had he fared? And Mel and Thera and Jord and all her other friends in stone houses with heavy slate shingles above their heads?

And, most of all, *Cam*?

She pushed her fears away and dragged her mind back to the group of children in front of her. She was keeping them busy with a lesson in rope-making while the adults began the work of cleaning up the village. The youngsters were working with the long cattail leaves that grew by the pond, learning the magic twist-and-ply moves that were the secret of bringing small, fragile fibers together in a way that made them strong. Their hands would be green tonight, she thought, but their parents seemed glad enough not to have them underfoot. For putting little things in perspective, there was nothing like an earthquake.

That night, some people went to their own houses, but many slept out under the stars in gardens and the grassy ring around the spring-pool. There had been some bangs and bruises and a few broken bones, and Seta Tailor had cracked her head rather badly, but no one had been killed. The ground was quiet now, solid and unmoving, like it was meant to be. Everyone agreed that things could have been much worse. It was days before they learned they were right.

Cam squirmed like a snake along the tree. The water rushed below him, just inches from his face. It seemed hungry, eager to suck him in and swallow him down. He was unwilling to be swallowed. He wanted dry ground and rock under him. And he was *cold*.

He wriggled around the jutting limbs of the half-sunken treetop, then straddled the trunk and scooted towards land, his legs dragging in the icy water. Pulling himself along, he began to realize just how battered he was. When he reached the root-ball yanked up by the tree's collapse, he dropped to the mud below and found his legs would not hold him. He crumpled and wept for a while.

When his sobs had calmed him, he began to take stock. First, he was shivering and soaking wet. He stripped off his sodden, tattered things, what was left of them. The dunking had washed away the copy of Keptha's map he had sketched on his under-vest. His belt knife was gone from its sheath. His boots and socks, too, had been stolen by the rushing water, and his feet were pale as wax. Fresh bruises, he saw, were just beginning to bloom all over his body. He thought he must have cracked a rib or two. He'd be black and blue tomorrow, and that was a fact. He began to realize how lucky he was not to have been knocked senseless in the water. A sharp blow to the head would have been the end of his story.

But his story hadn't ended, not yet. He would deal with whatever came next, which had better involve getting dry and warm. He shook the water from his hair like a dog and hung his dripping clothes on the roots of the fallen tree.

But the air was damp here, sheltered from the sun by foliage and moistened by the spray of roaring water. Nothing would dry, not for days. "I'll have to go back up...," and *that* was when it came to him that he was now on the far side of the river. He looked back across and saw the steep bank that led up to the road. On his side, he saw nothing but trackless forest. That was something to think about.

But later. First things come first. Fire would dry his clothes and warm his shivering carcass too— and that was when it came to him that his flint and steel and tinder were lost, gone with his pack. Well. He considered the state of affairs, but his thoughts moved haltingly, like syrup on a cold morning.

The water flowed off to his right; the pack must have been carried in that direction. Cam picked his way along the stream, scanning the edge, hoping to see gear fetched up against a rock.

Nothing.

He went back to his tree and found the walking had warmed him a bit. He was able to think better.

The pack was gone, either sunk to the bottom or carried away. That meant no blanket, no flint, no food. Well, water, at least, wouldn't be a problem. But what to do about getting warm? He could stagger off naked down the stream, trusting that it would run along the road and come at last into a town. But his short search for the pack had already taught him that walking along a watercourse was not the same as walking along a broad, well-traveled road. What with the twists and turns, the boulders, the mudholes, and the trees, it would take him days to cover just a few miles. A river is a clear path, but not an easy one.

Which brought him back to trying to get warm right where he was. He needed fire.

Like all the children of the villages, Cam had been taught how to kindle needfire for emergencies when no match or flint was at hand. That had been a long time ago, and he wasn't sure he could do it in such soggy air with hands that were shaking like unset jelly. But he could try. If he failed, he could always fall back on staggering naked through the woods.

So he set about making a fire-drill to spin the friction that could, he hoped, heat wood to a red glow. He found a likely branch for the bow, sturdy but green and springy, a little shorter than his arm. Then, to string his bow, he plied up about two feet of cord from the inner bark of the fallen tree, which had most obligingly retted it for him in the splashing spray of the water. Next, he needed a strong stick, rigid and dry, and a cupped rock that would fit into his hand so that the spinning drill would not bore through his palm. For the drill-bit, he broke a stiff branch off a pine tree; for the palm-rock, he found the perfect shape and size in the shallow water around the bend from his tree. He felt a little queasy even getting his feet wet to rummage around the water-smoothed stones. It would be a long time, he thought, before he made his peace with moving water.

The alarm had never been sounded in all the many months Len had lived in the village, not even on the night of the earthquake, which had sounded its own alarm. But Len recognized it right away even though, in her first Home Village, it had been voiced by a big iron bell. Here, it was a large ram's horn, but the urgency was the same, unmistakable. "Come running," it demanded in long, hoarse blasts, over and over again. "Come *now*."

Three days had passed since the quake and the village was getting back to normal. Repairs were under way. Bumps and scrapes were healing. The animals had come back and Goose was napping on the doorstep, the perfect place to get stepped on. Seta was doing well except for a headache. Thatcher was up, hobbling around on crutches. Walkers were beginning to trickle through from the upper villages, telling tales of damage, but not devastation. So Len wondered as she raced towards the horn with the others: What could possibly be the reason for this alarm, coming *now*? The path was solid, still and steady under her feet as she ran, just as it should be. Why the alarm?

As the running crowd closed in around the spring-pool, Len saw that it was Lia blowing the call, enormous gulps of air puffing out her cheeks as the great echoing peals rolled out into the sky. The villagers gathered around the midwife, jostling, shouting questions, pointing at the three young runners panting by her side. One of them was guzzling great drafts from the spring, letting it spill freely down his chest.

When the midwife saw that the village was well gathered, she let the horn drop to her side and waited, eyeing the crowd sternly until the hubbub died down. "These travelers bring news from Fourth Village Down," she cried. "Listen to them!"

"Three runners!" Len heard the man next to her mutter. What kind of news could be so urgent that it needed three runners to insure against mischance?

The runners — two boys and a girl — stepped forward, still dripping with sweat. So young, thought Len, so serious.

The dark-haired boy, somewhat less out of breath than his running-mates, called out, "Listen! There's news. The path is broken…"

The crowd forgot itself and broke out in urgent chatter. "What?" "What did he say?" "What did he mean?" "Where did they come from?"

Lia hushed them fiercely. "Listen to them! They've run a long way to bring us the news…"

She gave the young man a little push. He started again.

"Three nights ago, below our village, a great shoulder of the world fell away. The lower villages are cut off. Travelers that were caught on the path can't get home." A rustle of gasps was heard as people took in what it meant. Some families had walkers out on the lower path and couldn't know if they were below the break or above it. Some in the crowd were travelers themselves, making their way back to their homes in the lower villages. The news was most appalling for those from below Fourth Village Down, but of concern to everyone because of the friends, family, and trade that linked them all.

The runner went on. "They sent us, our village, they sent us to call on you for help. The path has to be mended, but our people can't do it alone. They said to tell you that, if it were just a matter of clearing away fallen stone, of course our people would do our duty— we've always tended our part of the path with care and we always will. But this is too much for us. Too much for any one village alone. It's not that rock has just fallen *onto* the path, it's that the path itself has fallen, carried away by the earthquake."

"It was that great slate plate, wasn't it?" Jee Mason asked. The runners nodded. "I know the place, not a half-hour's walk below Fourth Village Down. Good luck that it didn't take the village with it. How much of the path is gone?"

"We don't know," the girl answered. "So much fell away that we can't see the path on the other side. There's just a raw rock wall now, as if the path had never been." A rustle went through the crowd at this; almost all of them had walked the broad, sturdy ledge that had been the path between Fourth and Fifth Villages Down. Gone? As if it had never been?

The shorter boy, the one who had been drinking when Len arrived, added, "The slate cleaved off in the shaking, sheared clean like a layer of onion. Only there's this bulge of stone that blocks the view. Climbers were going up when we were sent out— no one knows what they'll find. But whatever it is, we'll need help to fix it. We're to call out all builders, carpenters, masons, and carvers to come. Help us. Advise us. Nobody knows what to do, but the path can't stay broken. Bring your tools and as much rope as the village can spare."

"Rope!" someone called out. "We can do better than that! Len Rope-Maker herself has come down from the cold to live here with us."

"That's good news; no one knows yet what we'll need in the long run— maybe some sort of bridge, or a new ledge carved out. Who can say? But whatever it is, it will take a lot of rope, to hold things together and keep our climbers and workers safe on the slate wall. Len Rope-Maker will be welcome in our village. Everyone will be welcome that comes to help us mend the path. The world can't stay broken forever."

Whether it's a spark struck from a flint or a tiny ember doggedly heated by the friction of a drill, if fire is to have a fighting chance, it must be caught by eager tinder, some kind of fine, bone-dry fluff that will feed it and give it plenty of room to breathe and grow. If the tinder is keen and willing, the smallest red glow will leap to life in a bright flame hot enough to set alight something a bit larger, a splinter of pine, perhaps. Then that splinter may give flame to a little pile of dry bark, which can light up a bundle of twigs. Then the larger kindling catches and soon you have a merry blaze.

That's if the tinder is willing.

Cam mourned his lost tinderbox. It had been fashioned from a cow's horn by his father's mother, with a pattern of raindrops and snowflakes on its tight little lid. Since he was first old enough to be trusted with fire, Cam had carried it with him, stuffed with the gauzy down of a cottonwood tree or a bit of cattail head. It had always kept his tinder dry in any weather, but now it was gone, and there seemed to be nothing in the world that didn't drip with damp.

Len had often told him, "First, do what can be done. Then, what can't be done may be easier." So he gathered firewood, of which there was plenty. River-washed limbs and logs were strewn everywhere, some unaccountably far from the stream-bed, some even lodged up in the treetops. He pulled these down eagerly; they would be dryer than anything lying on the moist ground.

To his great delight, he stumbled on several birch trees and helped himself to generous strips of their bark. If he could coax even the smallest flame out of some tinder, the flaky, sappy birch would light up easily.

He picked out his fireplace carefully, between two humps of stone in the hollow left by the uprooted tree. They would provide natural andirons, lifting his firewood and letting the air flow from below to feed the flames.

Always assuming there would be flames, of course. What-ever could he use for tinder?

As he gathered his wood and kindling, he kept his eyes open for something, anything, that might nurse a tiny coal to life. He saw a bird's nest and walked right past it, intent on finding the fuel he needed. Then he stopped.

He let his armload of wood fall to the ground. A bird's nest! He scanned the trees, found it again, and whooped for joy.

He knew that some birds lined their nests for warmth with down and soft plant fibers. He didn't know which birds did this, nor would it have mattered if he did, because he had no idea what kind of bird had nestled in the crotch of that large limb so high above. It was empty and waiting for him, up there so far away from the clammy damp.

He started to climb the tree, but a knife-sharp stab in his chest made him think better of it; he really must have cracked some ribs. Instead, he gathered a handful of pebbles and set about knocking the nest down. Heaving the stones jostled his poor bones painfully, but not so much as hauling his weight up a tree trunk.

After a few tries, there, it was down! It bounced on the ground, but stayed whole and he found that it was indeed upholstered with some kind of fine fluff, whether bird-down or plant-fiber he couldn't say. There could be no more perfect bed for receiving an ember. He would sleep warm tonight.

The rest was just hard work. He bent the bow to slacken the string enough so that it could be looped around the drill stick. He tested it; the stick rolled up and down the string smoothly, captive in the loop, which moved with it.

He set one end of the stick at the edge of a flat fragment of old pine, settled the cupped river rock on the other end, and began to saw back and forth on the bow as he pressed down on the rock to increase the friction. The looped bow string spun the drill stick, first one way, then the other, never stopping, until sweat poured off the fire-maker and a tiny wisp of smoke rose from the pine.

He kept going a bit longer, just to be sure, before he stopped. Finally, he set aside the fire drill and blew tenderly on the charred, smoking dimple in the pine until he could see a distinct red glow, no bigger than a gnat. He knocked the ember gently into the waiting bird's nest.

That night, a cheerful fire lit up the forest by the river, bouncing its heat off the big rootball and warming the little hollow underneath it, while Cam's clothing steamed and Cam snored, curled up under a great mound of fallen leaves and bracken.

That night, in Lia's kitchen, Fox had a lot to say about people who volunteered other people for things without talking to people first, and also about people who would even *consider* walking down four villages when they were already two villages below their limit. "And at your age, too!" she snapped.

"I'm not as old as all that," Len protested mildly, scrubbing away the congealed egg on one of the dishes she'd brought down from home village. "I'm not yet thirty-seven. That's not old. Not really."

"You're old enough to be a grandmother!"

"Well, you're old enough to be a mother!"

Lia, who'd been letting them fight it out on their own terms, snorted at their silliness. Fox giggled and then they were all hooting with laughter at the sad mess that love can make of logic. The baby laughed with them, bouncing on the midwife's lap, Lia's hands around her middle, her little legs working and pushing and wobbling towards the day she would walk.

"Strange things do happen," Fox admitted, as she wiped the tears from her eyes.

"Seriously, Fox, I don't think it will be any problem," Len said, handing her the dish to dry. "It's just Fourth Village Down..."

"Fourth Village Down for this village, but *Tenth* Village Down for us," Fox corrected her. "That's six villages below your..."

"But, you know, Fox, I'm not so sure any more about that business of limits. I'm beginning to wonder if a person can, maybe, get used to almost anything. When springtime first began to warm this place, I thought I'd perish from the heat and the damp. But it's not so bad now. I wear clothes that would get me talked about up in First Home Village, and I don't think I used to smell like this..."

"There's nothing wrong with a little whiff of good clean sweat," Lia interjected. She swung Jade out of her lap and leaned out of her chair, holding her so the baby's feet could feel the floor. Jade laughed and bounced against the rag rug, clinging fiercely to the old woman's hands.

"What I'm saying is, we've made do. We've adapted. Even me, the old granny. If distance is difference, maybe *I'm* different so far from home. I thought that I could never be happy or comfortable or at home this far down, but look at me now."

"You'd be even more comfortable if you'd let me chop all that hair off your neck."

"Maybe someday, Lia. You've been such a help, teaching us how to live here and be well and safe. I don't know if we could have done it without you. And there will be other folks down there to help, and I'll pay attention and do things the way they do them in Fourth Village Down. The world has broken in two pieces, and if I can help with putting it back together, then I have to go."

"Okay," Fox said, polishing the plate ferociously with the dish-towel, "but I'm coming with you."

"And that you are not," said Lia, looking up from Jade. "I try to stay out of other people's business, but that's the limit: You will not be carting this baby off to a village that's going to fill to bursting with workers from half the world, with no proper place to house them and no way to serve up good hot meals. No, you will be staying right here with me. Len's a Rope-Maker and you're a mother, and both of you have work to do, and yours, little Fox, is right here. The idea of it."

"And who would look after Goose if you came too? I'll be back soon, Fox. Now help me pack— we're leaving early."

Cam was in the dark, confused. Why were there leaves in his face and the noise of running water in his ears?

Running water. He sat bolt upright, and grunted at the pain in his ribs. And shoulders. And legs. It brought him back. He remembered the river and was suddenly awake.

Black night, and the fire had burned down to coals. It needed to be fed. He'd left a stack of wood nearby, though, to warm and dry as it caught the heat.

He heaved himself to his feet, groaning as he found each bruised muscle and wrenched joint. It was chilly and he was naked as a newborn. He tested his overshirt and trousers; not dry yet, but soon. His under-vest, though— that was close enough, and he pulled it on gratefully, although getting his arms through the sleeves reawakened the sharp stab of pain in his ribs.

He was stumbling towards the glowing embers when his eye was caught by a light, far off in the trees. He shouted. There was more than one of them— small glows, far away. Could they be houses? Food, maybe, and someone to set him on his way?

They were all around him. He rubbed the sleep from his eyes, but the lights were still there, like stars come down to flit among the trees. They came and went, tiny candles blown out and then lit again. What could they be?

He had never had a dream in which he had felt so entirely awake, or in which his feet had felt so cold. Had his pounding in the water shaken his brains loose?

He stood and gaped. The gleams were everywhere, even up in the tree-tops, and they were beautiful. He ducked as one swept past him. He saw they were not far away, only very small, like sparks.

The next one that flew by him, he chased and caught, timidly, because he feared to burn his hands. But it was cool. He held the fluttering radiance gently between cupped palms, and saw that it was a winged creature — a bug — with a little lantern on its hinder parts. The lamp glowed and went dark, glowed and went dark. He set it free, and it danced away from him, one crumb of light in the night.

"What a world of wonders!" He laughed until his ribs reminded him not to and then squatted by the little hearth and fed his fire, lighting up the night, while the living stars came and went around him.

The party gathered just before dawn. Aza Stonecarver was there with the heavy chisels and hammers of his trade. Jee Mason and the Carpenter couple, Dena and Tern, were leaving their apprentices to finish repairs in the village and join them later down at the rift in the path. Tris Baker had decided to go along, because she guessed that they would be needing to feed the draft of workers that would soon flood into Fourth Village Down.

"And," she said, "there's not much good I can do here anyway, what with the oven crumbled like a dry biscuit." The baker actually relished the thought of an outing for she had been without an apprentice for almost a year. For a baker without a helper, a broken oven meant a holiday.

Seven strong walkers would go with them to help carry tools and all the rope that could be gathered. Three of the carriers were travelers from the lower villages who had been out on the path when the earthquake struck and were on their way home, anxious to learn if all was well down below. One of them, a tall tattooed and shaven-headed man who'd been taking hospitality at Wren Smoker's house, was from very far down, on the other side of the break. His name was Nish, and Len knew him a little from the village, as they had traded. A few days before the earthquake, she'd given him a knife for one of the hammocks he was carrying on his way up the world.

Weeks before, while they were hanging out the wet laundry to dry in the bright spring sunshine, Fox had confessed to Lia that she was beginning to feel a little put out at Jade, a little irritated at the way she pulled at Fox's clothing whenever she wanted to nurse, "As if she owned my body. As if she were entitled to it. At any hour of the night or day. And of course, I love to feed her. I love to feel the weight flow out of my breast and into her little body."

"Not so little any more," Lia observed.

"No, but I mean, I really want her to have what she needs. It's just that she's always there, pawing at me whenever she's hungry. I should be ashamed of myself for saying this, but sometimes I just want her to leave me alone."

"No shame to it," Lia told her firmly. "There's no better mother in the world than a cat, is there? Always ready to snuggle down and give the little ones a good feed. But just you watch: When her kittens get big, and it's time they're weaned, suddenly she's not so patient. Sometimes they'll cry for her and she won't come running, or they'll nuzzle up to her and she'll swat them away with an ugly word. It's natural. Stands to reason: If she kept feeding them, why would they ever go to the trouble of learning to feed themselves? Don't you worry about it. It's the way things are meant to be. You're wanting your old self back. Jade borrowed it for a bit, but now she's growing one of her own. Weaning time is near; mark my words. Meanwhile, we'll get you and Jade each into your own hammock at night, so that she can dream her dreams and you can dream yours."

"Oh, Lia!" Fox hugged her, there between the flapping shirts, because, truly, she *had* been thinking she might be a bad mother.

So when Nish had come up through the village with his carry-basket full of shells and hammocks to trade, Fox had picked out an elegant pattern in red and purple shot with thin green stripes. Not at all what Len would have chosen for herself, but Lia had given her a talking-to about Fox needing to become her own person again, so Len had kept her mouth shut about the loud, clanging colors. And truly, the work was beautifully fashioned, with each cord smooth and tight. The weave had draped softly over her hand as she'd fingered the fine net of cords. Nish was a master of his craft. She'd willingly traded one of her sharp brass blades for the hammock, wondering how many hours had gone into preparing the fibers, plying the twine, and finally weaving the net. She'd asked about his materials, and had ended by taking him home that evening and giving him the hospitality of Lia's house.

They'd talked over dinner about fibers they had known, and compared tangle disasters. He was a good talker, though his word-hoard and the rhythms of his speech were strange to her ears. Distance is difference, as she always used to tell Cam, but that is what makes swapping stories with travelers such a treat. Each of Nish's tattoos referred to some wild, improbable tale of strange beasts, adventures, and the sea, which among his people was evidently believed to be covered by a deep, sloshing layer of water. He had given Jade a minnow-pendant to wear on a little cord around her neck, carved from some shell that shone like silver mixed with rainbows.

All in all, Nish had been good company and, on that chilly dawn when she joined the group of walkers heading down-world to the break in the path, Len was glad to see him adjusting the straps of a carry-basket before heaving it up onto his broad brown shoulders. She saw Lia pull him aside for a private word, no doubt telling him to look after the out-of-place Rope-Maker along the way. Lia, always taking care of people.

The early start and the many carriers were in the service of speedy travel. Leaving at first light, sharing out the load, and walking without stopping, they should make it to Second Village Down before nightfall. If all went well, a second day of hard walking would bring them into Fourth Village Down by the late afternoon or early evening. Then the work would begin. What that work might be, they didn't yet know, but they would be there to do it.

Fox stood with the others who had come to see them off, holding a sleepy Jade in her arms. She had already said "Take care of yourself" to Len in so many ways that there wasn't anything else to say. She shivered a little in the damp dawn air. Her partner came over for one last hug before shouldering her pack, and Lia joined them. Len wrapped her arms around them all, feeling the strength of each in its difference; Jade's soft baby-flesh, Fox's firm young muscles, and Lia's bones and cords. It was hard to pull away from their embrace, hard to see that Fox was crying.

For once, Len had nothing to say. She laid her hand on each beloved face one more time before she turned away, back to the tools, the walk, and the work. She would see them again soon— this wouldn't take long.

Nish grinned at her as they hefted their loads. "Down we go, eh, Rope-Maker? Down, towards the sea? Maybe you'll taste the hospitality of Nish Fisher someday?"

And she laughed and said yes. It startled her to find that she meant this. Once the path was mended, there was no place she might not go.

Cam woke up hungry.

His clothes were dry, the fire needed feeding, and so did he.

"First things come first," he told himself and threw the last twigs from his woodpile onto the fire. "I need to gather more wood if I don't want to have to start this up from scratch again."

He brushed himself off the best he could and climbed into his trousers, glad at least not to greet the day naked. But he was hungry... He pulled on his shirt, grunting at the strain of getting his arms, bruised and purpling, into the sleeve-holes. Keptha's old felted wool jacket was still damp; he turned it on its branch and let it hang a while longer.

Cam filled his belly from the stream, drinking crouched over the flow like Goose over her cat-bowl, only not so dainty, he reflected as the chilly water ran down his chin. He wiped his face on his sleeve and saw a dart of silver in the water.

It was a fish, an enormous fish, as long as his forearm. He crept out along his tree (it was a poplar) to get a better look. Lying along the trunk, he peered down.

There seemed to be a lot of them, larger than fish he had ever heard of or imagined. He could see them easily in the clear water, to the detail of their eyes, the black stripe down their sides, and the dark graceful fan of their tails. How did they hold themselves so still against the moving water? And then, when they *did* move, how did they move so fast— as quick as falling stars?

Cam knew that the finger-sized fish that lived in wells and springs could make a meal for cats and some birds. Would one of these huge monsters do the same for a man?

And how to catch one? They were quicker than rock-lizards and sleek. Probably slippery, too, he thought, though they wouldn't hold still long enough for him to test this.

He could throw rocks at them. Though Yarrow had been a hunter, his son had not inherited that talent. He had never been much good at bringing home meat, though he could knock a birds' nest out of a tree. But even if he could hit a fish through the shield of the water, wouldn't the rushing water just carry it away, like it had almost done to him? He didn't feel friendly towards the water and he didn't want to feed it; he wanted to feed *Cam*.

He lay on his tree and studied the fish. The stream burbled through the crown of the fallen tree, the mighty strainer that had saved him after almost drowning him. He shuddered, remembering how the force of the torrent had pressed him into the branches while the water flowed through, chuckling.

The memory made him queasy, but it gave him a clue about how to catch his breakfast: He needed a strainer, some kind of basket or screen or net that the water could go through but the fish couldn't. He looked at the tree-top, appreciatively now, and saw how it combed the water and snagged leaves and floating branches.

Cam had never learned the art of basketry, nor how to weave. But the son of Len Rope-Maker had made his first net when he was four, a little bag to carry around the feathers and twigs and stones he played with. The knots had been uneven and the gauge a little wild — acorns dropped right through it and were lost — but if he had it with him today, even that first childish effort would do to catch a fish. He would only need to open the draw-string wide and scoop the fish inside.

It wasn't as easy as that, of course; it took hours to turn more tree bark fiber into enough cord for a net, and then half again as long to tie the knots so the web wouldn't let the giant fish slip through, with his stomach rumbling and grumbling all the while. (He was beginning to feel very hollow inside.)

And then he had to find a long branch with a fork that would hold the net open for the fish.

By the time he had his fish-net, it was noon or later— he couldn't tell for certain because the trees blocked the sun, but it felt like well after lunchtime. He took off his outer clothing, not willing to risk another drenching, and cinched his belt tightly around his tree to give him something to hold to while he fish-hunted. Then there was a certain amount of splashing, of learning not to let a shadow fall on his quarry, of slipping the net through the shallows as quiet as a hunting cat, and of holding it still in the water until his prey had placed itself just so. And there was waiting. A lot of waiting.

Then there was the gutting — which was messy without a knife — and the cooking — over the fire, skewered on a green stick — which meant more waiting, hard to bear.

Cam's fingers were sticky with fish-blood; he washed his hands in the stream. He checked to see if his jacket was dry yet. Almost. He gathered more sticks for the fire.

Then there was the eating...

Len was limp, spent from the two days of hard walking. She let someone take her pack from her. She didn't care what they did with it. She was interested in only two things: water, and where she could hang her hammock and rest, probably for several weeks.

Before taking the path to Fourth Village Down, Len had assumed that the heat and the damp would grow only gradually, as they had between First Home Village and New Home Village. And she had been right, as long as the path cut back and forth under trees and through those astonishing groves of cane that pressed like walls on either side, thickets so tall and dense they blocked the sun.

But a little past Third Village Down they had turned a corner of the world and come to where the path zigzagged down bare slate and shale. Her sweat dried, leaving her skin tight and crackly. The black rock held the heat like a baking stone. Only short scrub and dwarf trees found a toe-hold in the cracks, nothing that gave shade from the sun or shelter from the dry wind, hot as a gust from an oven. Suddenly,

Len couldn't drink enough. Her water-jug grew light. She found herself lagging, leaning heavily on her stick like an old woman. Somebody helped her, took her jug, gave it back to her, heavier now.

I should have listened to Fox, Len thought. I've gone beyond my limit. Then she'd stopped thinking and gave herself over to walking.

Now they had arrived somewhere, evidently. Cane and thatch buildings. People crowding around. Talking. Shade. A village. A place to sit down. Someone was pressing a mug into her hand. Good. More, please.

"Slowly," Nish cautioned her as she guzzled the cool water. "You'll make your stomach sick. Let me pour some on you, cool your head. Bend over."

And this sounded good to her, so she bent and let Nish empty a gourdful of water over her head. When she straightened, she felt a little dizzy.

"Tonight," Nish said, "you let me braid your hair. Not a big heavy braid— too hot. Lots of little braids. Keep your brain cool. I'll show you."

"I know how to braid my own hair, thanks," she thought, but didn't say, because somehow, the idea of sitting quietly while his hands smoothed and plaited her hair seemed appealing. Instead, all she said was "Thank you," as the cool well-water ran down her neck, leaving her damp shirt to cool her back as it dried.

That evening, while the others walked down to inspect the break in the path, Len washed her hair. Though her body was tired to exhaustion, her heart felt unreasonably light.

"Wawa," Jade said, reaching for the cup. That night, with her fingers curled around her teardrop pendant, Fox cried a little because Cam wasn't there to hear his daughter's first word.

Before Cam went into the forest, the road and the river had run together for some miles. Just how far, he could not say, because his awareness of the "bee-tree" hum had dawned only gradually. But now he judged that his best course was to follow the rocky winding course of the water and trust that it would bring him out, somewhere.

He learned that it was easier to walk through the trees at some distance from the stream. He could follow it by ear without having to stumble along its rough and rocky banks.

It was pleasant walking, and eerie, for there was no path at all, just his own choosing whether to go to the left or the right around each tree, always guided by the call of the water. He picked his way slowly; he was barefoot and there were spiky hollies scattered among the softer-leaved trees.

Cam carried his fish-net over his shoulder, with his fire-drill riding along in its mouth. In his pocket, there was a handful of fuzz he'd saved from the birds' nest. And he had his belt and clothes. That was all.

He lost count of the days and simply walked, trusting the river for water, food, and direction. When he was thirsty or hungry, he came back to it. When he was tired, he stopped and rested by it. When it was dark, he made fire along its banks.

He came loose from time, walking along without path or landmark. One night it rained; he did the best he could worming into a hollow log. There were a lot of spiders, but he had had enough of being wet and cold, so he asked their pardon, squeezed in with them, and slept dry.

Once, while gathering firewood, he found a squirrel's trove, last year's nuts. It was too early in the year for fresh ones. Most of the hoard was acorns, which he left alone because soaking out the bitterness would take more time than he wanted to spend. But there were butternuts, too; that was a very good day.

The waterfall was another good day. He was picking his way over rocky ground when he noticed the river music deepen. He turned back to the left to find the water again, and saw the forest green brighten ahead of him. He broke out into open sunlight on a broad wrinkled sheet of stone under a cloudless blue sky. The river leapt over an edge and cascaded down a great wall. He squatted to watch, enthralled, as the lacy curtains rippled and billowed over the rock. After a time, he lay down in the sun and listened to the water's music. When he threw his arm over his forehead to shade his eyes a bit, he could blot out the view of the trees above the waterfall and pretend that he was home, where water flowed straight down from the top of the world to the bottom and no one was ever lost.

Just at the top of the falls there was an outjutting that broke the avalanche of water into spray, a rainbow of sparkling individual droplets that threw themselves high in the air before falling back into the stream. Together, then apart, and then rejoined.

Their hosts had given them the hospitality of a house of their own, the Dyers' place, right in the middle of Fourth Village Down. (Or Tenth, to Len. Where was her Home Village now?) Both of the Dyers had been out trading for dye shells in the lowest villages when the earth shook. It was hoped they were safe below the rift and would return, if the path were ever mended. But until that day, the Rope-Maker would need a workshop, and the dye vats could be pushed aside easily enough.

The Dyers' house is a very colorful place, thought Len, as she pulled her clothes on, that first morning. The rainbow room with the lavender walls was crowded with bright hammocks and it took some effort not to bump into Tris Baker as she swung in peaceful dreams. Tris had mentioned that bakers without apprentices never got to sleep late, and Len wasn't going to be the one to wake her after their long push. But she wanted to see, with her own eyes, where the path was broken.

So they'd need a world of rope, would they? She'd take a look, see what shape they were in. She filled her water-jug from the cane spout that fed the kitchen. It would be good to have a little time to herself— give her a chance to think, to size things up. She'd go now, before breakfast, before everyone was awake and about.

But it turned out that, except for the weary new arrivals, everyone *was* awake and about. Len joined the many jostling up and down the path, a long narrow shelf that trailed across the world's wall, the stone face on her right, the great fall-off on her left. Dozens of new braids, Nish's doing, swung and flapped around her head in a way that felt strange to her, and pleasing.

In about twenty minutes' walk, the path brought Len down in a curve around a swell of stone. Now, over the heads in front of her, she could see the break. The sight stopped her.

Big.

The earthquake had sliced a giant wedge out the world. The huge mass had given way cleanly, along the slate's folded planes, leaving smooth gray walls opening out from a straight sharp corner, like a great table-cloth opening from a fold. The path dropped into nothingness at the edge of the gap, wiped away like a smudge. If you kicked a pebble over the edge, it wouldn't stop until it reached the bottom of the world.

Len could see what the builders' problem would be; there was no place to build, not the slimmest ledge that could be deepened for the path. But there must be toe-holds for climbing, she realized, when she spotted a half-dozen tiny shapes in the distance— climbers out on the rocks already. The human forms gave her eyes the scale of the disaster; they looked shockingly small as they inched up and around the break, like ants on a wall. Some were already above the gaping rawness, up where patches of green still mottled the gray— small trees and goat-grass that clung to the world with stubborn fingers. Climbers up that far must have stayed out all night, hammocked to the rock through the darkness.

Builders of all sorts were scurrying around her, pointing and arguing. She heard snatches of talk about anchoring and cantilevering, how to get food and drink up to the climbers, what would happen when it rained, and the good quartzy granite up above the slate. "But what's below?" someone muttered darkly. "That's what I want to know." Two birds, big ones, maybe eagles, soared across the break in the world, trailing their shadows over the riven stone.

Len didn't need to go all the way to the edge, to push her way through these people who had work to do. She had seen enough. Some problems, she knew how to fix. This one, she didn't. But there were those who did. There had to be, because the world couldn't stay broken in two like this. Whenever they figured it out, whatever they figured, they were going to need rope. Lots of rope. Anyone could see that. And rope was something Len knew about.

She turned back towards the village. Time to get to work.

Cam strode along closer to the river now. Walking was easier. The land had smoothed out and the water's song was softer here. The foliage was different too— lighter, lower.

He came to a patch of brambles and tried to skirt it, but couldn't seem to get around it. The thorns snagged his skin and clothing. There were berries, too, as big as his thumb, weighing down the spiny branches. They looked like wineberries, but were black as obsidian. He squashed one and sniffed it inquiringly. It had a sweet, fruity fragrance. Smelling nothing to offend, he touched a juice-stained finger first to his lips and then, after a pause, to his tongue. Sweet! He smacked his lips and waited a few moments to see if any late-rising bitterness or tingling would warn him away from the odd black berries— nothing.

He waded into the thicket, heedless of the thorns, plucking fruit eagerly until he held a double handful, then stopping to savor the strange little jewels of sweetness until his hands were empty and he filled them again.

In this way, Cam ate his way out through the thicket at the edge of the forest, not stopping until he emerged into full sunshine, face to face with a sleek brown cow that gazed at him with mild curiosity.

By the time Len pushed through the billowing sage-green gauze that served the Dyers as a door-screen, she had a rough idea of how to get started.

Someone needed to take stock. Someone needed to know what they had in the way of rope, cord, raw materials, and know-how. And more will be coming in from the upper villages, she reminded herself, as the runners carry the plea for help higher and higher. Someone needed to bring it all together under one roof, measure it, store it, keep track of it, and check it for strength and flaws. She had a brief mother-flash of how she would feel if Cam were one of the climbers creeping up the pathless rock, inch by patient inch. Any rope can break — she knew that — but usually it gives warning to someone with the eyes to see, someone like her. She was the Rope-Maker and, until she heard otherwise, she would be that someone. Every foot of rope that went out to the work would first pass through her fingers and under her eyes to ensure it wasn't frayed or poorly crafted.

The rope would have to be gathered first, which might take some doing. She thought she would ask Nish to work with her. He could ply a fine cord, and she couldn't find fault with his knots (though she had tried, when she first decided to bargain for his hammock for Fox.) Yes, she thought Nish Hammock-Maker would be a good person to work with.

Over breakfast, which Tris Baker had cheerfully *not* cooked (though she did help with the washing up after), Len learned that the others had also made plans. Aza Stonecarver, the Carpenters, and Jee were all going down to the break. They wanted to see the rift before they gathered with the other builders to start thrashing out what must be done, and by whom, and in what order. Tris was going to offer a hand to Hal Baker. ("Probably my last morning to sleep in," she added ruefully.) Of the carriers, three would work on putting up a large sleeping shed for the helpers from the upper villages. The others would stand ready to serve as runners when something was needed down at the break, or when someone had to be found in the swarm that the village had become.

"And you, Hammock-Maker? Do you have a task?" Nish didn't respond, not a flicker, though he was looking her way. "Nish...?"

He realized she was talking to him. "I'm not Hammock-Maker; I'm Fisher. Nish Fisher." To make himself clear, he pointed to the bright blue tattoo that adorned his right forearm: a big minnow curved in an unlikely leap.

"But you trade in hammocks, and make them, too? You talked so knowledgeably...?"

He laughed. Nish laughed a lot. "Oh, yes. I make hammocks. But I'm Fisher. Hammocks are just fish-nets, made pretty, with colors, like this." He gestured at the table-cloth, bright yellow with maroon stripes. "I'm a Fisher who makes hammocks."

"Well, Nish Fisher, will you work with me on this rope business?"

"Yes, Len Rope-Maker, I will work with you."

Len felt foolish. She remembered now that he carved fish; he had given one to Jade, weeks before, when he had taken hospitality at their table. And last night, when he had done her braids, he had run a shell comb, shaped like a fish, through her hair. After, he had given her the comb as a present. She had demurred, tried to turn aside the gift because she had nothing to give in return, but his big hands had pressed it into her. "No. Not the trade, the present," he insisted. "You walk far, get hot, come to help. You need the present. Take it." And her fingers had closed around it.

"Thank-you," she said.

It was the first gift Nish gave her.

After so much time in the woods, Cam found the big village jangling. It was loud and crowded and, frankly, seemed a little dirty. He walked the streets, by turns cringing at the noise, jumping out of the way of carts, asking for work, hoping for hospitality, and stunned with amazement.

The town was huge. It seemed that many hundreds of people must live here, all piled together, though flat land spread out around it as far as his dazzled eyes could see. The place was cut in half by water, not the river of his acquaintance, or at least he didn't think so; this water was broad and brownish, with none of the restless rush of the stream he knew.

At several points, great arms of wood spanned the water, arching between pilings of stone. People, animals, and even wheeled carts could cross these, so Cam ventured out. He stopped in the middle to peer over the railing, down into the water. He could see now that this water, too, had a direction and a hurry to it; from a distance it had seemed smooth and still. No rocks blocked its way and churned it to a frenzy, but he could still sense it moving below him, rippling around the bridge pilings, more sedate than its forest cousin, but close kin nonetheless. "If there are any fish down there," he thought, "you would never know it; the water is too dark."

Raising his eyes to look out further, his faculty for amazement was finally overwhelmed. "Oh, look," he thought numbly, "there's a house floating away." The people coming and going around him didn't seem to care, didn't spare a look for the marvel that slipped below them under the bridge. Perhaps many houses break loose when so much water pours through a town. Perhaps it's only to be expected. The people on the roof of the drifting building didn't seem to be in distress or in any way bothered by their predicament, and their neighbors didn't care. If only his pack had been able to float like that house...

A woman pushing a wheelbarrow full of onions jostled him. He turned away from the railing and went on across the water.

Cam had come into the town bruised, barefoot, and without coins. He was rank and grubby from sleeping on the ground; he could smell himself. He wished he had taken the trouble to wash up before coming among people again. His clothes were rags— what the river had left of them, the thorn-bushes had seen to. And he couldn't speak very well.

But instead of recognizing him for what he was, a traveler in need of hospitality, the people of this place seemed not to see him at all. As they shouldered past him on the bridge, hurried and full of purpose, they spoke no greeting. No one met his eyes. In fact, their glances seemed to flit away, almost, he imagined, as if they were pretending he wasn't there.

He had nearly grown used to the unwelcoming ways of this world. Distance is difference, he kept reminding himself. But the aloofness seemed more chilly here. "Maybe it's a thing of the larger villages," he thought to himself. "Or maybe it's just that I feel it more, because now my need is greater."

Because, truly, all he owned was a fish-net and a fire-drill. It wasn't much.

Fox stood with Jade under the eaves of Lia's house and watched another string of walkers file downworld, bound towards the rift in the path. Some waved at her cheerfully. Others wore intent, purposeful expressions. All walked with the short, heavy steps of carriers whose pack-baskets were full.

Everyone is going to help, she thought. Everyone except me.

Out of the blue, Lia said, "They're only with you for a minute, babies are. If you blink, they're grown and gone. Don't waste it, Fox. Don't spend this tiny moment wishing you were somewhere else, doing anything besides what you're doing."

Fox's arms tightened around Jade, warm and solid against her heart. "Okay," she said.

But her eyes followed the last carrier until he disappeared around the bend. Her eyes lingered on the empty path. What news, traveler? What news?

That afternoon, Nish found Len in the smithy, where she'd gone to arrange to test some of the rope they had gathered door-to-door. Not all the coils they'd collected were made of fibers she knew, or Nish either. If they were asked, "Will this line hold this much weight?" she wanted them to be able to answer with authority.

So she had betaken herself to the Smith, whose sweltering, smoky domain included all sorts of ways to burden a snip of rope to its breaking point— anvils, in particular. She was also pleased to find that Smith had a fine collection of tackle: blocks, pulleys, rings, and hooks of all sizes. Those would come in useful.

Brock Smith was willing to oblige, though he warned her that she'd better be careful of her ropes around the forge-fire if she wanted to learn anything besides what kind of ash they made. She agreed to mind herself and her materials while she was under his roof.

As she was turning to go, Nish rushed up. "You want to see this, Rope-Maker! Come!"

She followed him out to a little house near the edge of the village terrace, smaller than the Dyers' house and without the bright bursts of color at each window. It had been freshly roofed, by the look of it. Len admired the clever way the big cane was cut and split into rounded shingles in this village. They overlaid each other like rows of little half-barrels running down from the rooftree, giving the eaves a fancy scalloped edge. The new green shakes were just now drying into the mellow gold of the other village roofs.

Large, tight screens of creamy woven mesh covered the windows. Len had noticed this sort of window treatment on all the houses in this village. There must be a matter of night-flyers here, she thought; those screens wouldn't keep out anything bigger than a determined cat. Goose could make mincemeat of one. She sighed.

"Spinner?" Nish called. "Rope-maker is here, come to see what you have."

"Come in, come in," a girl's voice fluttered.

The door-screen here was not a great waft of netting like the Dyers', but two long, overlapping sheets of un-dyed linen, each neatly weighted at the bottom with a short stick. Nish and Len slipped through the vent between them and came inside.

The Spinner was sitting at a flax wheel in the buttery sunlight softened by the window-screens. Her hair was the same color as the fibers on her distaff. "How pretty she looks there," Len thought, "and how young!"

The Spinner, whose name was Breeze, stood up to welcome them. "Will you sit?" she asked, offering some stools. "Will you take a cup of water?"

"Water is good," Nish agreed. "Rope-Maker is from the high villages, needs water, or she'll dry out and flop like a fish on the sand."

Len laughed. "He's right; I do have to drink a lot down here. I'd be grateful for a sip of water. But, as for sitting— maybe some other day. I'd love to talk sometime. You do lovely work," she said, fingering the fine thread. The girl blushed. "Nish said you had something I should see."

"I don't know if it could of be any use," Breeze started as she poured them each a horn cup of water. "But he said you were collecting all the rope and twine to help the climbers. I told him I didn't have any in the house to speak of, but I do have the makings." She waved towards the half-attic that overhung her workroom.

"The makings?" Len echoed.

"Yes. Do you want to see?"

"I believe I do."

Breeze led her up the ladder into the dim light of the loft. As soon as her head cleared the ceiling that was also the upper floor that spanned half the house, Len saw bales and bales of fine, straight stalks, stacked up to the rafters: Flax!

"I've never heard tell of linen rope, but...," Breeze said apologetically.

"Neither have I. But I don't see why not. And just think how strong it would be!" Len clambered up onto the rough wood of the attic floor to get a closer look into the shadows. Towering piles of sleek, perfect stems, each longer than her arm. The rope-maker looked at Nish, still perched below her on the steps. He grinned back. She stroked the golden bundles. "There's so much of it! Do you grow it for trade in these parts?"

Breeze blushed again. "No, I just like it. It doesn't grow here at all, except in some of the cracks in the rock, and those are sad little plants that bloom as pretty as you please, but never grow tall. So when I moved here to partner with Jory, I brought some. A lot, really." She seemed embarrassed.

"Where's your flax-break, then?"

"Out in back, under the eaves. It's a big one, heavy. Jory usually helps me."

"Good. Can you and Jory put aside...?" She fell silent. Big tears were leaking from Breeze's eyes.

"Jory's a climber." Breeze said in a small voice. "He's... out."

Out. Len took a breath. Her eyes again sought Nish.

"And no apprentice?"

"We're just getting started," Breeze explained, with a little shrug.

"Well, Breeze Spinner, Nish and I are going to send you some big strapping muscles to keep that flax-break going. If we need the fiber, we'll have it ready. If not, you'll at least have enough broken out to keep your wheel busy for years. And," — Len gave the girl's shoulder a little squeeze — "I will see to it that any rope that comes to Jory Climber from my hand will be as stout and safe as what I'd give my own son."

Cam walked more slowly now. Night was nearing. He wasn't so sure that he had bettered things by coming out of the forest. He wondered if he could find his way back to the brown cow and the brambles, go back into the woods where he could fish-hunt and sleep by his stream. No one in this town had offered him so much as a drink of water. In that way, at least, the river had been generous.

As the light faded towards evening, Cam was aware in a detached way that if he weren't so disheartened he would be intrigued by the very odd street down which he was walking. On one side of the road there were the usual buildings, all pressed up against each other with no space in between. (The people in this town must like each other very much to live so close together.)

The other side of the street was bounded by a wide board-walk along the water. And there, packed side by side as tightly as the other dwellings in the town, was a row of brightly painted floating houses, bristling with tall posts, clotheslines, porches, and railings. They jostled against each other, muttering restlessly, creaking against the great cables that held them fast, rubbing against the planks of the boardwalk itself, which were cushioned by enormous ornamental knots like long melons, frayed by hard wear. He stooped closer to see if he knew the pattern, then had to skip out of the way for a string of carriers staggering up the boardwalk with heavy bags hefted over their shoulders. A thick-bodied, leather-skinned woman came behind them, shouting directions.

She paused to yell something back over her shoulder. Cam seized the moment to ask, "Can I help to carry?" She turned back to him.

"Looking for work, are you?"

"Yes. Looking for work. Can I help?" The woman studied him critically from under the short, wild curls that almost hid her eyes.

"You made that?" she asked, pointing a stumpy finger at the fish-net he still carried over his shoulder.

"Yes. I made that." He handed it to her. "For...," and here his word-hoard failed him, "things in water." He made a fish-wiggle with his hands.

"Yes, of course. But what's this thing in it?" She disentangled the fire-bow from the net. Her hands were strong and rough, but she handled the cords with care.

"For fire," Cam explained. "For making fire."

"Oh." She considered it for a moment, turning it over in her hands, and then brought her gaze back to him. "Good with your hands, eh?"

He held them out in front of him, turning them over. The nails were black; the fingers, stained from berry-picking. "My hands— all I have."

She slapped him on the back, rattling his ribs painfully. "All any of us have, really," she laughed, and he thought, not really. You have shoes, bags it takes six carriers to handle, the coin to pay them, and a place to sleep tonight. And you probably know the word for "fish." But he didn't say this.

"Well, you're too skinny for this lot," she waved at the line of heavy-laden carriers up ahead, "but we could use a hand on the Duck starting tomorrow. Not much coin, but there's a place to sleep and you'll eat what the family eats."

Cam didn't have to think about this at all. Any offer that included the words "coin," "place to sleep," and "eat" was a good offer.

"Yes," he said, nodding with vigor. "Good. I will work for you. Hard. I will work hard."

"You bet you will," she laughed. "But in the meantime, you look like you could use some food. You want to come along, meet the rest of the crew, get some dinner?"

"I have no coins," he said sadly.

"I *told* you," she said, whacking his arm. "You eat what the rest of the family eats. Tonight we're eating fish." Cam looked blank at the new word; Genia made the fish-wiggle with her hand and he understood.

"Oh," he managed. "Fish. Good."

"I'm Genia Duck, by the way. What do you call yourself?"

"I'm Cam. Cam Far-Walker." Genia pulled him along through the town in her wake.

"The climbers have met! The climbers have met!" The good news rippled through the village.

The climbers from the high side of the break had encountered climbers coming upworld from below. In fact, one of the climbers from First Village Down was on his way now, following the ropes and anchors and platforms their own village climbers had laid out across the rock, coming to take counsel with the builders here and tell how things looked from the other side.

A feeling of satisfaction settled on them. Ram Climber would be the first person to come up into the village since the earthquake broke the path. He was proof that the world could still be travelled, if only by the brave and strong. But that was something.

It was darker than dark when they left the eating place. A heavy fog sucked up the starlight and dissolved all shape and substance from the town. Cam was blind lost the instant he stepped outside the tavern's friendly doors, but he followed

his new friends as they stumbled along together, guffaw-
ing at each other when they tripped over paving-stones and
walked into walls.

Cam had fallen in among warm-hearted people. He was
not clear about all their names, nor about who was related to
whom, and in what ways, but they had fed him. They had fed
him fish that was not speared on a green stick and cooked dry
over a smoky fire; instead, it was stewed up in a spicy soup,
hot enough to make his nose run. "Good," he sniffled. When
he had thought he could eat no more, a tray of fishcakes had
arrived, which they shared out, eating with their hands. And
then came what they said was the *real* meal: great slabs of
golden fish, batter-fried and stacked on a platter, with, Cam
noted, their heads and tails thoughtfully removed.

Now he was sinking into a stupor from a belly full of fish
and dark, syrupy beer. He had no idea where they were or
where they were going, but he would cheerfully trail along
through every puddle in this benighted town, for they had
offered him hospitality. They had learned that he had no place
to sleep that night. He was going home with them.

They dragged him along as they staggered down the light-
less alleys. Finally, somewhere near the river, they stepped
onto a porch where a futile little lamp lit up a globe of fog
about as big as a fruit-basket. Cam found he was having
trouble with his balance. Someone pulled him over a threshold. He stumbled down a short, steep flight of stairs. A cellar,
he thought, regretfully, but then the others clattered down
after him. If he was passing the night in a damp root-cellar,
at least he wouldn't be the only one.

Someone lit a candle and he saw in the swaying light that
this cellar was festooned with clothing and fitted out with
narrow beds built into the wooden walls, like shelves. One was
for him. He crawled in, banging his head on the bunk above.

Then cradle-comfort engulfed him. "The beer must have
gone to my head," he thought as he had the sense of being
rocked gently to sleep.

It was like wrestling with snakes.

Len was out in the Dyers' garden, hatted against the hot
sun, sweating, working side by side with Nish to ply four

ropes into a single cable strong enough to lift heavy tools and lumber up to the good rock above the rift. Len had never made a cable this heavy. Had anyone?

They both held a strong one-inch rope in each hand and had been plying silently for a while now, leaning back hard against the yards of cable they'd already produced to keep the work taut while they plied. (The completed end was anchored to a boulder behind the Dyers' house.) They'd fallen into a steady rhythm by now: Len would give a half-turn to the top rope, then bring it down and under the others, slipping it into her left hand while she released the rope she'd just been holding to Nish. At the same time, Nish would hand her the next top strand— take a rope, give a rope, over and over. Like a dance with only two steps. Do it again. Their fingers touched, dexterous in the exchange. Again. The ropes twined around each other, four into one. Again, always pacing each other to keep the twist and the tension even.

The needs for rope, all kinds of rope, were growing day by day. First, light, strong line had been wanted for pulleys to lift food and drink up to the climbers. Then there had been a call for rope stout enough to carry the builders, who were not as nimble as the climbers. Now they had been asked for cable bigger than any Len had ever heard of, to carry up the materials that would rebuild the path.

It's all the same twist, though, thought Len, the same twirl that Breeze spins into her spider-fine linen thread, the same that Nish coils into the cords he makes for nets, the same that I've put into a lifetime of ropes. It's the same thing.

"I remember when I thought this was all a trick," she said suddenly.

"What trick?"

"This, what we're doing— putting things together to make them stronger. I was around nine years old, visiting old Rize Rope-Maker, making a nuisance of myself. He had me pick out two bundles of fiber. 'Make sure they're the same size, now' he told me. So I did, and he took one of them and in about a second he'd twisted it into a simple two-ply cord, about as long as my hand. 'Still the same?' he asked, and I said 'Yes,' because I saw that he hadn't added or taken away any of the fiber. I remember it was like hair, like blond hair. 'You're sure?' I nodded. 'Well, then. If these two bunches of fiber are still the same, they should break the same, shouldn't they? I mean, the same weight or force should pull them in two, right? It stands to reason,' he said, and I agreed.

"Anyway, he handed me the first little bunch, the one he hadn't touched. He told me to hold each end in one of my hands and pull, hard. I did, and it broke in two, easy. He laughed and said, 'You're a strong little girl. Now try this one, just the same.' I took the bundle that he'd twisted into cord — just *twisted*, nothing else — and pulled on it with all my might. It held. I never did break that cord; it's still around, somewhere, up in my first Home Village.

"Rize told me that if I could ever tell him why the twisted fiber was so much stronger than the other — 'Just the same, remember' — then he would take me as his apprentice."

Nish twinkled at her. "And you know the answer?"

"I do. It took me a long time to figure it out, though. Nobody would tell me; I thought grownups knew, but it was some kind of secret. I bothered my parents about it a lot— they just told me it had something to do with the twist. I knew *that*; I had to understand what it was about the twist, how it worked. You know, don't you, Nish?"

"I know now. Not when a child. How did you learn…?"

"A weed taught me. Really. A strangle-vine got onto one of our apple saplings, and my mother sent me to clear it away. You know strangle-vines?"

"No. They do not sound friendly."

"Well, you could say they are *too* friendly, maybe. They wrap themselves round and round things. If you leave them long enough, they can make wood grow in spirals— pretty for a walking stick, but not so good for a fruit tree. Anyway, I was trying to pull this vine off a branch, and the harder I pulled, the harder it clutched. I was afraid I might break the little tree, poor thing— pulling just made the coils tighter. I had to unwind it, loop by loop."

"Smart vine. Smart girl." The ropes rolled easily now, from his hands into hers, from hers back into his, building this strong thing together.

"Well, I'd been worrying at old Rize's riddle for weeks; I had twists and twirls on my mind, I guess. Anyway, suddenly the answer was clear to me, as if I'd always known. I ran to tell my mother; I had to explain it to somebody. I felt like if I didn't put it into words it might get away from me again."

"What words did you put?"

Len paused a moment in the work, holding two ropes in one hand while she dragged her sleeve across her forehead to keep the sweat out of her eyes, then went on.

"First, I showed her the little spiral twig of strangle-vine. It kept its shape after I peeled it off the branch. I showed her how you could pull it and it would get longer, then spring back when you let go."

"Ah."

"When you tugged on it, the loops would stretch out long-ways, of course, but the important thing was that they got smaller *across*. It was so simple, once you saw it: The spiral got slimmer when you pulled. *That's* how it grabbed on tighter when I yanked on it and *that's* why it's called 'strangle-vine.' And *that's* what Rize Rope-maker did with his magic twists: He laid each fiber side by side and turned them so that they spiraled around each other. Just like the strangle-vine. Then, when I pulled on the ends, the spirals tried to stretch out. Just like vine. And the coils got a little longer, maybe, but the point was: They got skinnier, too. They pulled closer, supported each other. Helped each other not to break."

Nish nodded. "That's it. Upworld, downworld— the same. The twist— it puts little things side by side so that the heavy weight, the big pull, makes them stronger. They hold. Without the twist, they break alone."

"Exactly. And when I could explain it so that my mother understood, I knew I was ready to be Rize's apprentice. That was the beginning." She was silent for a while, rolling the ropes over, down, across, and under, and then went on. "Cam, my son, grew up knowing about the twist; I don't think he ever saw the power of it. But I never stopped seeing it. These four ropes that are blistering our hands right now— we put them together right and they'll hold more than the sum of what each of them could hold alone. That's magic."

Nish nodded, "Weak things, put together right, they get strong. But for me, the magic is *after* the making is done, when you throw line or net into the ocean, bring something up from the deep. That's my magic."

"Nish, I have to confess I never really understand you when you talk about the ocean and what you do."

"I fish."

"You make fish. Like I make rope."

He laughed. "No, fish aren't for making. Fish are for catching. Catch them and eat them. Catch them and dry them. Catch them and smoke them. Catch them and trade them with the far people. Catch them and carve their bones." He pointed to the bird-figure that dangled round his neck, shiny as a tooth, but Len was still stuck on the first point.

"You *eat* fish? There must be an awful lot of them..."

He nodded eagerly. "Many fish in the ocean. You'll see. After we make the big bridge, you come, Len— see where I live. Lean together, maybe, like these ropes that make each other strong." Without stopping the ply, he leaned into her, letting her feel his shoulders, giving her hip a little bump with his. "Throw out the nets together, maybe catch something big."

"Maybe we will," she laughed. Nothing seemed impossible.

They worked on, side by side, twining the ropes around each other, careful of the tension and the twist.

Cam woke up sick. He tumbled out of his narrow bed and stood swaying on his feet, looking around urgently in the dim light. The other bunks were empty now, though this was not easy to make out in the forest of boots and coats and trousers that swung, gentle pendulums, from hooks on every surface. He spotted the ladderish stairway and scrambled up and out the door.

He lurched to the porch railing and threw up over it, into the broad waters below. There was laughter behind him, and a big hand slapping him on the shoulder like a blacksmith's hammer. Genia's voice bellowed, "Good morning! Welcome to The Duck!" Too loud, too loud. Someone handed him a rag.

He wiped his mouth and gawked.

Their home had broken away during the night. It had been, he realized, one of those on the street of floating houses and now it was loose and drifting. In front of him, green fields slipped by like clouds on a windy day. Turning, he saw unbroken forest passing on the other side of the water. So much, so much— Cam's eyes couldn't hold it all.

He pointed, shakily. "We go?" No one else seemed concerned about this disaster. His legs wobbled under him, but it was the floor itself, rocking on the water.

"That's right. Can't all of us lie abed until noon, boy. We cast off at dawn." Genia waved her hand upstream, towards the town far behind them. "Seemed better to let you sleep, though. You're too stove up for heavy work anyway. We'll get some meat on your bones first." Here, she pinched his shoulder, hard, and clucked like a disappointed mother. "You'll do, soon enough. Have to see to the cargo now. Beans need to be stowed right and tight— looks like rain. Come a rain, beans get wet, they swell up and sprout, burst The Duck, and sink us all." She laughed merrily at the idea. "Wouldn't want her to go down, now would we?"

"No," he agreed, shaking his head fervently. "The Duck should not go down."

"You're pretty nervy, aren't you? Jump at the lightest touch, like you've been stabbed. Want some breakfast?"

"No." This he was sure of. "No breakfast. I'm sick." Somehow, the swaying of The Duck seemed to get inside of him, into his stomach, and wipe out any trace of hunger he ever had, or ever *would* have. The very idea of food…

"Best if you eat something. A full belly is a settled belly, I always say. Trust me." She strode off along the railing, looked back at him, and said, "Don't stand there and let the gulls nest in your hair, boy; come along to the galley. Let's get you fed."

He followed her doubtfully.

What he had thought was a porch (because it had railings) was in fact the roof of the floating dwelling. On top of it all, in the shade of a great white awning on a vertical post as tall as a tree, a smaller house was built. They walked back to this, with Cam staggering like a drunken man as The Duck rolled under them. Genia led him down a few steps to the tiniest kitchen he had ever seen. It wasn't much bigger than his bed.

He stood swaying, gripping the doorjamb against the sick-making dipping and bobbing. He tried not to look while the big brown woman dished out a glop of some sort of thick porridge and topped it with a wedge of butter and swirl of brown syrup that reminded him uncomfortably of last night's beer. He swallowed hard.

"Here. Take this up top. The fresh air will do you good. Eat every bit of it, then come back to the galley and get to work on these." She flung her arm over the scatter of dirty crockery. Cam took the bowl and scooted out before she could pound him on the back again.

That night, Len dreamed that the whole path of the world lay across her lap, a great bundle of silvery strands.

"It's too big," she thought, "too much. I can't get my hands around it all."

But then Nish came and helped her. They divided the path between them, their hands filled with silky filaments like the hair of the moon if the moon had hair, and then twisted it, together, into two-ply cord. Simple. So simple.

"Is it strong enough?" Nish asked her in the dream.

"I never did break that cord," she answered, and woke up.

That was the night that Len went to Nish.

He held the hammock open to her. She eyed the fine web that outlined his dark body in the dimness of the Dyers' upper room: rippling hints of blues and greens that swelled and surged as the hammock moved under him. "Is it strong enough?"

"It will hold," he answered, smiling.

They were very quiet; the house was full of sleeping friends.

Cam obeyed Genia. It seemed the thing to do.

He took his bowl of mush up to the porch-roof and settled himself comfortably into a coil of rope under the big triangular awning that billowed tight in the wind, but the tall one, Quoit came and chased him away; evidently ropes were held in such regard here that they were not to be sat or stepped on. This sign of respect for her craft would please Len.

He sighed and looked around for somewhere he would be out of the way, for there was a great deal of bustle on The Duck's hind end: heaving, grunting, and shouts of encouragement and command. Genia had a very strong voice, he thought, and headed the other way.

He slipped around the little house where she'd given him his breakfast and up to the front end of The Duck. It was pointed, like a wedge.

As he leaned over the rail, seeing his shadow reach out far in front of him, he saw that The Duck was in fact a long wedge cleaving through the water, pushed along from the rear by the wind. The ruffle of water around the pointy end showed that, though the stream was moving, The Duck was moving faster, elbowing the water aside in her hurry. The breeze of her passing tousled his hair. He propped himself in the wedge of railing and watched the ripples in the broad brown waterway glitter in the morning sun as the world of land glided past on either side.

He recognized a hawk, just like any he might see in the skies of Home Village. It rose boldly from the forest, not bewildered at all by the table-top flatness of the water and the wideness of the world. He shook his head, and took a reluctant spoonful of the mealy mush.

Genia was right; it did seem to settle his stomach. He could not say much for the flavor, though, which fell somewhere between "nothing much" and "none at all." "It's probably better hot," he thought.

He learned an important thing while he ate: The Duck family included a cat, a big orange one. She turned up her nose at the bit of porridge he offered, but was willing to lick a smudge of butter off his fingertip. In return, she allowed him to stroke her, though not for very long. If he really wanted to pet her, he would have to do better than porridge.

She was twice the size of his mother's cat. Would he ever again see Goose amble home at Len's evening call? And this brought his thoughts back, again, to Fox. When would he find her again? Not being with her ached like something missing, some part of him gone, something missing from inside his chest. He had meant to turn back a long time ago and head for the high villages, to cross the roof of the world in the strong summer sun. But midsummer had come and passed, he thought, during his long walk in the woods. He had followed the stream as it ran down, going always further down and deeper in, into this strange, strange world.

He wished— what? That he had not left her? No, not that, not if it meant that he had never walked into this world of giant fish and floating houses, Keptha's world and Anani's world and Genia's. No; he could never want that walking undone.

Did he wish that he had promised to return? What good would that have done? He'd intended to come back to her, promise or no promise. That was a fact, as solid and as real as any cord tied around a wrist. The only thing that would stop him would be if he died first, and even the Never-Ending

Braid can't put the fallen back on the path. It hadn't saved Len from losing Yarrow and it had hung on her arm forever after he died. No, better not to tangle people up in promises that could haunt and hobble them.

Did he wish that he had asked Fox to wait for him? How could that be fair, not knowing where he was going, how long he would be gone, or what dangers might find him on the way? And now The Duck was taking him even further, carrying him downstream and downworld, towards the sea and away from Fox. Far and farther on the unstopping flow as the fields and forests unspooled on either side.

Wishful, but not knowing what he wished for, Cam finished his breakfast and went to wash the dishes.

The rope work sorted itself out between the two houses, the Spinner's and the Dyers'.

The actual rope-making, the plying, braiding, splicing, and knotting, was done in the Dyers' workshop. That's where Len and Nish spent most of their hours.

At the beginning, it was hard for Len to trust anyone other than herself with the actual plying of a line that might hold a human life. But the demand for rope had increased to the point where she learned, unwillingly, that she must rely on others. (Though she still ran every foot of rope through her hands, inspecting it by touch and sight.) They simply had to have more rope-makers, and Len chose careful crafters like Nish for the work.

From the first, Brig Weaver had helped them clear away the Dyers' vats, dyestuffs, and finished cloth left to dry. Weavers tend to be tidy and precise people with a wholesome horror of snarls and tangles, so Len asked Brig to take charge of the rope they made and the rope they were given; more was coming in each day as the upper villages learned of the need. Brig measured every piece and marked them with knots at the end that told their length. He coiled them neatly and hung them from the Dyer's drying racks and hooks, sorted by strength. If no one could tell him how strong a rope was, he would cut a bit from the end, take it to the smithy, and load it until it broke. No one was allowed to take a finished rope from its place in the Dyers' workshop except for Brig Weaver.

The readying of the fibers, on the other hand, was handled at the Spinner's house. Breeze Spinner, the blushingest girl Len had ever known, received, prepared, and stored the fibers. Her little house overflowed with bales, coils, and bundles until a lean-to was added to make room for the materials that were being carried in from villages all along the path as they learned that rope would be needed for the mighty scaffolding that was being built to rejoin the world.

The builders had decided that it was best to repair the path in two stages. First, a scaffolding, some blend of boardwalks, ladders, and rope-bridges, would be anchored to the good rock up above the rift. This could be built fairly quickly. It would allow people to come and go, and give workers a place to stand while they whittled out the more permanent solution: a new path, carved by hand into the living stone. Nothing on this scale had ever been done by the villages. It was thought that the work would take more than a year to finish, if all went well. The labor would be long, but it was felt that the wood, rope, and cane scaffolding could serve as a short-term plan, while a new ledge hewn from the rock itself would answer for their children's children's children.

So, while Breeze kept her strong young helpers busy at the flax-break, a wealth of fibers poured in from the other villages, each sending what was native and abundant at their own levels. Breeze's Home Village sent, of course, more of the golden flax; Len's First Home Village, nettle-stems, still green, harvested a little early. Lia's and Jade's Home Village sent huge coils of green creeper, as big as barrels. The creeper vine came with word that Fox hoped to visit soon and reminders from Lia to wear a hat and drink plenty of water. First Village Up sent baskets full of the spiky spears of a certain plant that grew in the crevices of the hot rocks. Neither Breeze nor Len knew what to do with it.

"Do you think it's meant for the cooks?" Len proposed, poking it doubtfully. "It's pulpy, like a vegetable."

Nish laughed at them. "Boil it," he said, "in a big pot. Like yams. Get it all soft, all mush, and then scrape down the spears with an old blunt knife. You'll find the fiber in it sure enough, if you look. Sometimes, you have to do some work to get to the good— scrape away the surface. Go a little deep."

Even the highest villages sent help. The rawhide, Breeze gave to Len for braiding. The wool baffled them both. "What are we supposed to do with it? Knit sweaters?" This, Brig Weaver was able to help with. He had heard, when he was an apprentice, that in the very highest villages, where rope and rawhide grew brittle in the cold and snapped like twigs, that the world was held together by woven woolen bands. "Everything from a finger's width to a foot across— all woven of worsted wool." So Breeze and the spinners from neighboring villages spun the lot of it up into strong yarn and Brig Weaver took charge of it. Soon, Len was seeing children all over the village, leaning into back-strap looms anchored to trees and doorposts, doing their part for the mending of the path.

Later, Len heard from the builders that the woven bands were prized by the builders for two uses. Being not only strong but flat, they held loads of wood and cane together more firmly than rope. Also, when fashioned into the loops and belts that harnessed the workers to catch them if they fell, they were more comfortable over the long hours on the rock face. So soon even the gifts of the very farthest villages were woven into the work. The path was everyone's business.

For Cam, life on the floating house simply seemed to be made up of the same chores as any house, mostly scrubbing. While the others scurried about, jumping to adjust the big wind-catcher at Genia's command, Cam scoured dishes, floors, and laundry. This suited everyone well enough; Cam had been mastering these skills ever since Keptha first put him to work at the inn and he was quite handy at them by now. All along the path, he had earned his food and lodging by the work of his hands. He had become a mighty washer of dishes; the three meals a day eaten by The Duck's crew of five were nothing compared to the avalanche of crockery he'd dealt with at Rudily's glad gift-giving.

Laundry also fell to his lot, but Genia's family was not particular about wearing the same clothing, rough trousers and patched shirts, day in and day out, so this too was a fairly light duty.

What Genia *was* particular about was keeping The Duck clean. For such an easy-going woman, she was very keen on sweeping and mopping— particularly on *Cam* sweeping and mopping. Every inch of The Duck had to be cleaned each morning, before everything else. When Cam asked her why, she shook her head gravely. "Rats, boy. You let The Duck get dirty, next thing you know, you've got *rats*. They can eat your cargo while you sleep."

"And then no beans," Cam pressed her, hardly daring to hope.

"That's right. No beans. Wouldn't want that to happen, would we?"

Cam didn't say anything to this. It seemed like Genia must love beans dearly; whole rooms on The Duck were brim-full with sacks and sacks of the strange pale, pebbly things. They were round like peas, but bigger— as big as the tip of Cam's thumb. They reminded him of the tricky rolling gravel below Seventh Village Up. He wondered when he would scuff through that gravel again on his way home. It was very far away, but he seemed to be eating a bowlful of it every midday when Genia dished out bean stew for the five of them on The Duck. And then there it was again at supper, in the bean soup served with steamed bean-bread. And if you ground that gravel to sand, boiled it to mush, and served it up with butter, you would have something very like the daily breakfast on The Duck. For variety, sometimes the bean porridge came with butter and salt; other days, it came with butter and syrup. But always it was beans— unless someone caught a fish.

Cam learned to fish using a fine strong thread and a hook baited with bacon salvaged from the bean stew. In the evenings, sometimes he and Veydle and Lexo would sit on the back porch of The Duck and trail their lines in the water until a sudden pull told of a fish that wanted to be fried for breakfast. Then there would be shouts of encouragement — "Slowly, now! Careful!" — and someone would grab Cam's long net and scoop the fish onto the boat. And that is how Cam learned the names of the river fish, the spots and stripes and rainbows. Quoit taught him how to clean fish properly and, when he had learned, gave him a knife to replace the one the river had stolen. It fit the sheath he still wore.

It was through fishing that Cam finally made friends with the big orange cat that was named, as far as he could tell, "Cat." Cat was very interested in fish and fishing and would perch fastidiously on The Duck's railing, very still and alert, and watch when a fish was landed. After it was cleaned and sent to the kitchen, she would stroll over and take notice of the fact that there was a fish head on the deck, along with some of the mushy bits that people wasted. She expressed a willingness to help clean up the mess — only if they wanted her to, of course — and they agreed that this would be a good idea.

After Cam had paid his respects with his first fish head and guts, Cat finally accepted him as the newest crew member. That night, Cam slept with a warm, heavy purr upon his chest.

Jory Climber had worried about Breeze while he was out working on the new path, for that was what they were calling it even though it was little more than a set of hefty ropes fixed to rock-anchors at this point. Breeze was new to the village; he didn't want her to be too much alone. But up there, crawling around like spiders on a wall, few climbers could handle themselves as well as he could and see to the safety of others, too. He tried to come down fairly often, but he worried when he was not out there to watch over the work, and the workers, too.

So when that older couple, the pale upworld woman and the downworld man with all the tattoos, moved their hammock into the attic of the Spinner's house, Jory was glad that Breeze would have company. The bales of flax they'd stored there were mostly gone now: some stacked out by the flax-break, some broken, some hackled, and some already turned to fine linen rope. Jory was rarely at home, out working above the break for long days at a time. Compared with the crowding in the Dyers' house, the sleeping shed, and the other homes that were offering hospitality to workers from afar, Breeze Spinner's little house was roomy and private.

Len and Nish were mostly at the Dyers' house during the day anyway, so Jory and Breeze could steal some time together when he was home. But, to be alone, they had to chase away the Spinner's helpers as well. For Jory's shy young partner had taken on, not just one apprentice, but a whole gang of extra hands to ready all manner of fibers for the rope-makers.

Under Breeze's charge, they kept the flax-break going, boiled great pots of the spear-like leaves, and scraped away

mounds of slime to find the fiber at the heart of things. People
who had never even seen nettle growing in its patches along
the path up near Len's Home Village learned how to tease out
the strength of its stems. Breeze explained to Jory earnestly
how retting something for too long or leaving even the smallest bits of chaff among the fibers could weaken a rope, rot
and stem-shards being sharp as knives. "They can cut and
fray a line from within, and nobody knows 'til it breaks,"
she told him. No fiber went to the rope-makers until it had
passed through her hands and she knew that it was clean and
sound. She knew her work like her partner knew the hard
rock wall of the world.

Breeze wasn't an outsider any more. She wasn't lonely or
bored, and Jory's heart rested easier. When he worked on the
new path, snug loops belted his thighs and waist. He knew
a strong rope would catch him if he fell. Jory did his work.
Breeze did hers.

Genia learned that Cam couldn't swim when Veydle threw
him overboard and he sank.

Cam had spent the last half of the night on watch. All
in all, he liked this night duty up on the nose of The Duck.
Under the tiny night sail that allowed some of the crew to
go below for sleep, he would stand — "Never sit! You might
doze and let the The Duck be smashed to toothpicks. Wouldn't
want that to happen, would we?" — and keep an eye out for
things in the water: rocks, sand-banks, logs, or other boats
that might crash into them. As Cam endorsed the idea that
The Duck should not be smashed to toothpicks, he always
kept a careful watch. He enjoyed the cool darkness, the stars,
and the moon that rose behind them and raced The Duck to
the distant line where the sky met the land at morning. It
was restful not to have to say many words, only calling out
every now and then when he saw something, so that Genia or
tall Quoit, whichever of them was back at the steering stick,
could turn The Duck if needed.

After night-watch, he would join the others for a breakfast
bowl of bean-mush — "For if we don't take a bite of our cargo
now and then, how will we know if it's spoiling?" — and then
go down to his bunk for a sleep.

On the morning when he got thrown overboard, he had just woken up. He was clambering up the steps when he heard a ruckus above him, scuffling and shouting. He rushed out to find Quoit clinging desperately to the railing while Veydle and Lexo, each holding one of his long legs, were trying to twist him over the side. Cam flew to Quoit's aid, knocking Veydle away with the force of his rush. He turned his attention to Lexo, trying to break her hold on Quoit's leg, but then felt both his ankles seized and lifted. He let go of Lexo and scrabbled for the railing as he was tipped mercilessly over the side to the sound of laughter. He slid headfirst under the brown water.

He had thought the other river bottomless, but now he learned about real depth. He twisted and fought, but there was nothing to fight towards or against, no rocks, no bottom, no light, no foam. There was no air. No air. No air—

Then there *was* someone to fight against. ("Well, jump in after him and fish the boy out!" Genia had shouted at them.) Someone had an arm around his neck and was trying to throttle him while he drowned. Cam kicked against him furiously, but the strangler was behind him, dragging him down.

Then his head broke water. He gasped air, beautiful air, and Veydle was yelling in his ear, "Don't fight, idiot! I've got you."

After Veydle and Cam had scrambled back onto The Duck, Genia yelled at all of them: at Lexo and Veydle for horseplay when they should be working, at Quoit for encouraging them, and at Cam for not knowing how to swim. "The very next town we stop at, he starts learning," she growled. "And the two of you will teach him."

Veydle said he was sorry he threw Cam off The Duck. Cam said he was sorry he kicked Veydle in the groin while he was trying to save him. Genia said she was sorry she had such a duckload of fools for a family, and that they had all better get to work or Cam wouldn't be the only one thrown overboard that morning. The orange cat also looked disapproving, but it didn't say anything.

In late autumn, with Jade grown into a sturdy toddler and the harshest heat of the season behind them, Fox came for a visit. When she got to the village above the rift, she asked where Len Rope-Maker might be found and was directed farther down the path to the Dyers' house. "How will I know the place?" she asked.

"Oh, you'll know it all right. It's the *Dyers'* house." She walked on, a little puzzled, until she saw a large house screened with a different color at every window: lilac, rose, buttercup yellow, sky-blue. Weathered swatches of every color drooped from the eaves. A familiar form disentangled itself from the pale green drapery that fluttered at the doorway.

Fox began to run towards Len, then stopped and swung Jade down from the back-sling where she'd ridden for most of the four-day trip. To show off how much she'd grown, Fox set her on her feet, gripping her hand, for she was still wobbly. Mother and daughter took little steps down the path together.

Fox pointed. "See— there she is, Jade. There's Len! Can you call her? Call Len."

Jade said nothing. She knew Fox and Lia loved it when she said sounds for them. Her words excited them. She enjoyed this and found words could also be useful for their own sake: "More!" for example, and "No!" and "Juice!" But she was tired and had been in that sling for too long. She felt cranky and didn't intend to say anything at all until after she'd had a chance to try out her walking on this funny-colored ground. She took a few steps, holding hard onto Fox's hand. Good; it still worked.

Then a big person, with hair like little ropes, swept her up in her arms and squeezed her tight. Jade squealed and wriggled furiously to get away. The woman put her down and grabbed Fox, too. Jade clung to her mother's legs for safety. Fox was laughing, almost crying, and hugging the stranger, and pushing her away so she could look at her, then hugging her again. "Oh, Len— I love your braids!"

Len shook her head so the ropes flew and the beads clicked. "It keeps my brain cool. Nish said it would. There's so much I have to tell you. Fox, you have to meet Nish. And you too, Jade."

The big person squatted and said, "I'm sorry I grabbed you, Jade. You're not a baby anymore, are you, for anyone to pick up as they please? I forgot how long I've been gone. It's just been a few months for me, but it was a quarter of your whole life. What a big girl you are, walking and everything! But I bet you're tired and hot. I know I was when I got here. You want some water to drink? Or some juice?"

Juice? Jade peeped one eye out from behind Fox's knee.

Cam dreamed of Lexo's hand, her strong palm against the small of his back, supporting him as he learned to trust the water, as she taught him how to float.

"That's good," she crooned. His ears were full of water, but he could still hear her. "Relax. Let your knees bend if they want to. Fill your lungs with air; you'll float higher. You don't have to do anything but breathe. Just lie there. Breathe. I've got you."

And he floated, bobbing with the little movements of the water, lightly anchored by her hand.

He woke up grumpy, with vague resentment towards Fox because she wasn't there.

Goose felt hollow and restless, like something was missing. She paced around Lia's house, searching and calling out. It was too quiet now, not enough breathing. It wasn't food she was hungry for. Something else. She bawled out for what was lost, and finally sat crying under where the bony one snored softly. Lia finally grunted and stirred. She rubbed her eyes. "Missing them, are you?"

She patted her stomach and held the edge of the hammock open. Goose jumped and, with claws out to grab the tricky strings of the moving sleep-spot, she stepped delicately over the hammock and onto Lia's belly, the only really comfortable part for sleeping on the bony one. She curled around herself, kneaded a bit, and felt the welcoming hand settle on her shoulders, just behind her head, where thumb and forefinger could easily rub the comfort-spots just behind her ears.

Goose closed her eyes. Lia closed her eyes. A little purr.

"She just needs to get used to you again," Fox said apologetically. She took the wedge of bread that Len had just buttered and offered it to Jade, who wouldn't take it from the tall, rope-headed stranger.

"I've missed so much. She's grown up." Len sighed. "And how about you, Fox? What have you been up to since I came down the path? And Lia? Tell me about Lia."

"Well, Lia has been on the run a lot, just of late. It seems that a midwife's busy season falls about nine months after midwinter, what with the long nights and cuddling to stay warm and all. She said to tell you to drink plenty of water and eat pickles or you'll keel over."

"So— no change there."

"Always Lia," Fox agreed. "And me... mostly I've just been working with the Carpenters' son, Tap. With Tern and Dena both down here at the rift, Lia took him in to look after— he's only seven."

"Which meant, of course, that *you* did the looking after?"

"Of course. He was so sad, both parents out on the path without him, and for such a long time. So every day Jade and I would take him back to their house. He would brighten up as soon as he got into the workshop. It turns out that he's as good a woodwright as the Carpenters' apprentices, only some things are just too big for him to handle alone. So I'd help him, and we'd go around the village with our tools. The earthquake broke so many things. Tap was a good little teacher. We worked on the small jobs — broken shelves, doors off their hinges, things like that — stuff nobody else was getting around to because the big jobs had to be finished first.

"And we did them pretty well, Len— no slapdash fixes for us. I've learned how to use a hammer without hurting anyone, and a drill. And a saw, too, though my cuts could be straighter, Tap says. And I can plane a board and make rough wood smooth. It's fun, Len. And look what we brought you! We made it. Jade helped, sort of, with the sanding."

Fox was unwrapping what could only be one of Lia's dishtowels from around a slim bundle, about as long as her forearm. "I carved it with the knife you gave me back in our first Home

Village, back before Jade was born. Before everything." Len saw that the knife now hung from Fox's belt naturally, as if it had always been there. Where it showed above its sheath, the grip was no longer milky white but already ripening to a buttery cream-color. Someday that handle wouldn't be plain smooth bone anymore. It would be etched with the pictures and symbols of Fox's life and work. What would they be? Len wondered, but for now the knife was blank. Mellowing nicely, but still blank.

Len pulled her eyes from Fox's waist to the sleek reddish box her partner was holding out to her. It took her breath away.

"Oh, Fox!"

"It's a box."

"I know it's a box, silly." She took it in her hands. It was as smooth as polished soapstone. She ran her hands along the wood, savoring the craftsmanship of the even curves that narrowed to points at either end, like an overlong weaver's shuttle. The joining of the lid was so perfect it was almost invisible.

"It's for holding your knife, so the baby can't get at it."

Len didn't mention that she always hung her knife from a high hook, her hammock hook most recently, well out of reach of little fingers. Fox looked so... happy.

"Here, let me show you how it works. Tap helped me with the hinges and the latch. The latch was really hard."

She took the little box back from Len and showed off the workings of the complicated slide-and-peg fastener that was so secure against Jade that it was almost Len-proof as well. Len was impressed; the carving was very fine.

"You did this? You've come a long way from whittling sticks, Fox. This is really something."

"Tap taught me, Len. He's just a little boy, but he knows *everything* about wood. And *sandpaper*, Len! He taught me how to make sandpaper."

Len blinked. She didn't know what to say to match her partner's enthusiasm for sandpaper, so she just squeezed her tight and told her how much she loved her box.

"There's never been one like it, Fox. Never on the whole world."

That night, Len had an idea. Fox couldn't sit idle in the village, not while everyone else was toiling. All the food and sleeping space was needed for workers. After a short visit,

Fox would have to take Jade and go back to Lia's house. But Len didn't want to miss any more of the baby's growing up, or her partner's either, for that matter. So she went to the master carpenter to ask whether they could use another pair of hands in their shed, not experienced hands, but hands with some feeling for woodwork.

"She's never been apprenticed, but she can carve. And," she added, in case this were important, "she knows how to make sandpaper."

"But these hands, are they willing to work hard?" Lar Carpenter wanted to know. "This isn't fine carving we're about here. This is the heavy sweat-work of turning trees into planks. Sawing, planing, stacking… It's not for the work-shy."

"Work-shy, she's not," Len said, tickled by the notion of a lazy Fox. "Let me talk to her tonight. There's just one thing, though: She has a young daughter. I know you're working around the clock. I wonder if she could work at night, after the baby goes to sleep and I can watch her?"

The carpenter's face lit up. "All the better. We need more muscle on the night shift, but most people hate to get their sleeping and waking turned around. Send her over."

"Oh, and one more thing," Len added. "She likes to sharpen things."

Lar Carpenter grinned. "I like her already."

"Quoit! Look! Two waters!" Cam pointed excitedly.

"What? What is it, Cam? What do you see?"

"Two waters! One red, one brown."

"That's right; good eye, boy. During the night, the river we were on flowed into the Big River. Big River's red here; runs through clay country just above where we are now. Takes a while to mix up the waters. It runs like that for miles, a stripe of black-brown next to a stripe of red."

"That, before, was not a big river?" Cam asked doubtfully.

"No, that was just a little river. There's lots of them that empty into the Big. We call that one the Leg-Bone, because it runs so straight for such a long way, west and then west some more. Running down it, a man can get tired of having the sunset poke him in the eye every evening. Now we're on the Big River, we'll meander more, hither and yon, collecting the other rivers. The Big gets them all, somewhere or another. By the time we get to the sea, this river will show you what Big really means. You can barely see from one bank to the other."

"We're going to the sea?"

"Of course we are. What did you think? That's home, boy. We're going home for the winter."

"...cane as big around as my thigh, Len. I'm not kidding!"

"That's wonderful," Len said absently, probing for the last splinter from Fox's first night in the wood-shop. "Now, be still or I'll never get this." Jade looked on seriously. She knew about splinters. "Tonight, you wear gloves, my girl."

"Oh, and Len— you should *see* the tools they have there! Saws so big it takes two of us to use them, one pushing and the other pulling. And axes and adzes— they're different, you know. I wish Tap could see it. I wish he could have come down with me; he'd love to get his hands on this gear, only he's so little and it's all so big here, huge rasps and I don't know what all else— things I've never even heard of."

"I know. I know. But you have to sleep now. Jade, let's go get some breakfast. Fox needs to close her eyes. She worked all night, while you and I slept."

Fox lay her head back in the gently swinging hammock. She was bone-tired but oddly alert. Probably because it was morning. The sun was up. There was light all around her. She couldn't sleep.

She grabbed her tunic and threw it over her face to try to fool her body into thinking it was dark. It smelled of sawdust and sap. She breathed it in deeply.

She dreamed she was inside a hollow tree, rubbing its walls smooth with her hands. It was the box she had made for Len, red wood coming together into points above her head and somewhere far below where she stood. "It's getting very big," she thought.

"Not Carver," Nish explained patiently to Fox. "*Fisher*. Nish Fisher." He showed her the carved fish that hung from his big ear, pulling it towards her so she could see the fine work: fins, tail, eyes, and an open, eager mouth.

"It's beautiful carving, Nish. I don't know how you get the tiny details so perfect."

"The little things I do with fish-hooks, while I'm sitting in my boat. Waiting for fish."

"What's a boat?" she asked.

"Hard to talk boats if you've never seen the ocean."

"I have seen it, though. I know it's the floor at the bottom of the world, and I know it's the color of Jade's eyes." Fox also knew she was showing off a little.

"Let me see those eyes." Nish hoisted the child onto his knee. She went happily; he had blue pictures on his skin and little toys hanging all over him. Jade approved of Nish, and opened her eyes wide so he could see their color.

"Fox knows a lot; these eyes could be carved out of ocean. So, you know it's the floor of the world? Well, if the ocean is the floor, then boats are the shoes that walk on it. Without a boat, you're swimming. Or sinking. One or the other."

"But what *is* a boat?"

"Oh, the little Fox has deep questions. Questions too deep for this village. You come down to my village. You come, you see."

Nish talked in riddles sometimes.

"Just tell me what a boat is, Nish. Please?"

"You'll come, see. You'll see boats. Lots of boats. Then you'll understand. Okay?"

"Okay. Jade, no! That's too hard; don't pull on Nish's earring. You'll hurt his ear."

The big man laughed and guided Jade's attention to the fish that hung around his neck. It was a fantastic thing, with a graceful gigantic fin on its back.

Night-watch, with the orange cat for company, gave Cam plenty of time to think. The Duck was carrying him downstream and downworld. Unless he got off, it would take him all the way to the sea. And then the winter would catch him there, and it would be another year before he turned homeward. A year. Too long.

Or he could leave The Duck, get off at one of the riverside villages where Genia's family sometimes stopped to trade, and try to find a boat that was going the other way, back up towards the roof of the world. He quailed at the thought of wandering a strange town again in search of work and friends.

But even in this strange world, there was one thing he could always rely on, or two, those being his legs. He didn't believe there was any place they couldn't carry him. But who would show him the way? There were too many paths on this world and his copy of Keptha's map had been laundered away by the river, which had also stolen his boots. Going barefoot was not a problem on the smooth wooden decks of The Duck, but if he tried to walk back to the village of Keptha and Anani, he would need shoes. He thought uneasily about how fast The Duck traveled, much faster than a man on foot. If he turned back now, he would never make it back to the top of the world before the snows came again. He would still have to find a place to pass the winter.

That was it, then. Either way, another year. Nobody would wait two winters for someone to return. His eyes scanned the darkness, searching for shapes on the river.

Fox would give him up for dead. She would mourn him and make other friends. Someone else would walk with her, would prize her cheerful company. Someone would take her as his partner. Maybe they would have children together. Cam felt a little angry at Fox for that and his anger helped him say goodbye to hope. Both hands on the Duck's railing, he tightened his grip against the rolling beneath his feet. He turned his face to the cool river air, moist on his cheek.

That night, Cam surrendered his plans for their tomorrows. He let Fox go. But sometimes, down in his narrow bunk, he still heard her voice in dreams, echoing from somewhere above him (or maybe from below?), "Lower, Cam, further... All the way to the sea."

The scaffolding wasn't finished yet, strictly speaking, not *finished* the way the builders wanted it so that carriers with heavy loads could walk across on their own, without help or fear, and no more than the usual perils of the path. But though it wasn't *finished*, it was *complete*, in the sense that ladders, pulleys, ropes, and bridges ran from the path below the rift to the path above, without a gap. Guard-rails were still to be built around the platforms. Some of the footbridges hadn't yet been planked, so crossing them meant walking on the bare cables while holding to grab-ropes that ran at shoulder and waist height. Still, builders and climbers cat-walked back and forth regularly, wearing safety harnesses because a slip would mean a deadly fall.

Walkers who had been displaced by the earthquake began to ask if they could cross the new path as it was. "If we wait until they have it to their liking, we'll be too old to walk," Calla Dyer had whispered to her partner, for there was no private place to talk on the crowded sleeping porch of the tanner who was giving them hospitality.

The Dyers had been away from home for too long. Calla had counted one hundred and eighteen days since the earthquake had severed the path, too long to take hospitality no matter how gracefully offered. She was tired of hanging her hammock under somebody else's roof and tired of doing work that was not her own. Dyeing was not a useful skill in the mending of the path, so she and Sun helped to trim and carry the huge logs of cane that were hoisted up to build the new route. It was hot and sweaty work, not involving color except for the green stains on their clothing.

Calla and Sun wanted to go. They were willing to leave everything behind and walk without packs. They had both been good climbers in their youth and were not troubled by emptiness below them. So, when there began to be talk of crossing on the new path, the Dyers went to the builders and asked to go home. "Soon," Calla put in.

"Today?" Sun suggested.

"Maybe now?" Calla added.

And the builders said that they might pass, as long as they agreed to be belted into safety harnesses in case of a misstep. "And you need to understand," the crew-master told them, "that when you move from rope to rope, there will be times when you have to shed one harness and step into another before going on to the next stage. At those moments, in between safety lines, nothing will hold you on the world except your own good sense. So, stay awake up there! Now go on, say your goodbyes tonight. Start up the ladders before dawn,

so that you'll have a full day of light to make it across. Take
some food and drink, but nothing else. And you won't go at
all if it looks like rain." Which it wouldn't, this being the late
autumn dry time, before the storms of winter. But Calla and
Sun said they would do as they were told.

The goodbyes were not very sorrowful. The Dyers were
happy to be leaving and their neighbors were glad for them,
and glad too that there would be fewer hammocks crowding the sleeping porch. Tel Tanner said he would keep their
heavy trading packs for them, and loaned them a small, snug
climbing pack for carrying food for the trip.

They lay down early the night before they left, but got
little rest. They were as excited as children, whispering in
the dark in the big rainbow-striped hammock they shared.
They would sleep under their own roof the very next night.

The people of the village called them "the menders," all those
who had come down the path to help put the world right again.

The builders were not the only ones counted as menders,
though masons, stonecarvers, smiths, woodwrights, and strong
backs of every sort and level of experience were highly es-
teemed. The potters became menders when they made a new
kind of map for the builders: a clay model of the rift and the
world-wall above it so that the new path could be tried small
before it was built large. Climbers were menders too; who
else was nimble, tough, and heart-strong enough to brave
the pathless rock? The walkers who carried down offerings
of food from the upper villages— menders also, every one.
So were the cooks that chopped and grilled and fried and
roasted for the great common table in the shade of the new
sleeping shed. Tris rose before dawn each day and slipped
out of the Dyers' House so that the loaves the bakers had left
to rise through the night could slide into the giant oven and
bake before breakfast. Tris Baker was a mender, the old people
who cut the bread and laid it out on wooden trays for the
hungry workers were menders, and so were the youngsters
who washed the dishes after each meal.

But little Jade was too young to be counted as a mender.
Her gifts seemed to run more towards being a breaker. After

a bit of a mess was caused by inquiring little hands in the kitchen, Fox took most of her afternoon breakfasts on the front doorstep of the Dyer's house, under the shade of the eaves, where she could wake slowly from her daytime sleep while keeping one eye on her child.

That was how Fox came to be the one in the awkward position of offering hospitality to the Dyers when they came home and found their house full of strangers.

Almost dawn. In the hazy first light, Cam saw something.

"Genia, look. There! What is that?"

"Water-cow, boy. No more swimming lessons for you from here on down. Creatures in these waters, from now 'til home, they'd eat you for a snack and still have room for lunch. And not just the water-cows, either, there's fish, or at least folks call 'em fish, that are bigger than you and me put together, with teeth you could shave with."

No more swimming lessons. He would miss them; he liked the feeling of being swept along in the river flow, floating with it, learning not to fight it but work with it, arms pulling, legs beating hard to squeeze through it. (Kicking for swimming was very like walking, only faster and lying down.) And he particularly liked breathing. Veydle and Lexo were both good swimmers. They had shown him how to turn his head now and again for air. That had been very rewarding. He was learning not to fear the water so much, though he would never forget the terror of almost losing himself when he fell in.

Though they went more slowly now, night-watch was less restful. The Big River had more turns, more towns, and more traffic than the Bone. Boats of every size worked their way up and down its flow, pushed by the wind in their bellying sails or pulled by poles stuck into the water. Small ones, narrow as tree-trunks, poked their way through the lilies and rushes near the banks. Big ones that could carry The Duck as cargo with room to spare, zigged and zagged across the channel with the smaller vessels getting out of the way as best they could.

At sundown, lights appeared on every side. They reminded Cam of the fire-bugs in the woods. Stars wheeled above them.

Towns glittered along the banks. River bends were marked by bonfires tended by the river-keepers who lived off the tolls the boats paid. And lights moved on the river itself.

Genia said all the boats were supposed to carry lanterns at night; most did, but some did not. So Cam would strain to see through dark, still not favoring the idea of The Duck being smashed to tinder, though he understood now that the danger of this was somewhat less than Genia would lead him to believe. Genia was not a woman with the habit of talking small.

Fox welcomed the Dyers like she had been brought up to welcome any walkers on the path: She invited the strangers into the house and offered them something to drink. They followed her, tight lipped, into the kitchen where they found great loops of rope covering every foot of the floor; Brig Weaver was measuring a new line by wrapping it around the kitchen table, which just happened to be exactly six feet long, and didn't look up when they came in.

Calla finally burst. "What are you doing in my kitchen, Brig Weaver, and what is all this mess?"

Brig held up his hand for her to wait a moment; he was counting.

"Thirty-three, thirty-four, thirty-five!" he finished with a flourish. "The table is six feet long, which makes twelve feet on each pass — that's three hundred and fifty ... let's see ... four hundred and twenty feet of new rope. Welcome home, Sun, Calla. It's good to see you; it's been too long." Brig marked the end of the rope with four knots, side by side, with the last knot trimmed with a two-inch piece of white twine. He coiled the whole thing neatly, threw it over his shoulder and said, "Come on; let me introduce you around." They followed him silently, threading their way through their own rooms, crowded with strange gear and people.

"Where are all our things?" Calla cried.

"Oh, everything is safe and sound in the workshop. I packed it away in extra carry-baskets; more loads are coming into the village than going out of it these days. Plenty of extra baskets. I figured you wouldn't want the menders mixing up their stuff with yours."

"How many are staying here?" Sun asked, waving his hand at the long line of hammocks that had been unhooked in the morning and left draping down the walls so that there would be room to move around the house. Under each bright stripe of color was a large pack belonging to the person who slept there. Living so close together, they did their best to keep their things stowed away, but still, the room looked like an autumn forest after a bad storm.

"Let's see…" Brig gave the question some thought. "About fifteen, I'd say, unless Rill and Crenny headed back up the path this morning. Hard to keep track of the carriers." He looked around him, considering for the first time what it might look like to the Dyers' eyes.

"It's a little messy, I know," Brig said ruefully. "But, come see the workshop, and you won't find a hair out of place."

He led them into the workshop — *their* workshop — and it was too much for Calla. Their rainbow was gone. Their skeins of yarn and thread colored like flowers, their bolts of cloth colored like butterflies, their baskets colored like summer sunsets— everything was gone. Their dye-baths were gone. Their line of earthenware jugs full of dye-stuffs and mordants— all gone. In their place, stacked on their shelves and hanging from their hooks and racks, was a nightmare of raw rope and cord: rough, colorless, and orderly. It was sorted by size from the smallest linen thread (used by the surveyors, though Calla did not know this, to plumb the scaffolding which brought her home) to coils of cable so large that it would take three strong carriers to get them out the door.

"Len, Nish," Brig threw down the coil he carried on top of another just like it. "I want you to meet Calla and Sun. The Dyers. This is their house."

Cam dreamed the feeling of coming home. In his dream he was backing down that last steep pitch before Home Village, holding tight to the fat, weathered ropes, Len's ropes, that had been strung there to serve as handholds. Fox was with him, just above him on the path; he could see her brown boots and trousers as she stepped with grace down the well-worn footholds. They were giggly with homecoming, singing a silly old song about the moon falling down the chimney. His pack felt light on his back, nearly empty.

"I don't want to seem inhospitable. Or ungrateful, either, after all the work you've done." Calla looked at the faces around her, strangers' faces, faces tired from long days of work and short nights of rest away from the comforts their own homes. "But..."

"Of course."

"We understand."

"You've missed your home..."

"I can only imagine how you must..."

"And then you came back to all this..."

"We'll move out right away."

"It's just...," Sun started again.

"You don't have to say another word," Len interrupted. "We understand. I'll talk to the builders today, see if they can find another place for us to work." And store the rope, she thought uneasily. And sleep. Where could her helpers possibly go?

The village terrace was full to bursting. Two new smithies had been built, one for tools and the other to make the hardware for the scaffolding, the hooks and nails and pulleys and stakes needed to hold it all together. Stacks of lumber and cane had invaded the gardens. The clearing in the village center was no longer clear, as it held the big open shed where everyone took their meals and many of them slept. All the village homes were as crowded as the Dyers'— where could they possibly go?

But Len understood the tears that brimmed unshed in Calla's eyes. The Rope-Maker had felt home-hunger herself, more than once. She knew it was a need, like thirst or loneliness. So she patted Calla's hand and said, more brightly than she felt, "Don't worry about it. The builders will get us all sorted out. We'll be out of your hair in no time."

Calla looked at Sun with a question in her eyes. They each shrugged, at the very same moment, which made them laugh, a little weakly.

"Of course you won't," Calla said, taking Sun's hand. "You'll stay right here. Rope's the important thing now; dyeing isn't."

"Though I do think we could do something about that awful yellow-gray stuff you have in your hands," Sun said. They all laughed. "But… well, everybody just make yourselves at home." He shrugged. "We'll squeeze in here somehow. I don't suppose there's a room nobody's taken?"

Brig had to admit that there wasn't. At night, even the kitchen was crisscrossed with hammocks, hung high to avoid the dining table.

So Calla and Sun hung their big striped hammock in the workshop itself, and at night they swung gently together in a forest of pale yellow and brown rope, dreaming of the rainbow. They were home at last. During the day, they unhooked their hammock and let it droop down the wall like the others while they helped with the rope. Dyers, too, are fiber people.

Cam could feel it in the others, the homecoming feeling. It was a sort of rising of the heart, and a settling too. He recognized it from the many days when he had known that the next time he threw down his pack it would be at Len's doorstep. He remembered how it felt to walk the last steps towards sleeping in his own bed and eating across the table from his mother. He was well acquainted with the feeling. It was easy to recognize when it began to bubble up on The Duck.

In the same way that homecoming had always lightened his load and speeded his steps, it seemed to make The Duck's family more in tune with each other and more brisk about following Genia's shouted orders, dashing to the ropes, pulling together in time like people in a dance. Work began to feel like a game, the crew competing with itself only, to test how quick and keen they could be. There was a good deal of loud, hearty singing and Cam learned to join in on the simple repeating lines in the choruses.

In the evenings, while they fished, they told stories about their home, a big house on the edge of water that moved, not like the river, but like a cat's tongue, lapping at the shore. Bigger water, much bigger than the river. Water that went on forever.

Cam was gently skeptical about how any water could be bigger than the Big River or move in such a way. He had come to terms with the flow of rivers — it was just a case of how water, like pebbles, rolled downworld — but what would make water throw itself over and over against the land? It made no sense.

"Big water makes big waves, Cam." And they told him about the mighty water that caught all the rivers and gave them back again. "Where did you think the rain comes from?" Veydle demanded, when he seemed doubtful.

"From up. From the sky. Rain comes from the sky." Even in this flattened land, Cam knew this was still true.

"Right enough," Quoit prompted, "but how does it get there?"

"It grows in the clouds." Cam pointed to the rippling banks streaming over them, back towards the high lands.

"And where do the clouds come from?"

"Clouds come from the sunset. From the west."

Quoit slapped his thigh. "That's right. Clouds mostly come from the west. That's because the ocean is there, the sea, the big water. It gathers all the rivers, then breathes them back into the sky. Then the clouds make rain and rain makes the river and the river takes us...?"

"Home!" they all shouted (all except Cam). Then Lexo hooked a big fish and there was a deal of excited wrestling with her line and cheering, because there would be something besides beans for supper that night.

Len heard it from Tris Baker: The cooks were worried about the winter.

Autumn was here; winter was coming. It wouldn't be long until the high villages were closed in by snow and ice. Even below the snow country, rain would make the path slick and dangerous. Fewer gift-loads of food would come down the world, and the gardens of the villages closest to the rift could never feed the throngs of workers without help. Would there be a day when the crowd of hungry menders looked to them for food and they would have no food to give them? They were cooks, but if there were no food... What then?

And in the smithy, Len learned from Brock that the smiths were worried about the winter, too. Much of the coal that fueled their forges came from the higher villages, and winter would soon be upon them. Everyone relied on the smiths for the hardware of the mending, the rock-bolts and stakes and nails that held the scaffolding together, but without coal, what could they do? They had never needed so much coal as they needed this year; how would they keep the forge-fires burning when the carriers could not get through?

Over a big slab of brown bread and rosehip jam at breakfast, she heard Tern and Dena Carpenter fretting about the winter as well. How would the make-shift rig of catwalks and ladders that spidered across the rift stand up to the storms of the season? "Someone will have to check the joints after every big wind," Tern worried. "Maybe every day."

"And the cables, too," Dena added, her voice low. "The guy-lines are the weakest point, don't you think? Someone will have to look them over for wear."

"Sure enough." Tern took a bite of bacon and chewed it thoughtfully. "We need to catch any fraying before it has a chance to bring down a section. And the ropes could decay in the wet…"

(As if any of my ropes would rot in one season, Len harrumphed to herself.)

"And as to checking," Jee Mason joined in, "someone will have to cast an eye on those rock-bolts and anchors every now and again. The pilings are strong, no fear about that, but rattling and shaking can work loose even the strongest bolt. With the way of the winds in the winter, that has to be taken into account."

"What I'm wondering about the winter," put in Alten Stone-Carver, "is whether we'll be able to work at all. I've never passed a winter here, but up in my Home Village, we don't quarry in the cold months. That's when we move the work indoors. How will my people fare out on the new path, swinging picks and hammering chisels in the rain?"

The cooks talked to the carriers. The carriers talked to the smiths. The smiths talked to the carpenters, and they talked to the masons who talked to the stone-carvers who talked to the rope-makers. Questions flew in all directions.

The builders decided that they needed a time for everyone to talk to everyone, all at once, so that each could listen and speak for their own part of the work. And not just the teams working from the village above the rift, either: They would invite the menders from the village below the break, too. Everyone, together for the first time since the earthquake.

An autumn festival to celebrate the new path of wood and cane and to plan for the winter and the new path of stone.

So, the builders set a day when all the bridges and board-walks would be fully planked, with hand-rails so that they could be walked without safety harnesses, even by children. ("Sensible children, that is," Jee Mason added, looking sternly at little Geron.) That day the new path would be declared open and everyone would lay down their tools to take counsel and make merry.

Genia yelled at Lexo for letting the big catfish slash open her hand, because she, Genia, had — how many times now? — personally shown her, Lexo, the right way to handle a river cat. "Didn't I tell you, you hold its back-fin between your middle fingers where it can do no harm? And your thumb and little finger wrap round it *behind* those spears on its sides? Didn't I say that? A brain like a torn fishnet! Well, you'll remember now, if you live. Like razors, those fins, and slick with slime that will poison your blood and probably kill you." She stitched up Lexo's palm like a torn bed-sheet, after first scrubbing it mercilessly with tepid tea. Cam helped the patient hold her hand still on the table for the skin-sewing. She looked very pale under her river-tan, though Cam was not sure whether this was from the wound, the words, or the treatment. Genia was no gentle healer.

After being dosed with a powder against fever, Lexo was sent to her bunk with Genia grousing and grumping about being short a hand right when they would need her most, on the last stretch before Big River Town, where the water was clogged with boat-traffic. "So, Cam, you're a sailor now, and that wooden-headed Lexo will stand night-watch and handle the cooking as best she can. I only wish her hands were as hard as her head. But she can't get that paw of hers wet 'til it heals. Quoit and I will share the dishwashing. Veydle and Cam, you'll keep the decks clean. And I want that old catfish gutted and cleaned right now; any fish that misbehaves on The Duck had better turn up filleted and fried on my dinner plate tonight or somebody is going to wish it had."

So Quoit saw to the gutting and Cam put the grease-pot on the fire and they all ate fish that night for supper, even

Cat, who, in spite of its name, seemed to feel no constraining kinship with the catfish.

The day of the opening dawned quietly, absent the noise of builders bustling off to the new path with their tools and materials. Even the stone-workers took a day of rest away from the rock face where they were beginning to peck out the eventual route of the new path, chipping out a ledge along the faintest trace of an old goat-track above the rift. Everyone had been working from first light until sundown for many months now; they were glad for a morning to sleep late.

Though they had been awake for a while, Len and Nish didn't get up until they heard Breeze and Jory coming to life downstairs. Over the past few months, Len had gotten used to sleeping with Nish, to the way the sling of the hammock pressed them together. She liked the way their bodies sorted themselves out, head on shoulder, limbs entwined. She also liked waking to find Nish watching her, eyes so close that she could see the petals of pale brown and gold in his eyes, crow's-footed at the corners from a long life in the sun. He was smiling at her now. She nuzzled close and shut her eyes for a few more minutes of night.

She had come a distance. It hadn't been so long ago that she had slept in a feather-bed that didn't move, wearing a flannel nightgown, with quilts pulled up to her chin and no one to watch her wake.

"Food?" Nish crooned softly in her ear.

She wriggled in his arms. "Oh, yes."

"Then we should get up."

"We really should."

From below, Breeze called out, "We're going to see if the cooks want any help, what with company coming and all. We'll see you at breakfast."

"At breakfast!" Len and Nish called out together. They heard the door fall shut behind their young housemates and grinned at each other. The house was empty.

Being a sailor on The Duck turned out to be mostly a matter of pulling on ropes, the right rope at the right time. "Not that one, idiot boy, the one *above* it! Why do I even bother to show you? Do it now, or you'll have us over and the river-cows will eat us up." Genia hollered out to the river, "Duck stew with beans for supper. Enough for everyone!" Cam finally pulled the correct halyard the correct distance. "Right there! Now take a wrap around the cleat."

The purpose of pulling the ropes was to adjust the sails to the correct angle, that being the angle Genia wanted. Sometimes the sails would be so tight with wind, Quoit and Veydle and Cam would all tail onto a rope together to pull. They would heave until they heard a satisfied grunt from Genia, and then they would wrap the rope around a wooden peg, wrap it with a special twist designed to hold fast but shake loose quickly when called for.

Cam found the work interesting in a mysterious sort of way that reminded him of bread-making. Something and something, put together, added up to something, but he was completely in the dark about the hows and whys of it all.

During a quiet spell, Cam asked Quoit privately why they didn't just drift downstream like the leaves and logs on the river. It would take less effort and a lot less shouting, he thought.

"Up where the river's narrow we do it that way sometimes, but not here. Can't steer that way, not if you're drifting. Have to put some work into it if you don't want to pile up against the next boat or shoal that comes at you. The Duck has to go just a little faster than the flow so you can push against it. Wind helps us do it. Of course, we could always row; little boats do it that way. But I'd like to see the oars that would move The Duck. And who would pull on them, I ask you? Not I. No, better this way. Better the wind gives us a little push."

"But the wind... It's blowing the other way, up the world to the high places— where we come from, not where we go to. How can the wind help, blowing against us?"

"Well, that's the riddle, isn't it? How does the wind blowing towards the mountains help The Duck get down to the sea?"

"Yes. That is what I'm asking."

Quoit laughed and hauled himself to his feet. "You watch, boy. Watch how The Duck runs from one side of the river to the other. Watch how the wind fills her sails. Watch how she slips through the water. Nobody can tell you how a boat sails against the wind. But you can watch and you can learn. There's still a few days before we get to the city. But for now, we'd better look alive; Genia's about to bring this boat around and the quicker we're about our business, the sooner we'll hear the quiet again."

How did Quoit know what Genia was about to call for? Cam wondered. But just then, she called for it, so he had to put aside thinking for a while.

Len and Nish lazed the morning away in the little attic of the Weaver's house until an interesting smell of frying tugged them out of their hammock. They put on their tunics, which the Dyers had brightened for the occasion. Len's was the brilliant orange-rose of madder root; Nish's was a deep golden yellow that they got from boiled onionskins. It went well with his brown face and blue tattoos.

Nish put on all his jewelry. (While working with fibers, he only wore his earrings, arm-bands, and anklets; anything more tended to snag in his work.) After he had bedecked himself with little carvings everywhere, of fish and birds and children, he turned his attention to Len. She had never been garlanded before.

Nish tied strings of bone and shell beads around her ankles and wrists, then added a long strand around her waist which cinched in her red tunic and sat pleasingly on her hips. Then he draped a pendant around her neck. It was a fish with wings, she saw. "It's beautiful," she marveled, turning the delicate little bird-fish over in her hands. "You made this?"

"While I wait for fish," he said, puzzlingly. He tucked a handful of other dangles into his tunic pocket. "These others, we save for Fox and Jade," he said. "That one is for you— today's present. It's your fish. The flying fish. The other fish, they always tell the flying fish, 'No, no! You can't go in the air— you're a *fish*.' But the flying fish, she doesn't listen. Air, water; water, air— all the same to her. No limits. She goes where she goes. The flying fish is for you, your fish." Len closed her hand around the figure, feeling its strong silky wings press into her palms.

This was the second gift Nish gave her.

Cam watched, but he didn't think he was learning anything. Not, at least about his question: how the wind, blowing the wrong way, could help The Duck go the right way. By the time they got to the endless village, he had just barely begun to *see* what he was watching: the way Genia turned her cheeks to test the wind and eyed the bright bits of yarn fluttering from The Duck at different heights. The little twitches she made with the steering-stick as she squinted up at the sails. The way she seemed to listen with her feet to the ripple and flow of the river as The Duck turned its head. Cam noticed that whenever the very edge of the sail began to slacken towards a flutter, Genia was a moment away from changing something, either adjusting the steering stick or bellowing for the crew to pull at one rope or another.

Quoit was the same, though he was different in every way. He was taller than Genia, and leaner, and a man. He wore a long taut braid unlike her wildly whipping tangles, and was much, *much* more soft-spoken. But still there was something identical in the way that Quoit, when he took his turn at the stick, disappeared into the act of seeing-hearing-feeling, even seeming to *taste* the wind as he guided The Duck along a path Cam could not see.

From side to side of the river they went, at each turn swinging through a moment of flapping pause before the wind caught the sail again and nudged them one more step on their journey. Cam worked and watched, and if he did not exactly *learn*, he at least began to sense the unseen patterns in the flow of water and air and human work, patterns that could take a creaky little wooden house, sailing among other such houses, down its long path to the sea.

The ground under her seemed to be moving, not with violence like the earthquake, but with a gentle back-and-forth swing like a hammock or a cradle. Len thought she might be a little drunk. It had been a long time since she'd danced, and there was something different about the music down at this level of the world, something that seemed to make her tipsy. There were drums, for one thing. They'd brought them out after the day's long, tiring discussions were done: big logs, hollowed out with fire and scraping-tools. The drum-booms had gotten under her skin and made her jumpy, so she'd jumped, with the rest of the menders, and wiggled and shook and stomped until she was dizzy.

It was late, now, and dark. She was sitting on the sand between Nish's legs, leaning against his chest as if he were a chair-back. Jade was asleep on her chest. "I am the filling in a family sandwich," thought Len hazily, as the flickering light of the bonfire fringed the toddler's hair with gold. Len felt dampness on her breast where a little sleep-spit leaked from her granddaughter's mouth. She didn't mind; the orange tunic had seen its share of sweat and spills that night. She watched the dancers, her head nestled under Nish's chin.

By this time, it was mainly the young ones who were still following the music around the fire. As the night wore on, their elders had subsided in a loose circle around the cleared space near the edge of the village terrace, clapping and shouting encouragement to the dancers for a while, but now mostly talking quietly and enjoying the mellow finish of a great party. Fox was still dancing, flinging her arms in great free circles that seemed to follow the wailing of the cane whistles.

"The music here is different," Len pronounced.

"Different how?" Nish asked the top of her head. She giggled because, when he spoke, his breath and voice bounced her a little.

"It's more… You know…" She waved her cup at the drummers, pounding away on logs of all sizes. Some of her drink sloshed on the ground. It wasn't beer and it wasn't cider, but it was good. "It's more… like *that*." The cane whistles shrilled above the drumbeat and the dancers spun and shimmied in the firelight.

Nish chuckled, bouncing her on his chest again. "Yes, it is surely more like that. But what is music like where you come from?"

She thought about this. "I can't remember exactly, not with my ears all full of this. But I think it had more *words*, for one thing. And there were set tunes, with beginnings and ends, middles too, so you sort of knew where you stood. I think the players here just make it up as they go along."

"They follow the dancers."

"That's what I'm trying to say: The players follow the dancers and the dancers follow the players. Nobody really knows what's going to happen." She shook her finger at the night, nearly dislodging Jade. Nish wrapped his arms securely around the two of them. "It wasn't like that in my first Home Village. You knew the tune. You knew where you were and you knew where you'd end up. Here, you just dance."

"I think you are maybe a little drunk," Nish said.

"It's all this dancing," she explained, waving her cup towards the fire.

"You want to dance some more?" he asked her, gently taking the cup from her fingers.

"No, I don't think so. I think I'm a little drunk."

"Do you want to go lie down?"

"We'd have to stand up to lie down. Can we just stay here and watch? Fox is having a grand time, the first time I've seen her kick up her heels since… in a while. Let's watch 'til the dancing's done."

"Do you think it will ever be done?"

"No, probably not." She sighed.

"Here, give me the little one." Her back-rest leaned forward and propped Len up while he slipped out from behind her.

"Hey!" she protested. Nish lifted Jade off her grandmother without waking her, and then pulled Len to her feet.

"It's time to rest."

One arm around each other's waist, they walked away from friends, firelight, and music, following the well-known path back to the weaver's house. "So they have enough rope," Len said in the darkness. "They don't need us here any more, Nish."

"Our part is done," he agreed.

"And we're just two more mouths to feed, if we stay."

"Will we stay?"

"We can't stay. The Dyers need their house back. It's time to let things start getting back to normal. I saw a copper-breast today; they're flying down already, away from the cold. The builders want us to go home for the winter. But where…?"

He squeezed her to him. "To the ocean, Len. Come to my house. Learn to fish and swim and paddle a boat. Fox wants to know about boats, and she says that the little one grows stronger the lower she goes. Come to the lowest place. Come home with me."

"I'm not a Far-Walker, Nish."

"No? You've walked far already. Why not go all the way?"

"All the way, Nish? At my age?"

"It is easy, Rope-Maker— downworld all the way."

They climbed the ladder to their little room and, to keep Jade safe while they slept and Fox danced through the night, they hooked up the strong net that guarded the loft's edge.

It was two nights after the gathering had decided to send most of the menders home for the winter. Jade was asleep in her hammock, back in the Dyer's sitting room under the watchful eye of a houseful of friends, and Len and Fox had a rare moment of quiet together. The little bats swooped around them in the twilight as they walked towards the bathing place at the end of the village terrace where the water ran down the rock and was gathered briefly in troughs before it threw itself over the edge of the world. They were going to wash Len's hair.

"Do you remember how afraid I was of the bats when we first came down-world?"

"And Lia made fun of you about it."

"Lia made fun of me about everything." Len made a face. They set their things down on one of the benches. "I miss her."

The bathing place was almost empty, just a few people talking quietly, drying off, combing out wet hair, and turning home for the night. It was almost private.

"Here. Sit here in front of me," Fox said, dropping down onto a smooth rock beside the chuckling water. "You can lean back, if you want. This is going to take a while." Len exhaled deeply and settled back against Fox's knees. She closed her eyes. Well-loved hands began to unbind her dozens of slender braids.

She roused herself enough to remind Fox to save the beads and bells and bits of bone Nish had woven into her hair. "For next time," she said. "He always does the braids a little differently, but he uses the same bits to decorate them."

"Don't worry." Fox coaxed one of Nish's tiny carvings from a lock of Len's hair. "I brought a little bag."

Len sank and softened and emptied out. Knots of tiredness and tension, worry and watchfulness, loosened as Fox tugged gently at her hair, careful always not to pull too hard.

"This is wonderful," Len sighed. "You can go on forever, if you want."

"Your hair is pretty thick, but it's not a whole forever."

"That's too bad. I love sitting here. I missed you, Fox. This village is full of people — wonderful people — but I was a little lonesome before you came down with the baby. With Jade, I mean. I have to stop calling her 'baby' now that she's found her feet. She doesn't like it at all."

Fox's hands paused for a moment and rested lightly on Len's head.

"Nish is talking about us going down to his home village for the winter."

Fox said nothing to this, but picked up another braid and began untying the band that held it.

"What do you think, Fox? Winter by the sea?"

Fox kept plucking at the braid, but something had changed.

"Is it that time, Len? Time to untie The Knot?"

"What?" Len's hand flew up and grabbed Fox's wrist. "What are you talking about?"

"Remember, we talked about this, Len. That it might not be forever? We thought it might be me who would want to build a new partnership, if and when..."

"When Cam comes back."

"That's right. When Cam comes back. That's what we thought it would be. But that's not what happened. What happened is that you, not me, found somebody who's dear to you. Nish wants to take you home. And I'm happy for you. I really am. And I want you to know that..."

"Nish wants to take *us* home, you silly little bug. We're partners— we're adding Nish, not subtracting you!" Len turned and threw her arms awkwardly around Fox's neck. "Idiot!" she muttered, clasping her fiercely.

After a long and snuffly hug, Len drew back and looked at the younger woman. "Nish thought you'd want to..."

"Of course I want to. Going down to the very bottom of the world! I think I've always wanted... I just could never put it into words; I couldn't even put it into thoughts. But there was always this pull. I want to touch the ocean, Len. If I were alone— if there had never been a Cam or a Jade or a Len to hold me, I would have rolled down the path like a loose pebble a long time ago." Len was startled by her passion; Fox was actually panting a little.

"So, winter by the sea?" she asked again, and Fox nodded weepily.

"Let me finish your hair."

Fox untied all the bands, unthreaded all the beads, and unraveled all the braids, then brushed Len's hair until it sparked.

"I wish you could see it, Len, the way it ripples down your back." Fox pulled a few locks forward to show her the way they zig-zagged with the memory of the plaits even after they had been set free. "Here, try looking in the water."

They peered into the bathing trough. The smooth water mirrored back Len's wavy mane and Fox's short bob, with the bright evening star behind them.

Then they bathed in the water, which was warm— spring water that had run a way over the sun-baked rocks before pausing at this village on its way down the world. Fox washed Len's hair and, even after being washed and toweled and combed out, a faint ripple of memory still patterned it.

Later, when it was dry, she brushed it and the waves were still there.

Cam flopped onto his back again, banging his elbow on Veydle's bunk above. He couldn't sleep. The lashings that supported his thin pallet cut into him at his shoulder and hip, although they had been comfortable enough before.

The Duck's bunks were a clever arrangement, he had thought when he first studied their making: Beds like shelves, but floored with a tight web of cord— much lighter than wood. And, as Genia pointed out, much cleaner, too. "No place for mice to hide or dust to gather." But no place for sleep to gather either, not this night.

His mind kept running over the many beds he had slept in since he had first taken the path. The woven and netted slings of the low villages had been well suited to the heat there, without clinging bedding to soak up your sweat. A tug on a string, he remembered, would set them swinging, making a little breeze to cool your skin. And above the hammock-villages but below the feather-beds of Len's house — his house — there were several villages where you took your rest on thin mats on the floor: also cool, but *very* firm, to his mind. And further up, in the always-icy villages, he'd guested in cozy sleeping bags made of animal skins with their fur turned inward, nestled in long boxes of dry crackly grass.

And now this little lumpy pad on a shelf of rope, with the sleep sounds of his Duck-mates around him and the riffle of the river in his ears. Now this is home, he told himself. But he wasn't sure.

The trip down the river was almost over, Genia said. Tomorrow they would reach the biggest village of all, Big River Town, where they would trade their beans for coins, have a good dinner, spend the night, and then sail home for the winter. Would he stay with them, be a part of The Duck's family through the stormy season? They had made it plain that he was welcome. Or would he try to backtrack up the Big as far as he could go before the weather closed him in? Clearly, some traffic was still working its way up the river; they passed boats sailing against the flow every day, though he did not know how far they were going. And he could always walk, though it would be very far and he had no boots.

But he was to have a share from the selling of the cargo, he understood. "It won't be much, so don't get your hopes up," Genia told them all sternly. But Cam could see by the shine in everyone's eyes that the selling of the beans would be a good thing, and not just because it would bring a change in their daily menu (although that was not to be discounted.)

Maybe it would be enough to buy boots. He would see. For now, he would float with The Duck down the river.

But he wished that he could fall asleep.

Len dreamed of falling, like a pebble off the path. There was no end to the falling, so there was no breaking or brokenness.

In the endless falling, she is weightless, although it was her weight that made her fall. "It's a good thing I don't have wings," she thought. "That would mean such a lot of work."

In the restless night, Cat jumped on Cam's chest and settled there, circling head to tail. "Thank you," he whispered, making her ear twitch in the wind of his breath.

Staying with Len and Nish. Fox wondered if she was doing the right thing.

Tern and Dena had offered her a place as an apprentice. Evidently, some of the other carpenters had spoken well of her work. This pleased her very much and she knew little Tap would be glad to see her again. And there was Lia, too—going home with Tern and Dena would mean taking Jade back to the village where Lia could watch her grow, side by side with the other children she'd helped onto the world. And that would be sweet.

And learning more about wood-work— that would be sweet, too, wouldn't it? She loved wood, especially shaping and smoothing it into sleek arcs. Perfect corners were less interesting to Fox; she really liked shapes that bowed and bellied. You had to have a firm hand with them, but gentle too, or you could push things too far, lose the curve.

But so much carpentry had to do with straight lines and right angles. Houses were nothing but big boxes; shelves and chests, the same. Maybe she was meant to be just a carver of small things that could be held in one hand— things like Nish's fish-pendants.

But, truly, in the woodshop above the break, what had thrilled her most was the sheer size of the projects, the great beams, the massive stacks of heavy planks. The work had given her joy, but was it enough joy to bind herself to an apprenticeship? Enough joy to say goodbye to Len for another season?

Of course, Len might not mind saying goodbye for a bit, now that she was with Nish. She deserved a chance with him, and how could any couple, really, get started with a granddaughter tugging for attention and Fox trailing along just because she didn't know what else to do with herself?

And then there was Cam to consider. When (if?) Cam came back down from the snows and didn't find her in Home Village, the neighbors would tell him where she'd gone. Would he follow her down to Lia's village? She thought he would, if only to see the baby. But if he didn't find her in Lia's village, would he follow her to the rift? He might.

But if he didn't find her there? How far would he go?

What should she do? So many people to consider: Cam, Jade, Len, Lia, Nish... (But the sea. Not just to see it from some perch up above. To touch it.) Then there was Stone and Becca, too, she thought guiltily; they had never even seen their granddaughter. (But the sea!) She sighed and closed her eyes on the tangle for a moment.

In the darkness behind her eyelids, she could feel a nameless tug, something huge but unseen drawing her further down the path. Go lower, her heart told her. Get to the bottom of things, and then decide.

They did not hurry to leave the village above the break. There was little to do in the way of planning or packing; they would travel light. Len would take the knife-case Fox had carved for her and a few of her tools: her best blades, some combs, and a small hackle. The rest would stay with Breeze. Nish gave away most of his carvings as goodbye gifts, and left behind all of his hammocks except Fox's beloved stripes, Jade's soft lilac, and the big net of wavy blues and greens that he shared with Len. (Even with most of the menders going home for the winter, the village would still need extra sleeping places, especially when the work speeded up again in the spring.) Fox, her decision made, had nothing much that mattered to her except Jade. Jade had her own miniature pack; she kept putting it on and taking it off to rearrange her few small treasures: the string-doll Breeze had made for her out of thrums from the backstrap looms and the carved animals — a fish, a squirrel, and a parrot — Nish had given her to play with. Even of food they would carry little, trusting to hospitality.

But Len had learned that packing wasn't the only thing that a person needed to do to leave a place well. For her other moves, there had been no time to be thoughtful, to make arrangements, to say what needed to be said. Jade's birth had yanked her away from Home Village suddenly, like a leaf ripped from its tree. Then the earthquake had shaken her loose from Lia's village with the same suddenness and no time to consider.

But nothing and no one was rushing them now. The builders had merely said that the stormy season would slow the work to a crawl and it would be best if most of the menders went home until spring. Those from the high villages had better take the path before the snows fell, but Len's family was going down, away from the cold. There was time... for what?

For laying her hand on Breeze's belly and laughing with her when the baby kicked. For thanking Tris and Jee and the Carpenters for the way their village had opened itself to her, made her one of their own when Jade was born and she ventured down to Lia's village, so far below her limits, as she had thought then. They had helped her, shown her how to live and thrive in that new place, and then, in this one, become more than friends in their shared sojourn at the village above the break.

There were others to thank, too. Jory, all the climbers, for their daily courage on the dizzying walls of the broken world. The Dyers, for sharing their rainbow house with strangers. Tris, for getting up while others slept so that there would be fresh bread each morning. So many gifts to savor...

And, oh, time for a message to Lia. What to say? "Come and visit?" — when the one thing a midwife could not do was travel? "We'll come back to you" — when Len was no longer certain of where the path would take her? "Send word if you need us" when Lia was *always* the one who gave care, never the one who received? What could be said to Lia?

Finally, they just sent a message with their love and the simple facts: The way is open now and we are going to the sea.

Big River Town took shape around them gradually, like walking into a cloud. First, there were little clusters of houses along the left-hand shore. Lanes along the river. Wooden arms reaching out into the water, around which floating houses — boats — jostled and bobbed. Cam gawked as the boat-forest became denser and buildings on land pressed closer together until the left bank of the river was completely covered over: houses (floating and rooted), warehouses, carry-lanes, carts, and a strong smell of people, smoke, and cooking.

"Is it like this on the other side?" he asked, gazing off to the haze-hidden far shore.

"More or less. Folk over there are different, but the same: lots of them piled up close, just like here." Genia answered him without taking her eyes off the waterway in front of her which was choked with boats of every size, shape, and color.

"No thank you," she bellowed suddenly, waving off a long, low vessel speeding towards them. "As if The Duck would ever need a pilot to find her nest! NO THANK YOU!" she roared again. The smaller craft, daunted, peeled away.

"Is this it, then? The nest of The Duck? Home?"

"Not exactly 'home,' no. But it *is* where we drop those ever-farting beans and take on some nice bright coins in their place." This was surprising; Cam had never heard Genia speak of beans with anything less than deep affection.

"And then on we go, down through the marshes where the Big River splits into a hundred different channels. And maybe we find our way through, and maybe we don't and we get mired up and the biting bugs don't leave anything but our clean, white bones."

"Don't try to scare the boy, Genia. He knows you too well by now. Tell it straight: After we put our cargo ashore — and good riddance to it, I say — it's about two-three days to get through the marshes, depending on the tides and how smart The Duck is about choosing her path." (And here Quoit gave Genia a look that referred to some story Cam had not heard.)

"Then we turn south, inside the islands," he continued, "and right around the corner is our little cove. With the help of a few friends, we'll run the old Duck up on the beach to rest on her side for the winter, and then we're home."

"And that's when the *real* work begins. No more lolling about the decks, idle from sun-up to sun-down. It will break your heart to see The Duck's poor belly after a season on the river: weeds and worms and barnacles. Bring tears to your eyes. So there's the cleaning and the scraping and the painting— we'll barely have time to see to it all before…"

At this moment, Lexo and Veydle emptied a bucket of river-water over Genia's head and Quoit took the steering-stick while she chased them around the deck. A good deal was said, one way and another. But what was not said, but echoed loudly in Cam's mind, was the question: If The Duck is home, does that mean that Cam is home also?

Just a little past First Village Below the New Path, where they had taken two nights of hospitality, Nish stopped them with a sudden barring gesture. "What is it?" Len asked softly.

"Butterfly springs," he murmured, gesturing towards a small wet patch on the path ahead.

Seeing Len's blank look, he added, "Where butterflies drink. Children go first," he said. "Jade, time to walk."

Jade liked walking. Until she got tired. Then she liked bouncing along up high, looking over the blue pictures on Nish's shoulder. He talked to her and asked her questions and listened to her words and showed her things along the path. The picture man was never boring. She liked that.

He squatted and Jade obligingly reached up and clasped Fox's offered arms to be lifted out of the carry-basket on his back, where she rode now that she was a big girl and liked to stand on her own two feet.

And now he was letting her walk, letting her lead the way down the path, in fact. Even though Nish still held her hand and stood between her and the big fall-off, he walked a little behind her. He waved Len and Fox back. "Wait," he told them. "Watch. See."

So, puzzled, Len and Fox hung back and watched as Jade stepped out onto the wet stone of the seep. They saw, around her feet, first a flutter, then a swirl, then a storm of pale blue petals — butterfly wings no larger than the tip of Len's thumb, hundreds of them — rise like skyward rain. Jade stopped, shook off Nish's hand and spread her arms in the eddy of wings, rapt, reaching upward as if she too would fly.

Len squeezed Fox's hand and they walked forward together into the flower-storm of color, clouds of the little blue ones and a few larger, darker ones: black and iridescent blue speckled with gold. The bigger ones were slower to rise, and Len felt on her skin the breath of their passing.

On the path down to the sea, Jade came at last to the great stone where her story began.

First, they eased the heat of the day in a little pool below a gusher of water that broke from the rocks and dropped about twenty feet. Its falling had worn a cup in the rock, like a giant washtub. Grateful walkers had added rocks to a rough dam until, over the years, a pool had grown, a cool haven from the heat of the path, edged with fern and mossy stone. Birdsong mixed with the tune of the water, and butterflies danced out their last days in the fine spray raised by the cascade. Len turned to exclaim, and saw Fox's face.

Then she remembered. Before Cam went away, he had spoken of a waterfall, this waterfall. He'd been here, with Fox. Len squeezed her hand. What could she say? He'll find us. They had left word at Home Village, with Lia, at the village above the break. He would find them, if he walked the path. He would find them. If.

She said nothing, merely helped Fox to lay down her load beside the pool, help that the younger woman scarcely needed, but gave Len a chance to touch her, to let her hands say what they both knew: It's been so long. Years have passed, but he will find us if he lives. Fox smiled at her wanly, and lifted Jade out of her carry-basket .

Jade loved the water. She flapped her arms like a bird to make it splash around her, squealing with delight. The adults took turns, one tending her while the other two sat back-to-back under the falls, letting the power of the water knead their shoulders. Once, when Jade had gone silent for a moment, Len's grandmother eyes flew open from her blissful water-massage to see the child paddling through the water with a determined face, Nish's hand holding her under her belly. "Kick, little fish!" he coached her, and her strong legs dutifully stirred the water. "Look, Fox! Look, Len. Look at the Jade-fish, how fast she swims!" he called, speeding Jade through the water at the end of his long arm. So Jade got her first swimming lesson before she ever reached the ocean.

After she had played and eaten and napped on the cool moss, as the sun sank, they walked on down the path to

Jade's rock, Cam's and Fox's rock, the rock where Len first saw the sea.

"Listen, little Jade-fish!" Nish cupped his hands around his ears. Jade did the same. "You hear that?" She nodded. "The sound of winter coming."

All around them, dry leaves fell like rain, each one tumbling through the dry branches and hitting the ground with its own little clatter.

"And see out there?" He shielded his eyes from the sun. "The sky changing with the season." The endless blue was cluttered with long streamers of white, fuzzy like wool. "Those are clouds. Soon they pile up, bring us some wet walking, maybe before we get home."

Jade studied the sky seriously, from under the little hand at her brow, just like Nish. "Clouds," she repeated.

It was very quiet on The Duck. Moving through the marshes took a lot of watching and not much muscle, not at all like unloading the beans in Big River Town, which had needed hard back-labor and a lot of urgent yelling. But after their cargo was safely off and resting on the boards of the waterfront deck where The Duck was tied, then it became somebody else's work. As carriers began to truck the beans away in big rolling barrows, Genia grinned at her crew and jingled a pocket suggestively. "Is anybody hungry?" she wondered idly.

"Food!" they roared. They were weak with hunger, fainting, famished, perishing, puny from starvation. They had never worked so hard in all their lives. "One day of honest lifting and carrying reminds you quick of why you took to the river, doesn't it?" Veydle grinned.

And so they had settled on a crowded open-air balcony, with flowers tumbling over the railings, and bees and bright tiny birds darting about. When the stew came, the first bite made Cam weep real tears, it was so hot. They all laughed. Quoit handed him a glass of dark red drink. "A little spicy, eh? Here, try some of this." With her good hand, Lexo ladled him out a big bowl of steaming brown grain of a kind he had never seen. It had a pleasant nutty fragrance. "Grows in the marshes, hereabouts. It's good; try it. Just put a little of the stew over it, not enough to burn your mouth."

Cam followed her advice and found that he could enjoy the stinging flavor of the stew, just a little bit of it mixed with a lot of the grain. It made his nose water some, and the top of his head got hot, but it was an interesting and complicated experience. Still, he could not understand how the others could put spoonful after spoonful of it, pure and unmixed, into their mouths with clear pleasure. In eating as in speaking, he pondered, distance is difference.

They stayed up late that night, sampling the food and drink in several establishments near the docks before stumbling back to The Duck, with Genia threatening to get them up before dawn. "Shouldn't we show the boy the town before we head for home?" Quoit protested.

"Does he look to you like he wants to see the town?" she answered, throwing her chin towards where Cam walked, close behind Lexo, trying his best to stay out of the way of the throng that streamed around him. His head was down, watching his feet, because the paving stones gaped and bulged and were cluttered, even at midnight, with sellers and beggars. They all wanted something from the boat-people: food, a moment of their time to show their wares, a coin for the best beer on the river. Cam found it easier to keep his head down and pretend he couldn't hear them because he couldn't deal courteously with so many voices crying and hands grabbing for his attention all at once. He looked miserable.

"Maybe not," Quoit admitted.

"Besides, I want to catch the early tide tomorrow. We're not far from the neaps, and I'd rather get through the marshes now than get caught aground there and be stranded eating nothing but oysters and saltgrass until the winter storms come and blow us off."

"Oysters are better than beans," Quoit said.

The next day, Genia rousted them all out of their bunks too soon. Her talk of water coming and going made no sense at all to Cam — water only *goes*, goes downhill; he knew this for a fact — but he watched with the others as the crowded bank of Big River Town on their left slipped by, still draped by the half-lit early morning fog.

And now, here they were, in the marshes at last. They were moving very slowly, with just the little night sail to push them back and forth along the narrow, wandering channels. All around was grass, endless tall grass that whispered in the winds. Nothing else, except every now and then a tall bird standing, or a lonely orange butterfly bobbing past. No other boats. No houses. No form but flatness on the land. Which wasn't land so much as water, Cam realized as they eased through it. But, as Quoit explained to him, now that they were sitting high and empty, some water they could sail through, and some water they couldn't.

The two of them stood in The Duck's nose, swatting away the biting bugs while Quoit showed Cam what to watch for: hints of shallows or of sharp things that could tear out The Duck's belly. "See that... over there?"

Cam could see it. "That rock?"

"Yes, but it's not a rock, not exactly. But like a rock. Made of shells, big sharp shells, all stuck together. Rock or not, we don't want to hit it or any of its relatives. So we keep a good eye out. Lexo, up above, is mainly watching for the channels, which ones look like they go through and which ones narrow down and go nowhere. Nothing stays the same in the marshes. Have to find your way, new, each time. Lexo can see the far things better up there, but our business, yours and mine, is the near at hand, and Genia will have us for breakfast if we let The Duck get stuck in the muck."

They stood in rustling stillness, watching.

A butterfly landed on the railing of The Duck. Its wings rested open on the wood, with every now and then a weak twitch. Cam wondered if it was dying. Butterfly time was almost over.

"What's wrong, Cam?"

Cam looked up with a guilty start. He had let his eyes wander away from the important job of watching.

"What's the matter, boy? You've been worrying on something for a while now. I can't tell if you're sad or scared, but whatever it is... speak it out— I'll listen."

Far across the never-ending grass there was a line where green met blue. "I don't know if I can do this."

"Do what? Nothing to do in the marshes but stay awake and follow the water."

"I don't mean *this*. I mean…. I hate this feeling. My insides are…" What was the word? He tried again. "I'm a Far-Walker. I've walked to the end of the path, right off the edge of the land," — he threw his hands out to the marshes — "and now there's no more left. So have I reached my limit, Quoit? Is this my place? I want to feel at home somewhere, but I don't know if this is the where. I don't know what it feels like to reach your limit. I thought it would be more…. I mean, I know I am part of The Duck, but I don't know if I can rest with you for the winter. I don't know if The Duck can be my home. And there's this: Is there any place at all for me, anywhere, if not with The Duck?"

"You're from the Steep Land, right?"

Cam goggled at him.

"Place like a wall," Quoit went on. "Where you have to climb everywhere and carry everything on your own back? No rivers, nothing but cliffs?"

The younger man nodded dumbly.

"I always thought life must be very hard there, without boats or pack animals or carts or such."

And Cam rushed to explain that yes, his home was like a wall, but no, life there wasn't hard, it was easy: walking the path, up and down. Hospitality, friendship, and love. Simple. Easy. Understandable. He fumbled for words to tell Quoit about Home Village, a little terrace on the great world where honey-bees buzzed around the apple-blossoms that the goats tried to steal, and his mother twisted fibers to hold things together.

Quoit was quiet for a time. "You miss it, Cam? You want to go home? I mean, you're more than welcome to stay with us; you suit us. You take Veydle's mischief in stride and don't let Genia rattle you. But if your heart is calling you, why not just go?"

"Go how? It is so *far*, Quoit! Should I walk back up the Big River? How will I live, from town to town? And to cross the high place of the world, you need furs and food and strong boots. How will I get these things? And it will take so long. My friend Fox… It will take so long. Maybe I should just stay, make this my place?"

"And welcome, too. But why backtrack? Why go the long way? Why not just take a ship?"

Cam stared at him.

"You know, a ship— a big boat, like the tall fellows we saw on the river, only bigger. To go on the ocean. They ply up and down this coast all the time. The Steep Lands are just to the south of us, not that far, where the mountains run down to the sea. Maybe three days sail, if the winds are right."

Cam felt tumbled head over heels, like in the river.

A boat to go home?

When Nish told Len he lived in a cave, she was a little worried. To her, "cave" meant a hole in the ground. Damp. Dark. Cramped. Bats lived in caves. So did bears. Not human people. But Nish was so gleeful to be going home, that she hid her dismay and didn't ask about the details, in case her questions betrayed her anxiety.

So nothing prepared her for the grand airy gallery that was Nish's home: a long seam in the wall of the world itself, overhung by a rock ceiling, floored by a paving of mortar cobbled with shells. Their smooth rounded backs soothed her tired feet when she took off her boots after their final climb down the long rope ladder (made, she was intrigued to find, with a rich reddish-brown fiber that was new to her; a bit coarse, but interesting.)

She had also kept from Nish her worry that his home, so far down at the bottom of the world, would be too hot for her. In fact, it turned out to be cool and breezy. The friendly stone of the roof and floor could take all the heat the sun offered and still give back only a steady, pleasant coolness. And the wind from the sea was never still.

And, oh, the sea!

When they had first peeped over the edge of the great granite outcropping high above, the far-off jade-green flatness had brought tears to Len's eyes, not so much for the thing itself as for the fact that she had lived to see it. She, herself, Len Rope-Maker, a grandmother with a modest range of seven villages, had come to this place and seen the sea. It had been that strange truth that first moistened her eyes and made her heart big in her chest.

But then, as they walked down the switchbacks of the path, helping each other when the way grew steep and rough, it

was less her own accomplishment and more the sea itself that
kept making her catch her breath in wonder. It surprised her
at every new view. The shoulders of the world here embraced
a wide circle of it just below them, and outside that circle
there was a vastness that she could only take in bit by bit, as
if her eyes had to grow bigger before they could hold it all.

And when they were very low, drawing close to Nish's
home, she learned that it was no lullaby-tale he told when he
talked about water in the sea; she could see it with her own
eyes. The sea, she saw, was indeed something fluid, restless
and sloshing, rippling with movement.

And now, here they are, at home with Nish: no walls, no
windows, nothing between them and the sea and sky, just
a windswept rock balcony running the whole length of the
"cave." At one end, turning the light to lace, a swag of some
kind of vine hangs down with succulent green nibs instead
of leaves and yellow flowers like finger-tip suns. It drapes
like a drawn-back curtain around a stone basin big enough to
bathe in, filled by a steady trickling from above and spilling
over the edge and down the world outside. Ah, no wonder
Nish hungered so to come back here, to bring her, to bring
all of them here. And no wonder he was giddy with relief
that the earthquake had not crushed this place. How had he
been able to bear that close-in little attic for so many months
after living in this bright air? Once a person had lived open to
the sea, how could they ever live anywhere else? How could
they rest away from it?

Now Nish is kneeling with Jade at the low stone rim of the
cave. He points at something below them. The child gazes
downward, then laughs with delight. Fox stands by them,
her face radiant, looking out over the sea. The air rings with
the call and cry of birds.

Cam sailed home with them towards The Duck's nest, to
wait there until one of the great ships that sometimes put
into their cove for fresh water would carry him south to the
"Steep Lands."

On the way, he was sick again. As soon as they freed themselves from the marshes, the gentle sway and bob of The

Duck turned to stomach-churning lunges and plunges. Waves slapped the hull. The sails snapped in wind unthwarted by tree, house, or hill. "She smells home!" Genia exulted. But Cam's stomach found The Duck's excitement disturbing. With each homeward heave of the boat, his uneasiness grew, until finally he rushed to the rail and emptied himself over the side.

"Don't stand there like you're anchored, Lexo; hand that boy a rag! And you, Cam! Put your face to the wind. It'll set you right. Here, now, come join me at the tiller. If you're going to go to sea, you'd better learn a thing or two."

"He's worked a whole season and spent nothing at all, Genia; I think he can afford to go aboard as a passenger," Quoit said mildly.

"Our Cam? Sit idle while others work? I don't think so. He'll take a hand, even if it's just to empty slop buckets."

"Maybe. But I don't think he'll be steering the ship his first time out. Just doing what you're told and being quick about it— that's all you need to know to be a good shipmate on the big ones."

"No harm in him understanding a bit about how it all works together, though. You can do what you're told quicker if you're ready. Helps if you have some inkling of what it's about, the why of things."

Quoit shrugged. "True enough. And a hand on the tiller will at least keep him from turning his insides out before we get home."

"That's so. Nothing like steering to take the green out of a man's face. Come on, Cam. Stand in front of me, where you can see. No, not stiff like that— bend your knees. Springy, like, or The Duck will send you flying. She doesn't like stiffness in a man, not like some. Spread your legs apart, or she'll knock you over. Why do you think you have two legs? You're not a tree. That's better; now sway with her. Bend your knees. There you go. Now you can just lay your hand lightly on the tiller. No!— don't lean on it; it's not a railing. Just light as a feather, just to get the touch of her."

So Cam, in deep water far from anything he could hit or hinder, got his first lessons in sailing and his first feel for the quiver of life at the heart of The Duck. For he *could* feel her, a willful tug at the tiller, a mind of her own. He felt Genia's mastering hand and The Duck's resistance, then agreement that yes, perhaps Genia had been right all along. Over and over again, he felt this soft bargaining in the steering-stick, between Genia and The Duck and the wind and the waves.

And Genia was right, once again, about what would settle a sea-sickness. As she made him take note of the breeze and the sails and their path between the far coast on their left and the low, spotty line of islands out to their right, his insides settled. Cam was sailing.

"That one? That's a lobster. No lobsters up where you came from? Lobsters are very special, not like spiders; spiders have eight legs. Not like ants; ants have six legs. Not like cats; cats have four legs. Not like birds; how many legs on a bird? I forget. Lobsters have ten legs, five on each side, like fingers. How many fingers do *you* have on each side? Maybe you are a lobster; what do you think?

"Very wise, lobsters. Just like you. They grow and grow. They grow so big they don't fit inside themselves any more. So they break open, crawl outside themselves until they are naked in the sea, brave and careful in the sea, without any shell to hold them in at all. And, because they are so brave, the ocean gives them a new shell. Bigger. Stronger. With room to grow. And they grow and grow until the little Jade-fish eats them and grows wise with their wisdom and big with their bigness and strong with their strength. But the Jade-fish never wears a shell, so she always has room to grow."

Len sits in the warm sand in the shade of the big feather-duster tree. There is more sand here at the bottom of the world than on all the rest of it put together. Does it just roll down and come to rest here? She wonders, but Nish tells her that the sea chews on the land and spits out the sand. Wherever it comes from, it is very comfortable to sit on, though it does have a way of getting into folds and creases. Perhaps that's why Nish's people wear so little clothing: jewelry and hats to shade their eyes, mostly, and the men put on a sort of narrow diaper before they swim. "Don't want a big fish eating little Nish-fish," he explained as he wraps himself before one of their swims.

"Not so little, sometimes." She grins at him. He snorts.

They spend most of their time learning to play in the water.

Len still finds the first touch of the waves shocking, like sticking her head into a cold spring, though in truth the water here is not cold. But committing your body to the sea is *bigger* than just wetting your head to wash your hair. It's an all-over kind of thing. First there are the legs and feet, no problem, just shallow wading and the water coming and going like a cat's tongue licking your toes. But if you keep going, soon enough there's a great splash over the crotch that still makes Len shriek every time. Then waist, breasts, and finally the waves slap your face, leaving you sputtering and gasping. Nothing else on the world is like giving yourself into the sea.

Nish shows them, with Jade in his arms, how to squat and wait for the swell, then spring up and bob, lifted off their feet, for a moment or two in deep water. He teaches them how to hold their air in and bend down into a wave, burrowing under the frothy tumult and coming out the other side laughing. And he teaches them how to tease and trick the waves, acting as if they were heading out into deep water and then, just as a wave is upon them, at the very last minute turning to ride the crest in, sometimes all the way to the sand.

And he talks sternly to Jade about how sometimes a wave comes that is stronger than you are. "Then you find the bottom and wait. Just wait." He gathers their eyes to make sure that Len and Fox are listening as well. "You just take your pounding and hold your breath until it passes. Big wave comes, big wave goes, but the little Jade-fish is calm and waiting. No problem, no panic. Just waiting for your time."

So many hours of each day pass in wave-games that Len feels a bit virtuous to be doing some real work for a change. There are new plants here, new fibers to be understood. The prickly, pulpy spears she learned to scrape up at the village above the rift— those live here, and she finally learns the pattern of their growth: exploding from a single center like angry lettuce-heads. Right now, she is prying the husks off the giant nuts that come from the feather-duster trees that grow in the sand between the world-wall and the water. Their fiber is coarse and hard on her hands — probably the same material as the rope ladders — not fit for fine work, she thinks. The feather-duster trees also have enormous leaves that interest her very much. What can be done with those? Should they be worked dry or green? That's an important question because, while there's plenty of blow-down, it would be impossible to climb the long, smooth, unbranching boles to harvest from the top. At least, impossible for Len; the children of Nish's village shinny up and down the trees like happy squirrels.

Nish's village isn't a village in the sense that Len knows villages; there's no common terrace. It's just a loose collection of friendly families that lived in seams and caves around the circle of water. Some homes have fancy wooden porches opening out to the sea, but most just follow the natural shape of the rock. The people come down each day, to play, fish, eat, and work their crafts together, then clamber back up their ladders at night to sleep in their own places. Len asks Nish why they don't take advantage of the generous shelf of sand at the bottom of the world and build there.

"The beach — the in-between place — is good for play and work. Not a good place to live. Tides come and go — eat the land and give it back — and also, some years, a big wave comes, very big, and washes everything away. Cleans the sand off just fine, but if we live down there, it cleans us off, too. So we sleep up here and always keep one eye on the Far Away. Big wave comes, we run for the ladders. Maybe we lose a few boats; maybe sometimes even a few people. The ocean is a big neighbor, not always friendly, needs lots of room."

That makes Len thoughtful, the idea that the sea can wash everything away. While she is down on the sand, she keeps an eye not only on the line where the sky falls into the ocean, but also on where her beloveds are.

Right now, they are out on the water, sitting in boats, the strange cane-and-skin shoes longer than a person is tall that float on the surface and carry Nish's people out fish-hunting. Fox is learning to make her boat go, and spinning in great uncontrolled circles. Nish's boat is near her, circling her in a smooth arc across the water. Len can see Jade's little sun-hat in front of Nish's chest. Len imagines Jade is laughing at Fox's flailing efforts to paddle in a straight line. This is not an easy thing, Len knows from her own tries.

Then, suddenly, the little golden body launches itself from Nish's boat and hits the water. Len cries out; children digging for shell-animals near her look up to see the cause of her distress. She points, urgently, "It's Jade! She fell out of the boat!" They look where she is pointing. They laugh: "Yes, the little one! She's in the water. Swimming— see how well she swims for an upworlder? She's a fish!" And Len sinks back down onto the sand and settles her heart as the small sunhat doggedly makes its way from Nish's boat to Fox's, where she climbs in with her mother.

That afternoon, Nish and Fox begin planning to build a little boat for Jade.

"What will it be like, Quoit?"

The older man studies the moon, bulging towards full over the low scatter of islands off to their right, the West. He spits over the side, which Cam now understands is one of his ways of testing the wind.

"Bring her up a little... There! Just right." Then Quoit is silent again as The Duck slips along through the night.

"Quoit...?"

"It's a question, isn't it? 'What's it like out on deep water?' Kind of hard to say... One thing's for sure and certain: You will get seasick. No way around it. Nobody sails outside the Barrier Islands without their insides getting all shook around at the beginning. You get over it, though— some, pretty quick; some, it takes a while longer.

"The other thing is, you're a stranger when you come onboard. That can be hard for folks, you and your crewmates both. But you've eaten at that table often enough. Being a stranger hasn't killed you yet. You'll live through it.

"What else? It's close quarters out there, cheek by jowl with a mess of sailors who haven't had a bath since they said goodbye to their mothers. You'd think that with the ships being so big and all, it wouldn't be so tight. But the truth is that big ships take big cargoes and big crews. You live close and work close. Even as a passenger, you have to be polite and get along. Sea-sick, hung-over, or dog-tired from standing watch all night, you still have to get along. People get on your nerves and sometimes you have to step around trouble. You decide what's important and stand by that but let the rest go easy. Because you're stuck with each other, out where you can't see land. Maybe someone bothers you, just drives you crazy with how they chew their food or something. But then a big storm shakes up the ship and that person saves your life, maybe hangs on to you when a big wave washes over the deck, and real sudden, you don't care so much about chewing. Perspective, is what I'm trying to say. You get a lot of perspective when you're far from land. Watch what you're doing, now; you're starting to luff." Cam made a feather-light correction to the stick and the sail firmed up again.

"But what it's *really* like, Cam, I don't know how to tell you. It's big. Big water, big waves. Big sails. Big wind. And things you have no say in, not one bit, like the weather. Sometimes you just have to trust. Even if you know better. You trust your ship and you trust your captain and you trust your shipmates. Because that's all you've got, out there. Like on The Duck, I guess. But bigger. Bigger trust. I don't know how to say it."

Cam noticed though, that the Quoit of few words had actually said a good deal.

"It's not just about the seasickness or the crew or the hard, hard work. It's about being out there, out beyond…. You'll just have to go and see for yourself."

"When did you go to sea, Quoit?"

"Oh, me? I was about fifteen when Jazeley's Seagull took me on. And I stayed with her for eleven years. Saw a lot. Learned a lot. I liked the life. Hated it sometimes, too."

"What made you leave?"

"Hard to say. It was time. I lashed up with Genia for a while in Big River Town, and it seemed like I was ready to take to new water for awhile, learn something different. So that's what I did; no better teacher than Genia and the river's always new. The channel's always changing. The banks shift. Islands pop up where no island stood before. The same river, never same. Almost thirty years now, me and Genia, going up and down that river. Sometimes, home just happens to people, I guess. So stay with us, Cam, if it feels right. We want you, even if it's only for the winter. Or take the first decent ship with a good master that comes along. I'll see that you get a good berth. You find your way home, boy. It's worth it."

Cam adjusted the stick again. The wind was shifting. He could feel it.

"Tomorrow, we start by climbing up to where the cane grows."

"More cane?" Both Len and Fox eye the big bundles in the deep recesses of the cave, where the rock ceiling dips towards the floor. The crawl-space serves Nish as a store-room. Barrels, jugs, baskets, tools, nets, lines, and stacks and stacks of cane of various sizes line the crease in the rock.

"That's old cane," Nish says dismissively. "No good for shaping— too stubborn. Old things can get set in their ways. New boats need new cane: green, bendy. Cane that doesn't have too many opinions. Open to possibilities.

"And as long as we're passing through Second Village Up," he goes on, "I think we'll see if we can trade for some skins. Mostly it's good to tan your own for your own boat. See that it's done right, just the way you like it. But scraping and tanning hides takes a lot of work. Stinks, too. I think little Jade is turning into big Jade so fast, she'll outgrow this boat in a day or two. So no point in using up a lot of time on it. And besides, Jade wants a boat of her own now, not later. Isn't that right, little fish?"

Jade can always count on Nish to understand.

But even without the tanning, building a boat is a job of work.

Nish teaches Fox how to use his strange, long-handled saw that cuts on the pull-stroke instead of on the push like the upworld saws she's used to. It delights her how much easier it is to be precise with this tool.

And the precision is necessary; Nish is very picky about the angle of the cuts on the lengthwise supports of the boat. They must come together with its backbone in perfect points at the head and tail, he says.

Then, after trimming the cane, comes the bending, a complicated process of reaming out the pith, packing the empty core with sand, heating it over the fire a section at a time, then bracing the cane against a rock and pulling on it until the heat-softened part bows. "Why the sand, Nish?" Fox wonders, as his big arms oblige the straight rod to arch.

"I don't know. But without the sand, it breaks. Try it; I did— I wanted to save a step. I was a lazy boy. But saving a step isn't the same as saving work. Try it; you'll see."

"No, thank you. Let's just do it your way, on my first one."

While Nish holds the curve in place, Fox cools it with a rag dipped in seawater. "The way it cools is the way it stays," he tells her, in the voice of someone repeating wisdom he was given a long time ago.

They move on to the next section, and the next, until the "backbone" of Jade's boat rests in a graceful arc like a hunting bow, about six feet long.

"Now you see how to do it. Now we take turns," Nish tells Fox, and they do. Working with the lighter supports that run alongside the backbone, first he bends a cane, with Fox wielding the cooling rag, then he challenges her to make another to match it perfectly. "If not the same, then Jade's boat will be lumpy," he cautions.

Bending the cane isn't hard. Bending it to a certain curve is not as easy as Nish makes it look.

She learns to recognize the smell that tells them the cane is burning, not warming. She also learns some strong words to use when she pulls too hard too fast and hears the loud snap of something giving way. He chuckles and puts the splintered bits aside. "Nothing wasted," he tells her. "These make good fish-spears, good blades. Very sharp."

The work takes longer with Fox helping, but by the time they finish bowing the six slender supports that run long-ways and the nine shorter ribs that cross them and hold them in place, she knows a lot more about cane, curves, and camber than she did when the day started. She's also streaked with soot and sweat. Her hair smells like smoke.

"You say you want to know about boats," Nish reminds her.

When Nish begins to teach Fox how to lash the boat-bones together, Len is sorely tempted to join them. She walks towards them with Jade, to offer her help, but stops.

Fox's face is engrossed, captivated. Nish squats behind her, looking over her shoulder, coaching her as she twines the cord over the rib, under the backbone, over the rib on the other side, then under the backbone again. "Now, again, the other way," Nish prompts. "Keep it tight."

Over, under, over, under. That's a lesson Len's already learned. She turns away, leaving Fox to her new work.

Besides, she thinks, someone has to watch Jade or they'll never get done.

The frame of Jade's boat is soon done, just a skeleton of green cane lashed together. Nish whittles a smooth wooden cap for the nose and has Fox do the same for the tail, so the sharp cane-tips won't wear through the skin covering. Then he leaves it out to dry in the hot midday sun.

Jade is impatient. She is ready for her boat now. "When will it be done, Nish? Why can't we work on it today?"

"When the sun turns the cane to gold, we can work on it again. And the why: Green cane changes when it dries, so you have to give it time to mellow, find its shape. We cover that boat now, in a week it will be loose and baggy like old-man skin." He tugs a pinch of his neck to show her. "Better we wait, let the cane settle. Then we'll tighten up the lashings, cover the boat, and it will stay strong and close like little-girl skin." He reaches out to pinch her neck; she runs away squealing.

The next day, Jade runs to Nish. "It's gold! It's gold! The boat-basket is gold." He follows her to see. She points to the slight yellowing on the top of the sun-bathed green ribs.

"Oh, very good noticing; it's beginning to turn. That means it's drying out. And that streak of yellow that you notice with your good sea-eyes— we have to wait until that creeps around the whole cane and there's no more green left at all. Then we can cover it and send the little Jade-fish out in her own boat."

"We can't do it now?"

"Not now. Because now is for something just as important: paddles. Every boat needs two paddles—"

"Why two? You only use one."

"Oh, two because sometimes something happens. A paddle can fall out of a boat, or break in your hands. So we always have two. And right now, you don't have any at all, so we have to go on a great paddle-hunt."

"Where?"

"Along the sand, that's where the paddles are."

She looks at him doubtfully. Sometimes Nish speaks in ways that are different from ordinary truth. "There aren't any paddles on the beach. We walk on the sand every day. We don't see paddles, except the ones that belong to people."

"Are you sure?" he asks her. "Maybe they don't look like paddles. Maybe they are hiding inside pieces of strong wood, about as tall as you are, that need to be tickled with a carving blade before they'll show themselves."

So, while the cane tempers in the sun, checked and turned every day by Jade, they walk the sand until they find the perfect hidden paddles. Nish carves one free from the wood that cloaks it, and Fox releases the other. The child learns that Nish was telling the exact truth: Inside those two logs that looked so much like driftwood, there *were* two paddles, exactly the right length for Jade, with grips that fit her little hands just as if they had been made for her.

The Duck coasts through a near-invisible break in the green flatness. "Are we going back into the marshes?" Cam asked. He did not enjoy the marshes.

"No, that's just The Neck. You'll see the village in a minute."

And sure enough, as they slide along the grass-fringed channel, it widens out into a great openness, as still as a bathing tub after the heaving and dipping of the open sea.

"The Nest," Genia proclaims. Boats nuzzle each other by the piers and recline at rest on sand and grass. Many of them bear a family resemblance to The Duck: high beaks, fat bodies, and gently bulging bottoms, with tall masts to carry the sails.

A bell begins to ring, echoing strangely across the water. People pour out, calling and waving from the piers and houses that spangle the cove.

"Tide's not quite high enough yet. We'll have to sail around a bit."

"Good enough. Give them time to get things ready."

So The Duck zigzags around The Nest, showing Cam the sights: the best place to eat (which is different from the best place to drink), the sailmaker's workshop, and, best of all, "Home."

Four arms point like wind-vanes to a sprawling, weathered wooden house, silver-gray from sun and salt. It stands high on knock-kneed stilts and children are tumbling from the door and swarming down the front steps. Everyone is waving. Small shouts can be heard across the water. The Duck's crew whoops back and waves madly.

"Your house — all the houses — have *legs*?"

"Oh, my, yes. We build everything on pilings. Big winter storms blow in the water sometimes, swamp the town, no fun at all. The boats can take it; they just float it out, then lie down and go back to sleep. But the houses have to stand on tiptoe to keep their skirts dry. Settle down, everybody; we're coming around again. It would be a shame to run aground within sight of home."

On the next pass, they show Cam the boat-works. "And that's where The Duck was hatched, right over there."

Cam studies the tall double scaffolding where even now a small cousin of The Duck is being cradled, high and dry above the sand. "Where do you get the wood?" he wonders, for clearly there are no trees anywhere nearby, nothing big enough to build a big boat.

"Ah, now that's a good question. One of the great problems of life, that one is: Where the people know boats, there's no trees. And where the trees grow, there's no know-how. That's why the River is such a great thing: What one has, another needs, and the River ties it all together. Take those beans of ours. Up in the high country, folks are up to their noses in beans. Have so many they feed them to the hogs. But down in Big River Town, the ship people will pay good coin for them— those beans can go to sea in barrels and never sour nor spoil. (Unless the rats get at 'em, of course.) The River puts the need together with the have. Same with the wood; some places have more trees than they know what to do with, have to clear 'em off just to have a little room to farm. You should see it, boy— in the springtime when the waters swell up with snowmelt: great rafts of floating logs working their way down from tree-country, crashing and grinding, getting stuck and then breaking free again, heading on down to the sea. Boatwright buys up the best of them in Big River Town and hauls 'em over here in barges. The river holds it all together."

"With a little help from The Duck," Genia adds. Cam falls silent, pondering the ways of the river and the path.

When Quoit told Cam that "a few friends" would help them pull The Duck ashore for her winter's rest, he'd understated the excitement of the entire town whenever one of their boats came home for the winter. Everyone turns out, and their animals too: great hunch-backed bullocks yoked together as if to pull a cart. Only the cart they pull is a boat, up a long soggy trench at the highest moment of the tide. Ropes and cables stretch from every knob and hook on The Duck as people and animals heave together, sloshing in the water, until The Duck has gone as far as muscles and pulleys can take her and Genia bellows, "Stuck fast!"

"What happens now?" Cam asks Veydle, who stands beside him, waist-deep with the rest of the throng.

"Home, and a bath, and a welcome feast until low tide. Then, we come back with the rollers and carry her the rest of the way."

Cam looks up at the bulk of The Duck. "Carry her?"

"Don't worry. We'll have lots of help. Coil up that rope and throw it over the side; we'll need it later. Meanwhile, a bath; you stink, boy!" Veydle hits the water with his hand like a board, splashing a great gout of water in Cam's face. Cam splashes back, and soon a water-fight spreads to the whole group of Duck-haulers, while the bullocks look on placidly.

The mass of small bodies that bubbles out of the big rambling house on stilts are not *all* Duck children, Cam is relieved to learn. (Such a *lot* of children!) It seems that, in this village, much craft is done outside the home, in great shared work-places like the boats, the boat-yards, and the sail-making sheds— places where little hands might come to harm. So the care of the smallest villagers — those under five or six years old — has come to be its own craft, just like carpentry or soap-making. The Duck house is the workshop where this skill is practiced, and everyone who lives there is expected to take a hand. So during the storm that keeps them from working on The Duck's exposed and sadly mossy bottom, Cam finds himself an informal apprentice in child-craft.

Genia teaches Cam what she says is the basic, the funda-mental job: how to clean a baby's bottom. Bottoms are required to be as clean as The Duck's, only you can't scour them as hard and you can't use scrub-brushes at all, which makes the task more difficult than you'd expect.

Lanya, daughter of Quoit and Genia, shows him how to feed porridge to the little ones who are past their weaning but can't yet be trusted to find their own mouths with a spoon. (And then there's the face-cleaning, and the neck cleaning and ear-cleaning after feeding. The Duck family is much taken with cleanliness.)

Veydle teaches him the important task of chasing the children around the house, a vital but underappreciated part of the work, he says, because without the chasing, children would not take naps— a dire outcome for the adults who need the rest period to gather themselves for the afternoon.

Cam also helps Lexo and Aven instruct the older children— the four-, five-, and six-year olds— in the essentials of how to take care of themselves: how to wash themselves and their clothing; how to cut and carve with a knife and keep it sharp; the safe and skillful use of tools, levers, and pulleys; how to start and tend a fire; how to cook and bake; and — Cam's specialty — how to wash dishes.

So, while he waits for a southbound ship to visit The Nest to trade for water, Cam becomes an expert bottom-cleaner, a passable porridge-feeder, and a good-enough child-chaser (though no one outshines Veydle in this area). But it's teaching that he enjoys the most. Soon the children of The Nest are all wearing little bracelets of cord they made for themselves, fastened on their wrists by fat button-knots hooked back through the loop where the ply begins. Just like the one Len had helped him make when he was small, out of the nettle fibers that overflowed their house.

It's the first real storm of winter. Nish sees it coming the day before, the big bank of clouds hiding the horizon out past the curving walls that embrace their circle of the sea, past the lumpy bits of world far out in the water where the birds nest and raise their young. The waves begin to grow and growl with a new sound. They no longer remind Len of a big hand stroking a big cat, ruffling up and down its fur over and over again. The water now throws itself against the land with some high passion: hunger, maybe, or fury. And that's the day *before* the storm.

During the storm, they don't go down to the sand at all.

Nish rolls down the cane mats that are fixed like curtains above his balcony and lashes their lower edges to stone knobs near the floor. When the big wind comes, they struggle and flap but shield the family from the rains that fall like an unending avalanche. Several times, Len tries to peer out between the bellying mats to see the tumult of the waters roaring beneath, but the rain blinds her. She moves to the back of the cave with the others, where the ceiling drops lower and she keeps hitting her head. It's quieter back there, a little away from the growl of the wind.

They sit on their low wooden folding chairs around the storm-hearth and talk and work like families do in the winter. Len's hair is combed out, beaded, and braided, with Jade helping Nish as she begins to learn the pattern: over, under, over, under. Shell and bone are carved and polished, and wood, too, because Nish says it's softer and easier for learning. (And mistakes can always be fed to the hungry fire.) Fibers are twisted into cords in the old familiar moves that need no watching and no thinking— except if Jade helps, when a goodly amount of care is called for. And stories are told, by everyone, even Jade, whose short lifetime has already yielded a bounty of that fruit.

Fox asks whether she can leave Jade with them on the next clear day; she wants to go walking. Fox seems a little shy about this request, a little apologetic, not looking up from her whittling; the roar of the gale nearly drowns out her careful, planned words. Len is touched by a wisp of memory: Lia reassuring Fox when it was time for her baby to sleep alone. Perhaps this is another step: Fox wanting to go walking. For some reason — more than just the pleasure of Jade's company — this makes Len very happy.

"Of course, of course!" she answers her eagerly. "How high do you think you'll go? Should we pack some food for you? Maybe some clothes?" It's a little hard to remember that the rest of the world wears clothes, now that they've gotten so used to wearing nothing but hats; Nish's people don't even wear the Never-Ending Braid, not even the couples she knows to have great-grandchildren together. During storms, they keep warm in long swaths of soft goat's wool— that's all. If Fox is heading back up to the clothed world, she'll have to…

"Actually, I'm not going up the path; I want to walk along the sand, maybe get to the end where the wall reaches right out to the water. I'd like to see what's around the corner."

Nish nods. "It's a good walk, especially after a storm. A big blow carves up the sand, new shapes. Things blow ashore, sometimes good things. Useful. Or strange. Take a bag, maybe," he suggests. "But around the corner, no— can't be done. Can't be seen. I tried, back when I was young, more than once. Even tried climbing up the world to get around: too smooth for climbing there. But you go anyway. See the end of the sand. See where the big waves crash on the rock. We look after the little one. Maybe Jade helps us gather driftwood. 'Which fish is always hungry?'" He asks the child, sweeping his eyes towards the flickering glow on the storm-hearth. "Who eats and eats and never gets fat?"

"The fire-fish!" Jade cries out.

"That's right. And tomorrow will be lots of food for the fire-fish, all up and down the sand, and people gathering, gathering, so that the next storm that comes, our fires will be healthy and strong. Will you help us, tomorrow, gather food for the fire while Fox goes walking?"

The child nods solemnly. "But I need to hear the story again. The fire-fish story and how the water-world came and..."

Len finds that she listens to Nish's stories in a different way now. The flying fish— she's seen it skim across the water with her own eyes. The shell-creature that makes pearls— she's eaten it, fried and in soup. The flowers that grow below the surface— she's stroked them with her own hand and seen them jerk shut at her touch. What she once thought were dreams and fables have turned out to be the exact and literal truth, now that she's come to live where Nish lives. The sea is real, it's made of water, people move about on the water, and Nish fishes this water for his food and art.

Len understands about fishing now. It's when you take something you already have and offer it back to the sea at the end of a hooked line or in a basket-trap, and the sea takes it from you. Maybe the sea gives you back nothing at all, but often it trades you a fish to grill at night on the sand with your neighbors or to smoke and stew later at your storm-hearth while the winter rain falls. Fishing is a blind swap, and this is how Nish lives. It's a good life, she thinks, as her fingers braid four slender strands into a strong new fishing line to feed her family.

And now Jade is running up and down the beach like the little birds that hunt in damp sand but hate to get their feet wet by the waves. She brings Len sticks like old bones, and asks, "Is this good fire-food?"

"It will make the fire roar," Len tells her. "It will drive the night out of our home. Such fire-food has never been seen before!"

In fact, Len wonders about the driftwood. Where does it come from? It can't all have fallen down from the world above, for there are no trees to speak of until many villages up. And the wood is weathered strangely: naked of bark, but not rotten. Smooth and silver-white. Very much like bones, she thinks again, as she watches Jade's little golden body dart away and back to her with a new fire-morsel in her hands. Such a gift! Such *life*— so far from the weak, froglike sprawl of her when she was a baby. Now strong muscles ripple under her smooth, full child-skin, and her eyes are everywhere. She likes hunting for firewood. She likes hunting for anything. Yarrow was a hunter, too. Perhaps he lives in her sea-colored eyes.

When they swim out to the undersea towers to search for the giant crayfish that are so good to eat, Jade dives as deep as Nish now, peering under secret ledges, darting like a minnow through the rainbow-colored arches and caves. Nish calls her "Jade-fish"— this is who she is. It frightens Len sometimes to see how free she is in the deeps.

Len herself has learned to swim, to let the salty water hold her weight, to trust, and then use her arms and legs to direct her going. But diving.... She can bend down and kick, with her eyes firmly fastened to one of the big meaty shell-creatures they relish, but as her body begins to cry out for air, she loses confidence and turns back. Jade flashes below her and then bobs to the surface with the giant sea-snail. It will feed them that night and then turn into one of Nish's quicksilver carvings. Fox adds it to the net bag she tows behind her, buoyed on a little float of cane.

And now dragging another net behind her, filling fast with Jade's firewood finds, Len thinks this place is good for them. She can see Fox, tiny with distance, far ahead of her on the arc of sand ringing the water, walking at last. We made the right choice, she tells her partner silently, if you can call it choice when love and earthquakes and early birth force your steps. She looks down at her own body, naked and brown in the sun. A little sinking of her breasts, maybe, a little soften-ing of her belly, but her legs are still strong, she thinks. Her legs can still carry her. This is a good place.

Behind her, she hears Nish's strong ax breaking up a tree-top that washed ashore in the storm, too gnarled and branchy to use for building and too large to ride up in the pulley basket. Like the harvest of firewood, the ax-head makes Len wonder. It's shining metal of a kind unknown to her. Nish says it comes from over the sea, though she may not have understood him correctly about this.

Nish keeps them on land for several days after the storm; the waves are still rough and willful. He himself goes out to fish with some of their neighbors, not the smallest children or the elders past their strength. Their boats work together, hauling in large nets heavy with the harvest of fish driven in by the storm. Len gathers driftwood and storm-borne shells with Jade and watches the little boats, far out in the bay, tossed like leaves on a wind.

Fox spends the time walking. She brings back shells and word that, in both directions, the sand finally narrows away to nothing, until at last the waves crash right at the foot of the world, tearing at it, sending up mighty fountains of spray. She stays out one night, watching the water blast against the rocks, waiting to see if low tide will free enough beach to let her pass. The ebbing water allows her to go just a little bit further before surf on stone turns her back.

Of course, being Fox, she tries to clamber up the rock face above the water and work her way further, but it is as Nish said— at neither end of the beach can the world be climbed to see beyond. The stones that break the water are wet and slick with sea-life, and the wall above is without holds for hand or toe.

"I couldn't go on, Len. There was just no more path— it ends, Len. It just ends, right here."

"I imagine that further along it's just more of the same: waves breaking on stone." Len notes with interest that, instead of being frustrated, Fox seems enlivened, exhilarated.

"It is." Both women look up at Nish, gawking at his certainty.

"Better put your eyes on what your hands are doing, Len." She looks back down at the griddle. Nish is teaching her to make the soft flatbread of his people. It burns fast if you don't pay attention.

"Now, loosen the edges with the blade," he directs.

"But you mean" — Fox is not distracted by the skin of batter that wants to burn, stick, and bubble up, all at the same time — "you've been outside, into the big water?"

"Yes. A long time ago. Others, too, have gone. Careless people— the wind can suck a boat right out the big door, and then they're gone. Or sometimes someone hooks a big fish and gets too excited, gets pulled outside before they can cut the line. And people who are old or sad, and feel no need to be on the world anymore. But I wasn't careless or caught, or old or sad; I was just young. Young and stubborn and stupid. I wanted to go out to that rocky place outside. Where the birds nest." He pointed at the closest of the stony crags, like little worlds, that could be seen between the jaws of stone that enclosed their ring of bright water. Even from a distance, they could see the birds that boiled around it.

"It's not far and I was just a boy. I wanted their feathers to decorate my carvings. Eggs too, but mostly feathers. And just because nobody else had ever paddled there and come back— what did that have to do with me? I was Nish." He laughs. "Nish I still am, only not so stupid.

"Young Nish thought he was clever, thought he could outsmart the big water. I waited for a day with no wind, for what is it but the wind that sweeps people away? And I set out, with my mother watching with dark eyes from this same balcony. But when I went beyond, into the open, I learned that there is a wind down deep in the water that carries you, even if the air is still. I had to set my course far to the south, off that way…," he pointed, "to fight the north-pull of the water, and paddle as hard as I'd ever paddled in my life, but I got there." Len can see a glint of the prideful young man in Nish's eyes, even now.

"I came ashore, walking where birds' nests are so thick on the ground that I had to mind my steps or crush them. Eggs and babies and parents everywhere, fearless and untroubled by my gathering the feathers they had let fall. Finally, when the tide was turning — I had planned this, too, see — returning on the rising tide — I turned my boat back towards home, my bags stuffed with glories of blue and green and rose and white. But the water-wind was too strong for me, stronger than my strongest paddling, and swept me to the north no matter how far I set my course to the south. Soon, I was fighting straight south, just to keep the gates of home in view. That's when I saw the world outside, how the walls fall straight into the sea and the sea crashes against them, like an ax at the foot of a tree.

"My arms got tired and it came to me that I was going to lose, that I would be carried away. But I saw my family's boats put out, and others too, and I paddled as if each pull were my whole life. But my strength was not enough (and, remember, I was young then; I was *very* strong) and I was swept past the opening. But my father and my sisters had come in their boats. They clustered just inside the northern wall and threw cane buoys on long ropes out into the current that had me. It was one of these lines that pulled me back; I was exhausted. I caught it and held it. They dragged me home like a fish on a line."

"You made it," Fox breathes.

"I did *not* make it. I didn't make it *home*; that's what counts — mind what you're doing there, Len; it will be raw and sticky where it bubbles up like that — I had to be rescued. And that was on a calm day in summer, and me a big young man at the height of his strength." He looks at Fox closely. "And if I ever see you, any of you, going too close to the mouth of the ocean, I will break your paddles across my knee. Do you understand?" Len has never heard Nish sound so much like a father.

"But you got there, just with the strength of your two arms. Two people, paddling together, or three... We could go together, Nish. Outside— back to the bird island, to gather the feathers. Outside..."

"Yes, we thought that, my friends and I, when we were young. But strong is heavy, and the boats won't hold together with more than one heavy body in them. Me and Jade, maybe; but me and you, no. Fox, the waves are bigger out there. You can see their white hats from here. Out past the gates, sometimes the nose of my boat would be going uphill while the tail was still going downhill. The bones and skin of our boats aren't strong enough. You would need something harder, that wouldn't bend in the waves. But what is that strong that doesn't sink?"

"Something…," Fox begins to say, but a definite smell of burning batter interrupts them. Len has been distracted by the spark in Fox's eyes — more than just the reflection of the cookfire — and now the griddle has to be scraped clean again and Nish has to make a few more jokes about the difference between flatbread and rope.

The next day, Len notices Fox and Jade racing little "boats" — leaves, bits of wood, segments of cane — across a big shallow swale that the storm left stranded, high on the beach, cut off from the sea.

Len watches as Fox begins to build boats.

First, they're just chips of wood with no particular plan nor shape. Fox and Jade race them across puddles and swales between the storms. Then, after Nish puts the tools in her hands and makes sure she knows how to keep all her fingers, he sees that Fox has a talent for carving. But her joy isn't in making the little fish and birds and butterflies that take shape in Nish's hands. Her passion is to carve little toy boats during their long storm-bound days around the fire, then carry them down to the beach and test them in the water to see which ones come soonest to the end of a measured course and which ones can stay upright in a riffle. She tries narrowing their prows so they cut through the water more cleanly, deepening their keels so they won't skid sideways, broadening their bottoms so they stay upright. She trims them with feathers and leaves to catch the wind. She even, working with great delicacy, attaches little sleds outside the hulls, like Nish put on Jade's child-boat so it couldn't roll over.

When the weather allows them to climb down to the beach but the water is too rough for wave-play, mother and daughter race boats for hours on end. Len watches them from the shady ledge of Nish's cave where she is lazily knotting cords together into a fish-net. Although Nish is out on the water and no one else is at home to hear, she says aloud, "I believe we will be going out to visit that bird-rock." She lifts her eyes to the open water beyond the walls of the world and the white-frosted stone hummocks out there, seething with wings. "Probably sometime in the spring."

Cam feels the wind pounding on the house, hears it sucking at the roof and moaning around the chimney. The room he shares with Veydle and Glax is just under the eaves; there isn't much between him and the storm. Before, the one small window showed him the ring of lights around Nest Cove, sharp bright needles stringing their wavery reflection across the water. Then, as the weather closed in, the lights sank to a dim glow that barely hinted that The Duck family was not alone in the world. Now the window shows nothing but rattling, splashy blackness.

Cam rolls over in his bed — not a thin pallet now but a proper mattress stuffed with cat-tail down — and studies the dark square, lit every now and then by lightning. Some sunny day, no telling when, that window will show a sail out beyond The Neck. A great shout will go up in the town — the ships pay well for water — and boats will pull ashore to fill their casks from The Nest's deep wells.

And if Quoit approves, for he has strong feelings about some of the ships — "Not The Sandpiper, for all its sweet name; that crew always looks starved and mean to my eyes" — if Quoit knows the ship and trusts the master, then the boats will row back carrying not just water, but one Cam Far-Walker, going home.

Fox dreams the taste of salt: sweat that slicks down her face while she works hard in the sun, scraping away the core of some fallen thing, opening an emptiness that can hold them all. She licks her lips and tastes salt. She tastes the rime that dries on Cam's collarbone, tastes it with tiny tongue-tip-touches, like a sweat-bee. She tastes tears. She licks the salt-stone her mother puts out for the goats and presses her finger-pads down on a sprinkle of white grains on Lia's kitchen table. She licks her finger-tips and tastes the ocean.

Cam isn't dreaming. He really is perched on a barrel in a boat much smaller than The Duck, low and heavy in the waves. The barrels slosh and gurgle. The boat carries water out to sea. There is so much water there already, but it's full of salt, he's learned, and people need to drink.

In front of him, a double line of rowers pull on heavy oars in a steady, solemn rhythm, each matching the other, adding strength to strength as they round the crook in The Neck and he sees the great ship, the bare masts that will soon fill with sail and take him where his legs can't carry him. They will take him home.

Outside the shelter of The Nest, the swells build and the boat climbs and falls like any boat in open water. Cam isn't seasick, though; he turns his face to the wind.

Fox whittles boats. Len watches. Nish shakes his head.

A carving is not a boat. Nish knows both carving and boats, and they are not the same. Boats are light, made of air boxed in by skins stretched over cane. Cane is tough, but Nish has seen what big waves can do to cane. Fox is making pretty toys out of driftwood, strong enough, he admits, but no wood that drifts is big and sound enough to carry the muscles it would take to go out to the open sea and come home again. The ship-people come from a place with big trees and tools sharp enough to slice them like cheese. There is nothing like that here.

Fox is young, though, and Nish knows how much trouble youth can find when it tries. No harm in her sharpening her craft by carving boats— though they will hardly serve as trade goods up in the villages where no one has ever seen or dreamed of open water. He watches her carefully for signs of the kind of risky madness that once lured him out beyond the circle of the world.

One day, he sees her light a small fire on top of one of the storm-tumbled feather duster trees. The next day, there is a small scorched stain of black on top of the big tree-trunk. She scrapes the burnt wood away with the sharp edge of a shell. He comes over to watch as she builds not one but several small fires along the top of the log.

"Like the drums, up at the village above the rift?" he asks. "Hollowed out by fire?"

Fox grins at him. "Like the drums."

"It will take a long time," he says. But the next day, he lends her his sharp iron adze. "For scraping," he says. Len watches them and feels new life bubbling up inside her.

Cam sits, braced against the plunges of The Plover, and takes rope apart.

This is the strangest thing of all, more strange, even, than the sails bigger than any house billowing from logs taller than any tree. They want him to take rope apart.

When Quoit haggled for Cam's passage (a complicated bargain involving how much he'd pay and work balanced against how much he'd eat and drink) he'd boasted of how good Cam was with his hands. He showed them bits of tackle that Cam had made and pointed casually to the drape of a net Cam was working on with his young charges at the Duck house. But it wasn't until he mentioned that Cam was a rope-maker's son that there was a sudden warming to the idea of taking him onto The Plover. They assured Quoit that they had *just* the job for him with an enthusiasm that Cam didn't quite trust. This job they had for him seemed to be one they would be very pleased *not* to have to do themselves. But Quoit promised him (with a worrisome glint of amusement) that rope-picking would be just the thing for him.

"But what *is* rope-picking?" Cam asked. And now he knows.

Rocking with the creaking ship, he sits with a small iron spike amid baskets of old rope, frayed and rotting. He pries out the strands, and then strips them apart by main force. Even ripped apart, the component strands hold the spiral memory of the twist some faraway rope-maker plied into the line long ago. So he plucks them apart, until rope is once again a chaos of tangled fiber, then he crams the whole mess into great woven bags. When these are full, he stitches them closed. He never knows the why of any of this until after the storm that reminds him afresh how to be sea-sick and also drives the ship to seek open water, out of sight of any world. It's strange to Cam but, in hard weather, sailing people feel safer in deep water and far away from the rocky dangers of land.

After the gale is done battering the ship and the sky is blue again, the ship-menders tear open the great bags of fiber. He helps them to mix the tangles and tufts with hot, smelly black tar. (It isn't easy.) He helps them carry the heavy buckets into the dark parts of The Plover. As they caulk the seams between the planks loosened by the storm, Cam thinks about how sometimes, to hold the world together, the fibers must be torn apart.

The first time Fox sees one of the big boats, her eyes can make nothing of it. It is too big, too big to be a boat at that distance, so far away, beyond the stone piles and the bird islands where the waves crash outside the shelter of the world. At that distance, a real boat would look like a wood-chip in the water. It would play hide and seek as the waves first lifted it up and then lifted themselves around it. The great shape outside the circle, she first takes to be one of the islands. But it moves. Clearly, it moves, its white mass shifting across the mouth of the bay as it advances. It slides behind one of the bird islands, then shows itself again on the other side. It's as big as an island. But it moves.

She looks up and down the sand, then runs to Nish to ask, "What...?"

The second time Fox sees a ship, she understands. It's a boat, bigger than many houses put together, built where trees are so big and plentiful that they are cut to be burned in fireplaces, a story-place as far away as the sea itself was when they lived in First Home Village, as far away as the snow-line is to Nish's people: impossible, but real.

She understands now that the ship is built of many planks, though she wonders how they can be joined to keep out the water. (Sometimes, planks don't even keep out the rain.) And how do they, the builders of these mighty floating villages, get the wood to curve into the smooth, cutting sleekness that she is beginning to understand as the secret soul of boats? And — oh, dear! — how do they make them move? Too big, too big for paddles...

More questions for Nish. What he can't answer, he sends her to learn from Fand, so old and knowing that he lives in the lowest cave, closest to the sea.

The third time, Fox knows that great cloths, like giant bed-sheets, are hung there like laundry to catch the wind and push the boat across the water. Wind is a very strong thing— even more outside the encircling wall of the world.

This ship is much closer than the first two, and Fox can actually make out the fat creamy fabric swelling like a pregnant belly. Also, she can see the ship people on the flat roof of their floating house and crawling about up in the sail-hangers. Their figures help her eye discern how huge the whole thing is. One of the sails falls, and she catches her breath.

Nish, standing by her, looking out to sea, says, "They must need water; they're coming in."

Fox's hand flies to her mouth like a child's. Her eyes get big as the ship seems to lay an egg in the water, and a baby ship begins to make its way through the narrow mouth into the circle of their bay.

The adze drops from her hand. She pounds down the beach and into the waves. When it gets too deep to run, she launches herself into a long flat dive over the pressing swells and begins to swim.

The boat that comes in for water is bigger than any of the boats of Nish's people, but not impossibly bigger. Not dream-sized, like its floating-island mother, waiting outside while the daughter-boat runs the errand. It makes Fox think of a water-trough, a winged water-trough— one crammed with heads and shoulders and reaching arms, all weighed down with clothing like in the upper villages.

She swims on her side now, a resting stroke she learned from Nish, to hold her head above water. She wants to keep her eyes on this wonder. Others are following her with excited shouts. Sleek sun-browned bodies, swimmers and paddlers, all aiming themselves at the strange boat, to welcome the traders from the other side of the world. She hears calls of "What news, travelers?" from the swells behind her and answering cries from the newcomers, words she can't quite understand.

The boat is broader, maybe four or five times broader, than the cane-and-skin boats she is learning to craft. It would wallow, she thinks, if those long paddles didn't push it so straight and hard through the rougher waves at the mouth of the world. But it comes on fast and true.

Soon she can study its curves, more pudgy than sleek. She strokes closer to see it better and hears a voice call her name.

Now they've pulled in the long paddles and are shouting and beckoning her to come close. She sees how the narrow boards come together at the front of the boat, shaping themselves to meet each other in a graceful, lifting point.

And there he is.

Cam, gaping down at her over the edge of the boat.

Fox's feet forget to kick and she goes under. Cam here? She sinks, eyes open, below the surface of things, into the green-lit water. Down, she's going down to the bottom of the world.

It's still and quiet here beneath the surge and she sees the black belly of the strangers' boat above her, off to the left. Her hair drifts like water-weed. Below her, the jade world dims and darkens into night. There is a long, slow moment of decision. Then Fox remembers herself; she wants to breathe again. Her legs wake up and push her back to the surface. Her legs have always been strong and now they cut the water like sharpened scissors, up through the wavering bars of pale sunlight and back into the air. She gasps, treads water.

And there's Cam. Still Cam.

Long arms haul her in like a caught fish, and she suddenly understands why the boat is so broad and stubby: so that it doesn't overbalance easily.

But there's Cam. Why? Why is he here? Why now? After all this time, when she's just beginning… His face is browner than before, but his eyes are the same. Cam's eyes. Cam.

He crushes her to him in a hungry hug, twines his fingers in her dripping hair. "Fox." *Fox*?

Over his shoulder, she sees how the boat people begin to haul again on the long wood and how the paddle blades cut and pull against the water, pulling them towards shore. "This is how you make a fat boat fly," she exults, as Cam pulls away to look at her again.

He rips loose the ties on his shirt, strips it off, and drapes it around her dripping body. (Everyone else on the boat is wearing clothing.) She shrugs it off; "We don't do that here," she tells him.

Every village has one, some way to call and gather in its people, some signal: a bell set high in a tree, a heavy iron triangle, a trumpet, a big drum.

For Nish's people, nesting in crannies and seams above the circle of sea, it is a great horn, made by cutting off the tip of the shell of one of the big meaty conchs they often dine on.

Nish has tried to teach Len how to sound it, as everyone — even small children — are supposed to be able to sound the conch in emergencies. She's blown and blown until her cheeks are tired and her lips are raw, but never got more than a sad, rude blatting out of it.

But she knows the sound when she hears it, even though it is dimmed by wind and surf: a long lowing, like a lonely cow. She looks up from the spear-plant fibers coiling in her hands.

A seagull squawks past the open porch of the cave that is her home now, sounding for all the world like the rusty hinge of a door creaking open. She knows now that the fearless winged thieves glide by on purpose, scouting for any bit of food or brightness they can snatch. Seabirds have made her a better housekeeper, after more than one thing she thought was hers was carried off; it would be good to have a cat here.

She looks around the open cave protectively and then stands to look over the rocky ledge, down to the circle of sand, to see what the conch-call was about.

First, she sees the great ship far out, past the opening of the
waters. Then, the swarm of brown swimmers and paddlers
flowing out towards— what? Another boat, larger than the
boats of Nish's people but much smaller than the far-off vessel.
It is pulling towards the beach, with great wings beating
down and heaving against the water.

It's coming to them. This must be one of the travelers from
the other world Nish has spoken of. And it's coming in.

She tucks the loose work into a basket and covers it with
a gull-proof lid. Then she starts down the long rope ladder
to meet the strangers.

This is as close to a crowd as ever happens among the people
who live at the end of the path. Many of them are in the water
already, boats and bodies streaming towards the strangers,
welcoming them with shouts of greeting. Others are standing in the shallows, sea-foam chasing back and forth around
their legs. All eyes are on the squat, duck-like boat laboring
towards the sand.

"What's happening? Why are they here?" Len asks Arl.

"It's the ship people — The Plover, if I'm not wrong — come
in to fill up their water-barrels. They bring trade from the
other side of the world, for the water, and for other things.
They have goods we don't make here. Steel, for one thing,
good blue steel. You want a new knife or shears, Rope-Maker?
This is your day." Len touches the bone hilt of her old knife,
hanging in a leather sheath from a braided band that sits low
on her hips. A new knife?

She watches the boat get closer, full of people wearing
sun-faded clothing and looking very uncomfortable as they
sweat through the work of pulling the boat in. With this
sweet sea-breeze cooling her skin, shirts and trousers here
seem wildly out of place to Len now.

And Len sees that one person in the boat is naked, like
all Nish's people, except for the braid around her waist for
her knife sheath and another around her neck for a little
water-green pendant. It's Fox riding the strangers' boat in
and, there, beside her…

Len Rope-Maker, sensible and strong, faints dead away
on the sand.

The ship people are gone now, after a trade-fair on the beach. While the barrels were filled at the springs and falls of fresh water around the cove, there has been a welter of wrangling and exchange: shiny crystal for steel blade, fine shell carving for spice, fish-net for grain, hammock for wooden chest, rope for dried currants. But all that is done now. The strangers have sailed out of sight around the edge of the world and people have carried their new goods up to their homes. The sun is sinking towards the open sea.

For Nish, the homecoming of Len's son, Fox's beloved, and Jade's father is a time for feasting greater than the usual welcome of a traveler. Though they might deny this, the women have grieved Cam and secretly thought him dead, except for the little one, who hasn't thought of him at all. And now here he is and his death has to be undone.

So Nish goes out with his spear and his floating basket to the underwater towers and brings back lobsters and crabs, sea vegetables, and a big dog-fish for the grill. He climbs Eran's ladder and trades some of yesterday's clams, already cleaned and stuffed with meal, for a jug of palm wine.

But when Nish comes back to his own place, merrymaking is not the way of things.

Len is still in a babbling fog of joy, touching her son often, as if to make sure of him. Cam answers her questions willingly enough, but all his stories seem to trail off, his voice uncertain about how to bring them to a close, his tone lifting with what sounds like a hidden question.

Fox listens and with lowered eyes. Is it shyness? Is it anger? Jade sits unnaturally still and quiet on her lap with one hand in her mother's hair, fingering a lock, twirling it round and round as her eyes flit from her mother to her grandmother to this cloth-wrapped stranger they call her father.

Nish sees that Len is blind to the odd weather here. He uncovers the banked embers on the hearth and feeds them some bits of wood, setting a boiling pot in its niche. While the water heats, he cleans the fish and keeps his eye on the strange clouds of love around him.

Why can't she look at him? She's spent two years, two long and lonely years, hurting to see him again, to put Jade into his arms and watch him fall in love, but now...

Now he's here, right in front of her, sitting on Nish's mat, learning to eat lobster. And she can't meet his eyes, can't even drag her gaze up from his hands banging inexpertly at the lobster shell with one of Nish's special cracking stones.

Right in front of her. Wasn't this what she'd dreamed about all those restless nights? But what had she wanted? What had she possibly wanted from this man? What had she wanted to say?

After they finish the unfeastlike feast and wash their dishes, Nish takes Jade from her mother's arms and tells Fox to go down the ladder. "Take Cam with you. You two need to fight. Climb down to the sand and walk around the cove to the left. Out to the dunes. That's a good place when you have to fight. You can say what you have to there. Say it loud. Nobody hears you. Yell at each other— no problem. Lots of space there, good soft sand for fighting. Push somebody there, somebody falls down— no bruises. Get up, push back. Push hard. Nobody gets hurt, just sand in your mouth. Go there. Get it out, whatever it is. Fight."

And when Fox starts to argue, looking a lot like Jade on one of her stubborn days, Nish says, "Not here. Not with me. Fight with *him*. Take him down to the water, don't come back 'til it's done."

And when Fox opens her mouth one more time, he interrupts her again and says, more gently, "Like bending cane for a boat."

Her lips quirk. "You mean, you have to heat it first?"

"And if you skip a step, it breaks."

She sits silent for a minute and then gets up without looking at any of them. She starts down the ladder alone. "You coming?" she yells, after her head has sunk from sight. "Or am I supposed to do this alone, too?"

"Well?" prompts Nish, looking at Cam.

And Cam jumps up from the mat and follows Fox down to the sand, the salt, and the water.

Standing there by Nish, Len watches Cam's head sink into the night as he climbs down after Fox. For her, it's so simple: He's home. Her son is home.

But it's not simple for Cam and Fox. Len can see that now.

She reaches for Nish's hand. His fingers settle into the grooves between hers. The evening breeze flaps their robes. She brings their clasped hands up where she can see them in the firelight, see his darker skin interweaving with her lighter tan. She squeezes his hand. The four slim blue fish tattooed between his second and third knuckles all swim towards her.

This is what she wants for Cam, for Fox. This. Exactly this.

She can't give it to them, though. They have to make it themselves.

Jade doesn't wake up when Nish slips her into the lavender cradle of her hammock. Her grandparents put away the clothing they don't need and bathe each other in the big stone basin under the drape of vine that perfumes the night air with its yellow blossoms. The water carries away the sand of the day so that when they come together, skin-to-skin in the big hammock, there is no grit to chafe them.

This, Len whispers. This.

After, Nish dreams he's riding the swells of the sea in a great boat, not a fat and heavy one like the rowing boat from the big sail-ship, needing a dozen strong backs to move it. No, the boat in his dream is slim but strong enough to hold them all: Jade, in the front, with a full-sized paddle in her tiny hands, then Fox and Cam, then Len, then him, sitting where he can see them all, see how beautifully they lean and dip and pull like music, see the waves mound and sink around them. The paddle in his hand is long and broad; he understands this is so he can steer them safely through the big water. They are going to the island of the birds. They will walk wisely there, careful of the eggs, and take only the feathers that the birds no longer need. In his dream, although he is still at sea, he can glimpse the feathers already; not just the greens and blues and pinks of his memories, but colors like at the Dyers' house, colors for which he has no name.

Fox leads the way along the beach towards where the sandy land broadens out and sinks and swells like waves. Cam doesn't know what to say and she doesn't speak. They scuff silently along the strip of sand where the water pounds the land and the rolling blows of the waves are the only sound. The waves are smaller here than out where The Plover sailed, but still a force to be reckoned with.

Cam is uncomfortable with how naked everyone is here in this lowest village. At dinner, his mother and Nish clothed themselves in flowing lengths of undyed goats-wool, claiming the evening breeze was chilly, but he suspects this was just a courtesy to him as an outsider, to help him get used to how they do things here. But Fox sat stubbornly uncovered, leaning against a backrest carved from dark wood. Jade warmed her like a little furnace in her lap, she said.

Of course, he's seen Fox unclothed before, but that feels so long ago. A different life. A different Cam, a different Fox, a boy and a girl who grew up together, walked the same path— no reason to be shy. They were never prissy about covering themselves, not like the people of the high villages.

That night, though, when they'd clambered off the path onto that crag and discovered each other— then their nakedness had changed. But that, that new nakedness had been shared. So very shared.

Now there's this. Here he is, cased from calf to neck in sweaty garments long past fresh, as stiff as canvas from old sea-salt. On board The Plover, water was too precious to fritter away on laundry or bathing. He hopes he doesn't smell bad to her.

Fox is striding along a little ahead of him. She glows faintly, as if the moon-silver that picks out the sway of her hips comes from somewhere inside her. It's a relief to be able to look at her without meeting her eyes. And a pleasure, too: Her long strong back. Her neck. Her legs. Her ankles are frosted by sand her heels kick up as she walks, and the sand glitters like tiny stars.

In the moonlight, with her back to him, all the ways she's changed fade away: her skin, much browner now; her arms, sleek with muscles where she was soft before, her breasts... At dinner, he tried not gawk like a fourteen-year-old boy, but his eyes had a mind of their own. And his body too— Fox's breasts are a woman's breasts now. If they're really going to fight, she has him at a disadvantage.

He pauses a moment to settle himself and looks away from her, back along the way they came. Their tracks trail across the sand, one line because he walked in her footsteps. The lights of Nish's people gleam up and down the cliff.

The dunes are tufted by dark grasses taller than Cam, stalks that murmur and bow in graceful curves echoing the slopes of the sand. The sand itself glows with a pale diffuse light, giving back the thin moon.

They've come this far in silence. He doesn't know what to say. Walking behind Fox, he's had a chance to study her back, expressive as any face. There's something angry about the set of her shoulders, a sort of stiffness, a sort of tension.

Why is it like this? He's dreamed of her, ached for her: the old ease, the playfulness, the touch. The comfortable touch. And the fiery touch. All of it. Where is it? It must be there, somewhere. What they had, how could they lose *that*, now that they've found each other? And if it's lost, how do they find it again?

"Fox," he says at last. She keeps walking.

He speeds his steps to catch her, lays his hand on her shoulder. She whirls to face him in the night.

How do they find it again?

"Fox," he says again. "Why are you so mad? You're the one who said no. I asked you to come with me, but you didn't want to. You said..."

You have to heat the cane. You can't skip a step.

They are resting now, lying together where Cam has spread his shirt under their heads. They are very sandy.

She is looking up at the stars that play hide-and-seek between banks of cloud still silvered by the unseen moon. He is looking at her. "Do you want to fight some more?"

"I guess," she says, but takes his hand. "I'm still mad."

He breathes in, slowly and deeply, all the way down. "What else?"

She takes a moment, searches the darkness, wrestles with words. "It's just that... you got to see the boats, the big boats. You lived on one. You *cooked* on one." Her voice is plaintive, accusing. He misses it, doesn't catch the tone. He misses the point.

"The Duck wasn't really that big. I thought it was, at the time. I thought it was a house, actually, right at first. But I never even saw one of the really big boats until we got down near Big River town. They load up cargo there, and then go off, who knows where, out into the deep water." His voice trails off.

"And you got to see them. And travel on them. I" — her voice catches — "would have liked to see them."

"You saw Jade," he reminds her quietly.

She doesn't say anything for a few minutes. She doesn't tell him what she is remembering: Birth and nursing and the awful night when they climbed too high. Hours and days and weeks in Lia's rocking chair, going nowhere. The first word and the first step and saying "no" and cleaning mashed fruit out of little ears. A little head peering about with interest from its perch on Nish's back as the downworld path unfolded before her. A whirlwind of butterflies with Jade at the center. Cam can only guess about what she's seen. Maybe she'll tell him some day. Maybe not. Finally she answers: "I guess we still have some fighting to do."

"I guess so."

"This isn't over. I'm still mad."

She lets go of his hand and rolls towards him to dust some grains off his shoulder, presses her lips to it, then bites it hard, right over the bone.

"Hey!" he complains.

"I told you: I'm still mad at you. But I need a swim first. Then we can go at it again."

She jumps up and runs towards the water. Stripping off his trousers takes him a moment, and then he chases her through the muddled moonlight and into the silver surf.

It's good that they've both learned to swim.

Not far away, a tree-trunk rests in the sand. Its fire-blackened topside shows clearly in the starlight, and you can even see where the scorch marks have been hollowed out, deep bites into the smooth log. It's less easy to see that the skin of the wood itself has been scored with guide-lines where one end will be chiseled to an upswept point, curved to cut through water without struggle. That end is aimed down towards the shoreline, where tongues of water speak, and speak again.

Jade has her own little boat now. Fox made it. Nish helped.

Now Nish is helping her learn to paddle it. It's easy, much easier than paddling the grown-up boats where the edge is too high and the paddles are taller than she is. You don't just have to pull on the paddle, you have to pull on it just right, because the way you pull tells the boat how to go. And you have to turn with it, twisting from your waist, using your belly and back muscles so your arms won't get too tired.

Her arms are a little tired now, so Nish comes over and lays his paddle across both their boats so they can rest and talk for awhile. She likes it when Nish talks. He knows lots of things, not just about boats and fishing. Sometimes, to get him started, she points to something, a bird or a plant or one of the blue pictures on his skin, and asks, "What's that?" And he tells her about things.

Today, as they bob in the quiet morning waves, he gives her some fruit and some water from his drinking-ball. To get him started, she asks, "What's a father?"

There is a child. Or a fish. At this moment, it is very hard to tell.

It basks in seawater. It doesn't breathe. What is breathing? It doesn't hunger. What is hunger? It doesn't want. And yet, it dreams.

The child dreams. Its eyes twitch and move. Eyes that have never opened to the light of day still see. The child doesn't dream of *things* — what are things? There are no things, because there are no words, just the hum of that ever-changing voice, and the other voices, too, further away but also interesting. And the beating double heart of the world, of course, but that twining rhythm is so near, so always, that the child-fish doesn't hear it. It is the voices, coming and going, that are interesting. In its dreams, the child kicks out, takes a strong step towards the voices.

Len rubs her belly and thinks about the spring.

Our titles are available at major book stores
and local independent resellers who support
Science Fiction and Fantasy readers like you.

EDGE Science Fiction
and Fantasy Publishing

**Our titles are available at major book stores
and local independent resellers who support
Science Fiction and Fantasy readers like you.**

Alphanauts by J. Brian Clarke (tp) - ISBN: 978-1-894063-14-2
Apparition Trail, The by Lisa Smedman (tp) - ISBN: 978-1-894063-22-7
As Fate Decrees by Denysé Bridger (tp) - ISBN: 978-1-894063-41-8

Black Chalice, The by Marie Jakober (hb) - ISBN: 978-1-894063-00-7
Blue Apes by Phyllis Gotlieb (pb) - ISBN: 978-1-895836-13-4
Blue Apes by Phyllis Gotlieb (hb) - ISBN: 978-1-895836-14-1
Braided Path, The by Donna Glee Williams (tp) - ISBN: 978-1-77053-058-4

Captives by Barbara Galler-Smith and Josh Langston (tp)
  - ISBN: 978-1-894063-53-1
Children of Atwar, The by Heather Spears (pb) - ISBN: 978-0-88878-335-6
Chilling Tales: Evil Did I Dwell; Lewd I Did Live edited by Michael Kelly (tp)
  - ISBN: 978-1-894063-52-4
Chilling Tales: In Words, Alas, Drown I edited by Michael Kelly (tp)
  - ISBN: 978-1-77053-024-9
Cinco de Mayo by Michael J. Martineck (tp) - ISBN: 978-1-894063-39-5
Cinkarion - The Heart of Fire (Part Two of The Chronicles of the Karionin)
  by J. A. Cullum - (tp) - ISBN: 978-1-894063-21-0
Circle Tide by Rebecca K. Rowe (tp) - ISBN: 978-1-894063-59-3
Clan of the Dung-Sniffers by Lee Danielle Hubbard (tp) - ISBN: 978-1-894063-05-0
Claus Effect, The by David Nickle & Karl Schroeder (pb) - ISBN: 978-1-895836-34-9
Claus Effect, The by David Nickle & Karl Schroeder (hb) - ISBN: 978-1-895836-35-6
Clockwork Heart by Dru Pagliassotti (tp) - ISBN: 978-1-77053-026-3
Clockwork Lies: Iron Wind by Dru Pagliassotti (tp) - ISBN: 978-1-77053-050-8

Danse Macabre: Close Encounters With the Reaper edited by Nancy Kilpatrick (tp)
  - ISBN: 978-1-894063-96-8
Dark Earth Dreams by Candas Dorsey & Roger Deegan (Audio CD with Booklet)
  - ISBN: 978-1-895836-05-9
Darkness of the God (Children of the Panther Part Two)
  by Amber Hayward (tp) - ISBN: 978-1-894063-44-9
Demon Left Behind, The by Marie Jakober (tp) - ISBN: 978-1-894063-49-4
Distant Signals by Andrew Weiner (tp) - ISBN: 978-0-88878-284-7
Dreams of an Unseen Planet by Teresa Plowright (tp) - ISBN: 978-0-88878-282-3
Dreams of the Sea (Part 1 of Tyranaël) by Élisabeth Vonarburg (tp)
  - ISBN: 978-1-895836-96-7
Dreams of the Sea (Part 1 of Tyranaël) by Élisabeth Vonarburg (hb)
  - ISBN: 978-1-895836-98-1
Druids by Barbara Galler-Smith and Josh Langston (tp)
  - ISBN: 978-1-894063-29-6

Eclipse by K. A. Bedford (tp) - ISBN: 978-1-894063-30-2
Elements by Suzanne Church (tp) - ISBN: 978-1-77053-042-3
Even The Stones by Marie Jakober (tp) - ISBN: 978-1-894063-18-0
Evolve: Vampire Stories of the New Undead edited by Nancy Kilpatrick (tp)
  - ISBN: 978-1-894063-33-3

Milkman, The by Michael J. Martineck (tp) - ISBN: 978-0-77053-060-7
Moonfall by Heather Spears (pb) - ISBN: 978-0-88878-306-6

Of Wind and Sand by Sylvie Bérard (translated by Sheryl Curtis) (tp)
   - ISBN: 978-1-894063-19-7
On Spec: The First Five Years edited by On Spec (pb)
   - ISBN: 978-1-895836-08-0
On Spec: The First Five Years edited by On Spec (hb)
   - ISBN: 978-1-895836-12-7
Orbital Burn by K. A. Bedford (tp) - ISBN: 978-1-894063-10-4
Orbital Burn by K. A. Bedford (hb) - ISBN: 978-1-894063-12-8

Pallahaxi Tide by Michael Coney (pb) - ISBN: 978-0-88878-293-9
Paradox Resolution by K. A. Bedford (tp) - ISBN:978-1-894063-88-3
Passion Play by Sean Stewart (pb) - ISBN: 978-0-88878-314-1
Petrified World (Determine Your Destiny #1) by Piotr Brynczka (pb)
   - ISBN: 978-1-894063-11-1
Plague Saint, The by Rita Donovan (tp) - ISBN: 978-1-895836-28-8
Plague Saint, The by Rita Donovan (hb) - ISBN: 978-1-895836-29-5
Pock's World by Dave Duncan (tp) - ISBN: 978-1-894063-47-0
Puzzle Box, The by Randy McCharles, Billie Millholland, Eileen Bell, and Ryan
   McFadden (tp) - ISBN: 978-1-77053-040-9

Reluctant Voyagers by Élisabeth Vonarburg (pb) - ISBN: 978-1-895836-09-7
Reluctant Voyagers by Élisabeth Vonarburg (hb) - ISBN: 978-1-895836-15-8
Resisting Adonis by Timothy J. Anderson (tp) - ISBN: 978-1-895836-84-4
Resisting Adonis by Timothy J. Anderson (hb) - ISBN: 978-1-895836-83-7
Rigor Amortis edited by Jaym Gates and Erika Holt (tp)
   - ISBN: 978-1-894063-63-0

Silent City, The by Élisabeth Vonarburg (tp) - ISBN: 978-1-894063-07-4
Slow Engines of Time, The by Élisabeth Vonarburg (tp)
   - ISBN: 978-1-895836-30-1
Slow Engines of Time, The by Élisabeth Vonarburg (hb)
   - ISBN: 978-1-895836-31-8
Stealing Magic by Tanya Huff (tp) - ISBN: 978-1-894063-34-0
Stolen Children (Children of the Panther Part Three)
   by Amber Hayward (tp) - ISBN: 978-1-894063-66-1
Strange Attractors by Tom Henighan (pb) - ISBN: 978-0-88878-312-7

Taming, The by Heather Spears (pb) - ISBN: 978-1-895836-23-3
Taming, The by Heather Spears (hb) - ISBN: 978-1-895836-24-0
Technicolor Ultra Mall by Ryan Oakley (tp) - ISBN: 978-1-894063-54-8
Ten Monkeys, Ten Minutes by Peter Watts (tp) - ISBN: 978-1-895836-74-5
Ten Monkeys, Ten Minutes by Peter Watts (hb) - ISBN: 978-1-895836-76-9
Tesseracts 1 edited by Judith Merril (pb) - ISBN: 978-0-88878-279-3
Tesseracts 2 edited by Phyllis Gotlieb & Douglas Barbour (pb)
   - ISBN: 978-0-88878-270-0
Tesseracts 3 edited by Candas Jane Dorsey & Gerry Truscott (pb)
   - ISBN: 978-0-88878-290-8
Tesseracts 4 edited by Lorna Toolis & Michael Skeet (pb)
   - ISBN: 978-0-88878-322-6
Tesseracts 5 edited by Robert Runté & Yves Maynard (pb)
   - ISBN: 978-1-895836-25-7

Warriors by Barbara Galler-Smith and Josh Langston (tp)
-ISBN: 978-1-77053-030-0
Wildcatter by Dave Duncan (tp) - ISBN: 978-1-894063-90-6